Praise for the novels of *New York Times* bestselling author Heather Graham

"Graham proves that she is still at the top of the genre with the latest Krewe of Hunters book.... Evil lurks in the background and readers will be trying to figure out the motives of the killer while flipping the pages to see what can possibly happen next. Another great book to add to this long-running series."

—*RT Book Reviews* on *Fade to Black*

"Graham's lead characters are always empathetic people who want to stop a killer, find justice for the dead, and restore order."

—*Lesa's Book Critiques* on *Echoes of Evil*

"Graham takes us on a thrilling ride... A bone-chilling read."

—*Fresh Fiction* on *Pale as Death*

"Sizzling chemistry, murder, and ghosts deliver another fantastic case."

—*Caffeinated Book Reviewer* on *Pale as Death*

"Delivers plenty of suspense as the madness behind such seemingly random killing is uncovered. Once again, setting becomes its own character, with places like Fall River coming to life with vivid details and dramatic imagery."

—*RT Book Reviews* on *Dark Rites*

"Enough twists, turns and downright surprises that will keep you glued to the pages... The romance hits just the right notes because in the midst of tragedy and fear it only seems fair that they find a little happiness."

—*Fresh Fiction* on *Dying Breath*

"Graham is a master at world building and her latest is a thrilling, dark, and deadly tale of romantic suspense."

—*Booklist*, starred review, on *Haunted Destiny*

HEATHER GRAHAM

THE
STALKING

mira

mira

ISBN-13: 978-0-7783-0811-9

Recycling programs for this product may not exist in your area.

The Stalking

Copyright © 2019 by Heather Graham Pozzessere

www.Harlequin.com

Printed in U.S.A.

THE
STALKING

Prologue

The jazz band played a mournful tune under great oaks that swayed in the breeze, dripping moss as if the trees themselves cried.

The priest moved forward, silent and somber, leading the funeral procession. Though it was the traditional funeral that should accompany the farewells for any member of Janine's family, it all seemed so very wrong to Cheyenne Donegal.

Step by step, they neared the cemetery, the Louisiana "city of the dead" where the body of Janine Dumas would soon lie in the family tomb of her ancestors, ashes to ashes in the fierce heat of the Louisiana sun, in a year and a day, as they said.

This was a special city of the dead, begun as a private family cemetery, with an old mansion that was considered to be the most haunted for miles—perhaps in the state. It had a reputation for evil and death, and though that reputation had originated way back when, legends and myths never died. They just grew.

The procession had not had to come far; the funeral parade had begun at the old Justine Plantation building, where Janine had lain for viewing for a night and a day after leaving the county morgue, and where, they said, the haunts of the old cemetery— begun by the Justine family in the early 1800s— came out to welcome the newly dead.

Still, this area had been Janine's home, where she had lived and loved and believed in a spectacular future for herself, adventure and excitement to come.

No more.

Janine had been just sixteen, a young and beautiful girl, full of energy and love and enthusiasm, a flirt, a tease, perhaps, yet so full of life that her death still didn't seem possible, even though her family and loved ones had seen her lying in her coffin, had seen her mother scream and cry and try to pull her body out.

The coffin, drawn along in an old bier by two white mules, arrived at the cemetery. The jazz band, the pallbearers and the mourners entered the great ironwork gates of the cemetery and followed the path between the multitude of family crypts, coming at last to the one belonging to the family Dumas.

Cheyenne Donegal stood at her mother's side, along with their neighbors, teachers, friends and family as the rest of the procession entered the cemetery.

They took their positions at the Dumas family grave as the priest stepped out of the line of mourners.

Cheyenne heard her friends whispering to each other.

"You look so bereft… Janine wasn't perfect, you know," someone whispered at her side.

"She was so young," Cheyenne murmured, turning to see the boy at her side—Christian Mayhew. He'd been in Janine's class, three years ahead of Cheyenne.

"She knew how to take me down a peg or two," Christian murmured. "She could be…cruel."

Cheyenne didn't reply; her mother was staring at her, frowning. At her mother's expression, she sensed something was wrong—and then she remembered what.

Christian Mayhew had died.

Heartbreakingly, by his own hand almost a year ago. Cyberbullied and picked on at school, he'd apparently been able to take no more. A slew of drugs had been found by his bedside. He'd lain there, rumor had it, as if he'd chosen a long nap—and taken it.

But that couldn't be right. Because here he was.

As the priest continued to drone on, Cheyenne heard another voice.

"Christian, I was never mean to you. Yes, I might have teased you a little. But I was never mean to you on purpose."

It was a voice she knew well.

Her cousin Janine's!

Cheyenne managed not to scream, shout—or collapse.

Instead, she turned slightly. And there was Janine, next to Christian. Janine looked so beautiful, but then, she had always been a beauty, blessed with big dark eyes and sleek hair in the deepest brown, almost black.

The priest was still talking, his voice rich, his speech powerful, and still Cheyenne couldn't discern his words. How could Christian and Janine be there, standing slightly behind her, watching as she watched?

"Great funeral," Christian told her. "Mine was… not."

Janine didn't seem to hear him. She was staring across the crowd, across the neat rows of tombs, some a picture of decaying elegance, lost to time, others meticulously maintained, kept up by those living but destined to join their family members within the mausoleums. Her gaze traveled past angels and cherubs and Madonna statues, beautiful funerary art that could haunt the living and the dead. Janine was looking, Cheyenne thought, back toward the old plantation, now a mortuary chapel.

Cheyenne could have sworn that her cousin clutched her shoulder, that she felt her hand.

But of course, she did not. Her cousin was dead. Her earthly remains were being put into the family tomb, and there she would lie and decay, a year and a day in the blistering heat, down to bone and ash, scooped into the holding area, leaving room for the remains of family to come.

"That's him!" Janine cried. Her voice seemed to tremble. The hand that touched Cheyenne's shoulder was shaking. "That's him."

Him?

Cheyenne knew the police believed that Janine,

her beautiful young cousin, had been killed by a man they called the Artiste.

His victims had been between the ages of sixteen and twenty-two, pretty, precocious and energetic. The first three had been working girls—vivacious, bright young women who had worked for an escort agency.

The fourth had gone missing after telling friends she was meeting with a drop-dead gorgeous man she had met through an online site.

The fifth had been a runaway, living in New Orleans.

And the sixth had been Janine.

Cheyenne looked at the man who was standing on the trail between the old plantation house and the tombs. She knew who he was. Ryan Lassiter, a substitute teacher, sometime guitar player with various bands in New Orleans and all the way out to Lafayette, New Iberia and beyond. He was young, cool and hot. The kids loved him.

"Mr. Lassiter?" she said aloud.

"Cheyenne, dammit, don't you think I know what happened to me?" Janine asked, a catch in her ghostly voice. "I was so stupid! I thought I was so cool. Yes, I flirted with him. I had a ridiculous crush on him, and I thought he was… I thought I was so hot, and I was flattered, since for sure I had to be something…something for him to want to be with me."

Christian was looking at her. "Oh, Janine," he said. "We saw it…so many nerds saw it. Jody Baylor said that you told him you were meeting with Lassiter—here, as a matter of fact, to do research on the old plantation house. Jody said that it was sick, gross. He's—older. You're still a kid, Janine… You *were* still a kid. And he took those pictures of you… in life and then he fixed you all up and took the pictures of you…in death."

Janine heard his words but didn't reply. She stared straight ahead, at the man she claimed was her killer. "I was a fool…so ridiculously filled with myself and my infatuation. I thought he was going to wait for me to graduate, and then he'd marry me, and… You have to stop him, Cheyenne," Janine pleaded. "Tell them, tell them that he did it, that he killed me, that he stole my life, that he left me…there!"

Janine pointed to her casket and added, "I could be so careless of others… I could be self-centered, I know—selfish. But I would never want what happened to me to happen to anyone else, not my worst enemy. Cheyenne, don't let him get away with it— don't let him get away with what he did!"

She was looking at her cousin's killer—and a man who acted so concerned, so kind, so giving with others. But he had done such cruel and horrible things to others, he had tortured women, mentally and physically.

How could she prove it? No one else could see Christian and Janine…her friend, the suicide, and her cousin, the murder victim. Would they just say that she was crazy?

"Do something, Cheyenne!" Janine begged.

The priest was still speaking; the members of the funerary jazz band were preparing to start up with another song. The cemetery workers were waiting for them all to leave so that Janine, in her coffin, might be sealed into the family tomb.

Ryan Lassiter was looking toward *her* then. Or was he? Here, just outside Broussard, the landscape curled and dipped. The old plantation house was up a very small rise, with a smokehouse, original kitchen, carriage house and other structures seeming to fall away just behind it; the cemetery sat down the hill and to the right of the sweeping entrance to the house.

Cheyenne looked around: her parents were there; Janine's parents, teachers and friends; Mr. Beaufort, the gym teacher; Mike Holiday, captain of the football team; Nelson Ridgeway and Katie Anson, seniors, a class ahead of Janine, but friends with whom she had studied and partied; Mr. Derringer, the organist from the church; Emil Justine, hereditary owner and operator here, tall and dignified, caring and capable; and many others who had come to pay their respects.

Who was Lassiter looking at? Was it someone who looked back at him, as if they shared a confidence, as if someone else knew?

"Cheyenne, it's up to you!" Christian whispered. "You have to do something."

"Please," Janine said softly, and then she turned to Christian, tears appearing to sting her eyes. "You could have been glad for what happened to me," she said. "I wasn't always so nice to you."

"You weren't my friend, but you didn't do this to me. It wasn't you, it was many things," Christian told her. "And I certainly forgive you. I hope that I am forgiven, too." Christian stared firmly at Cheyenne again. "Now, Cheyenne. You're the only one who can help right now."

"Please!" Janine said again.

Cheyenne thought about what had been done to her cousin…and the other young women. They had been kidnapped; they had been kept alive. Pictures had been taken of them and sent to the newspapers— he'd forced them to smile. And then he had killed them, and dressed them up and set them in strange death poses, and sent those pictures to the papers, too.

And still, what can I do?

Something, anything!

She looked up for a moment at the massive winged angel kneeling above the family tomb. In a matter of minutes, the rite at the graveside would be over.

And Ryan Lassiter would have watched the spectacle, chuckling inwardly over every tear shed, and walked away, handsome and charming, never a suspect…

Free to kill again.

Cheyenne really didn't know what to do. And so she lifted her arm, pointing toward Lassiter, and she began to scream.

"That's him…that's the man who had Janine!" she

said. She didn't know how she would prove it, but more than one of their friends had seen Janine with him and they'd gossiped that it was disgusting, the older man going for the teenage girl. "Ryan Lassiter is the —the Artiste!"

The priest stopped speaking. Cheyenne heard discordant sounds as the musicians one by one stopped playing and turned to look at her.

"Cheyenne, Cheyenne," her mom said, turning to her and clutching her shoulders, eyes wide with surprise, worry and confusion. "Cheyenne—that's just Mr. Lassiter, the substitute teacher and musician, honey, he's not a— "

"He is—he's a monster. He seduced Janine—he had her meet up with him. She didn't want anyone to know. She had a thing for him, and you should have seen the way he looked at her! Mom, he killed her. Stop him! Stop him!"

Lassiter, with his flashing dark eyes and a sexy brown lock of hair falling over his forehead, stared down the aisle between the tombs, gaze hard on Cheyenne. Then, he pointed at her and mouthed the words, *You're dead.*

But he was seen, and the trombone player set down his instrument and went after Lassiter.

The musician, one Jimmy Mercury, was tall and handsome—and built like an ebony battleship. He shouted something to the guitar player next to him, another tall man, maybe eighteen or nineteen, with dark hair and tawny skin, and built like a brick house. Lassiter began to run, but he was no match for Jimmy, a former linebacker for Louisiana State, who now had him trapped. The dark-haired young man, already past Lassiter, doubled back to see that he didn't escape.

Lassiter went down hard. The musicians held him with knees on his back.

Soon the sound of sirens blared through the cemetery, all but shaking marble angels and cherubs.

Once the police were there, chaos reigned in the middle of the funeral, as other young people who had been friends with Janine stepped forward, shouting accusations.

Ryan Lassiter protested all the while. There was no physical evidence—not there, not then. This was hysteria, he claimed. But for his own safety, the police assured him, they were taking him in. They would get to the bottom of it.

Cheyenne didn't really know the outcome that night. Her parents called one of their friends—a fellow who had retired from the FBI just a year earlier—and he came over to keep an eye on her if Lassiter got out.

Her father had been a hunter in his younger days; he still had his shotgun.

Cheyenne didn't see her cousin or Christian again that day; they had disappeared in the melee.

It wasn't until the next morning—when she was barely awake—that her mother came to sit by her, eyes filled with concern once again.

"Cheyenne, they got a search warrant and a warrant for Lassiter's DNA and…you were right, he was a killer. He killed all those young women… He killed our beautiful Janine. The DNA isn't back yet, they told me, but they're sure they'll get matches. He confessed! He confessed! And…oh, my God, Cheyenne, he was holding another girl. They were able to get to her before…before he killed her. She was locked away, out in a storage shed. He—he would have killed her. He'd already sent her 'living' picture to the police. How—how did you just see him there in the cemetery and know it was him?"

Cheyenne carefully hid any expression from her mother. "I—I had heard kids talking. All the girls thought he was fine, cool…sexy. Janine wouldn't have gone with just anyone, but I know that she did think he was an amazing poet and…" She paused, smiling, and yet with the sting of tears in her eyes. "It was almost as if Janine was there with me…right there, in the cemetery. And, Mom, I couldn't let him get away with it."

Her mother accepted her words.

Ryan Lassiter was tried for all six murders.

He received the death sentence, and began his long route for appeals.

The years went by. When Cheyenne was eighteen and about to leave New Iberia, Iberia Parish, Louisiana, for the big city of New Orleans and an education at Loyola, she went back for a final visit to the cemetery and the family tomb.

The surname Dumas was chiseled into the arch at the top; it was Cheyenne's mother's maiden name. When Cheyenne's time came, she would have a place waiting for her here, too. Her dad was what they called "English," even though he was a mix of Irish, British and more—all American. Her mom had been born in Cajun country, and was Cajun to the bone.

Cheyenne loved her heritage, her hometown, but she was ready to move on. And while home would only be about two and a half hours away, she felt that she was leaving. And she had to say goodbye to Janine.

She stood by the tomb, her hand upon it, and spoke softly. "I'm heading out this afternoon, moving into my dorm. The big city—well, however big a city NOLA might be. Janine, I'll never know how, but…you did it. You got that man into prison. The cops had DNA and fingerprints, but even though Lassiter was substitute teaching, he'd managed to submit other fingerprints than his own into the system, so he wasn't flagged that way. Because of you— and Christian—he was caught. I have a scholarship. I'm going to major in forensics and criminology. I want to help others, and stop others from dying." She hesitated. Her cousin had been gone for five years now; she still felt the overwhelming sadness when she was in the graveyard. "Like you did!" she said softly.

She nearly jumped a mile high when she felt a touch on her shoulder.

Janine was there, still so beautiful, her eyes alive and dark and flashing. And Christian was at her side—standing just slightly behind her, as Janine rather liked others to be.

"You're still here!" Cheyenne whispered.

Janine smiled, slipping one of her ethereal arms around Christian. "No, no, no—we're not *still* here. We don't hang around in the cemetery—there are many, many places better to be."

"Especially at Halloween," Christian said. "So much fun to scare the bejesus out of people at the haunted houses."

"He's still such a child," Janine said, rolling her eyes in mock horror, but with deep affection in her voice. "We go all over."

"We're here today for you," Christian explained. "The living apparently think that the dead hang around in cemeteries and graveyards. I mean, seriously?"

"Am I really seeing you?" Cheyenne whispered.

Janine laughed softly. Cheyenne felt spectral arms around her, as gentle as a whisper of air. "Cousin, I am here, and I am somehow ridiculously free. I've got Christian and…thing is, we don't know exactly why we're still here."

"We just want you to know that we're watching over you—when we're not at some big social event that Janine just has to attend!" Christian said.

Janine bopped him on the shoulder, and then her face became sad and serious as she said, "I'll be there if you need me, Cheyenne. Oh, Cheyenne, remember Maw-Maw?"

Janine was referring to their grandmother, gone now for a good decade.

"Of course," Cheyenne said.

"She always said someone would have the *clair-sentience* in the family. It's you—and it's strong in you. You gave me justice. I will be there for you."

"*We'll* be there," Christian corrected.

They faded away, and Cheyenne stood alone in the old cemetery, amid the rows of tombs and marble angels, St. Michaels, and weeping Madonna statues.

Night was beginning to fall. In the distance, she could see the old plantation house, high up on its hill, well maintained but still haunting in the looming dark with its columns, cupola and Victorian gingerbread balconies. To an unfamiliar observer, the very house could seem dark and evil.

But the house was not frightening to Cheyenne, nor were the darkness or rising mist—or the row upon row of tombs that graced the cemetery.

It was not the dead who threatened the innocent.

It was the evil in certain human beings who were very much alive.

1

"Whoa—what's that one?"

The question was asked by a boy of maybe sixteen or seventeen visiting the museum with another young man about his age, and a young lady who was, it seemed, his girlfriend.

The three stood just feet away from Andre Rousseau, staring at the same display.

The creature in question, seen rising above terrified teenagers paddling down the bayou in a pirogue, was monstrous. His chest was huge, his waist drawn in, and his creator had given him odd and ominous proportions, like a dangerously starved canine of a paranormal variety.

Andre couldn't help but answer. "That, my friends, is the rougarou, closely related to the loupgarou, or werewolf. He can be depicted many ways, but I'd say the museum has done an excellent job here. See how he stands so menacingly above the couple, fangs shimmering as if covered with dripping anticipation. That's part of the legend—beware the moon, beware darkness, and don't mess around at night."

The three of them were looking at him wide-eyed. Andre supposed that he had spoken rather dramatically.

Finally, the girl laughed. "Like many a legend—or a fairy tale by the Grimm brothers—the rougarou helps keep people in line, huh?"

"I do imagine so at times," Andre agreed.

"You know all about it," the girl said.

Andre shrugged.

Beneath the tableau were plaques explaining that the creature was known to inhabit Cajun country, that it had found its way to southern Louisiana along with the French colonists who had first come to settle the region, but in time had come to be the primary creature of the region feared by children...and that might still haunt the minds of adults by night in the darkness and shadows of the bayous, islands and swamps.

"Ah, well, we have our myths and legends everywhere," Andre said. "I happen to come from an area of Louisiana where the legends are strong."

"You're from Louisiana?" the boy who seemed to be with the young woman asked.

"I am, sir."

"But you have all your teeth!"

He had to wonder at first if the young man had been joking.

He had not.

The words were not spoken with any mean intent

at all—the kid was truly surprised. Andre lowered his head, half wincing, and half smiling.

"Yeah, I know how my region has often been depicted on TV," he said pleasantly. "But please, trust me—most of my friends have all their teeth, too."

"And you're so good-looking!" the girl gushed. "For an older man, of course."

An older man. Well, he had just turned thirty-one.

"Thank you," he told the girl.

He pointed to another display. "Honey Island Swamp Monster—that one can be found down in southern Louisiana, too. We, as human beings, have often needed monsters to explain terrible things happening, and we're great at making up things when we're afraid of shadows by night. Enjoy the exhibit."

He waved as the kids grinned at him, thanked him and moved on.

Andre did think that it was a great exhibit—the rougarou was created so realistically that it disturbed him. Not that he believed in such creatures, but the very name had a bad taste due to past associations with it in his area of southern Louisiana.

Kids—especially middle school and high school kids—loved cemeteries and creepy old plantation homes. Nothing like hiding out in them and telling tall tales, daring one another to step into whatever family tombs they might find open.

But Andre's hometown had had a real monster to go with the fairy tales—the Rougarou. A man, but one who had ripped several women to shreds, as if he had been a fanged and clawed beast.

And later, the Artiste, the man who had imitated the Rougarou—one Andre had come to know about all too well.

There would always be those ready to imitate monsters.

He gave himself a mental shake.

The displays around him were full of imaginary creatures. The American Museum of Natural History had allotted a massive exhibit hall to a temporary exhibit on the Legends of America, and there were tableaus and displays of mythic creatures from all over the United States—along with the cultures, peoples and places with whom they were associated. The Abominable Snowman was there in his many guises, along with the Jersey Devil and many more.

"Hey—not a bad day for you, my friend," Angela Hawkins teased, heading his way. "Not only did the young ones note that you do have all your teeth, but you're also really good-looking—for an older guy." The blonde woman smiled at him.

"Ha ha. Maybe I've convinced someone to question stereotypes about Louisiana," Andre said, grinning.

"Good job," Angela agreed. "So, have you ever met that guy?" she asked, indicating the rougarou.

Angela was one of the original members of the Krewe of Hunters, a specialized unit of the FBI Andre had joined early in the summer. What cases they accepted filtered through Angela, who was also married to Jackson Crow, the field director of the unit.

She was a brilliant woman, in Andre's estimation.

One of those people who did not believe in micro-management, who trusted her coworkers, and was also ready to dig in and help at the drop of a hat. She managed to incorporate a tremendous ability at organization with a deep understanding of human nature—so necessary in their work. She had a way with people.

Yesterday, a docent had run screaming out of the museum, swearing that one of the creatures—a rougarou—had come to life, and was out to get her.

Adam Harrison, a wealthy philanthropist as well as creator and director of the Krewe, was a major contributor to the museum, and since he was able to do so, he had sent agents in.

Andre had just closed a case in Colorado, one settled very nicely because of a phenomenon that almost never occurred—a dead man's ghost had led them straight to his killer. Andre was glad of an assignment that was basically a little R & R. While this had seemed almost silly—none of them actually believed that a museum creature was coming to life—he and Angela had come to investigate the situation.

They had quickly discovered the source of the terror—a faulty wire in the animatronic rougarou had caused the docent to panic, certain that something was wrong, something was haunted…and something dire was about to happen.

The Krewe of Hunters hadn't really been needed—an electrical engineer could have easily solved the problem. But in talking with the docent, they had learned that she had gotten her promotion and was supervising the staff for the exhibit because a coworker had recently died, and she had felt guilty, certain that she had stolen the job from a dead man.

Angela had talked her down while Andre had arranged for one of the engineers to repair the creature.

Now, situation solved, they were enjoying the exhibit on legendary creatures of America.

"Did I ever encounter a rougarou? No, I never did," Andre told her. "Of course, I did hear plenty of stories, but then…" He paused, shrugging. "I've been gone a long time. I grew up near Lafayette until I was about fifteen, but then my parents moved to New Orleans. When I was a kid our camp counselors loved to tell tall tales. But you and Jackson know New Orleans and environs well, right? Didn't the Krewe of Hunters form and have its first case in New Orleans?"

"Yes, it did," Angela said. "Adam Harrison managed to convince the powers that be that he should head a special unit. Because a congressman's wife had supposedly been murdered by a ghost, we started out right in the French Quarter. But you and I both know there's a world of difference between New Orleans and the countryside, which is part of the charm of the state—you have so many cultures and peoples coming together within not so many miles."

"I've been gone from New Orleans for a while now, too," Andre told her, though he had a feeling Angela was the kind of agent who would read up on a partner before an assignment. "I was with the NYC office before joining the Krewe."

"Do you still have family there?" Angela asked.

"Cousins spread throughout the state. My parents have a small house on Bourbon Street close to Esplanade, but they spend most of their time in Florida now, down south on the west coast of the state. Don't get me wrong—I love New Orleans." He turned to look at her. "But I have never felt that I'm more where I need to be than when I'm working with the Krewe."

"It's a good match for all of us," Angela stated. "Let's go see that *hodag* thing—monster from Wisconsin."

"Sure, let's take the time we have," Andre agreed. But he found himself pausing, looking back at the rougarou. He'd been looking at the damned thing half the day. And still—faulty wire or no—it was still disturbing him.

He lowered his head grimly, shaking it. He had certainly never encountered a rougarou out in the bayou.

But once, something akin to a real monster had existed. Long ago, Civil War era—way before a man might be called a "serial killer," there had been one at work in his area. Victims had been strewn across southern Louisiana. But war had been raging. A few more deaths might not be noted. He'd had some odd habits, though—perhaps he'd been an artist coming latently into his talent. He'd left pictures, and he'd been known as the Rougarou.

And years later a killer had imitated him, right in

Andre's backyard again—this one becoming known as the Artiste—killing across southern Louisiana.

"Andre?" Angela called to him from the doorway to the next exhibit.

"I'm on my way!" he said cheerfully.

But even as they played tourist types at the museum for an afternoon, he was disturbed to experience a strange feeling. He needed to shake off the rougarou. *Coincidence—or a bizarre premonition?*

Because he and Angela didn't go home that night; they were summoned back to the offices in Alexandria right as they were leaving the museum.

At five o'clock, he was sitting in Jackson Crow's office. Not that such a thing was unusual; the Krewe didn't necessarily keep nine-to-five hours. Then again, neither did many of their traditional counterparts. And it was natural that Angela should head back—she was married to Jackson Crow, and would have met up with him at headquarters, anyway.

Angela accompanied Andre into Jackson's office, perhaps a little surprised herself since it seemed that something was going on that she didn't know about yet.

Jackson urged them both into the chairs in front of his desk. Yet even as Andre entered the office and saw Jackson's work board, he knew the feeling the rougarou had given him had meant something.

Jackson perched on the edge of his desk and began to talk.

"I received a call from Keri Wolf, the researcher recently involved in the case at the Miller Inn and

Tavern, and now living in Alexandria, Virginia, with Joe Dunhill. A few years back, she worked on a true crime book that had to do with a serial killer, a man named Ryan Lassiter who was caught over ten years ago now. Keri usually worked on historic crimes—as in crimes from centuries past. But because this was solved, for one, and because it also correlated back to crimes that took place well over a century ago, she worked on a book detailing the murders. Keri had been taking a special term of classes at Loyola, and there she heard all the stories. One of her college roommates had been directly involved with the case—the girl Keri roomed with had a cousin who was one of the Artiste's victims."

"Very sad," Andre murmured. Yes, he knew the case. The entire country had heard about the Ryan Lassiter case, and you couldn't have missed it in Louisiana and across the South. But Andre knew it better than most; Jimmy Mercury had asked him to play with him that day for a jazz funeral. The very service for the final victim, and the day Ryan Lassiter had finally been caught.

The deceased had been the victim of a serial killer who had plagued the Gulf coast of Louisiana.

Before being apprehended, Ryan Lassiter had been known as the Artiste—he had tormented families and friends by sending pictures of his victims to the press once he'd imprisoned them.

And then again, when they were dead—and prepped for burial.

Andre had read Keri Wolf's book—one of her

first, and the one that made her work known. She'd done an excellent job of research. Keri had a tendency to wind up at "haunted" locales, finding all the known facts, putting forward theories, but never stating a definitive solution. She covered crimes that had not been solved—and most probably never would be.

Andre liked Keri very much as a person—she'd interviewed him a few years ago in New York City as part of her research. It had been good to see her again at Krewe headquarters recently.

He'd never imagined, however, that an old case that had been closed years ago might be something that would come up again now.

He stared at Jackson, wondering if his field director was aware that he'd been more involved in the case than anything in his file might have told. Probably. Keri knew Andre had been there that day apprehending Lassiter. She'd likely told Jackson.

"Keri's book was very thorough. No one today really knows about what went on in the 1800s," Andre told them. "The first case dated back to the Civil War. They never caught the killer. Back then, they called *him* the Rougarou. The bodies of eight women were found in various stages of decomposition in and around the city of New Orleans and out in Houma, Lafayette and New Iberia. Sketches of them had been found—looking beautiful and alive, and then there were sketches of them all laid out in coffins. As you can imagine, things were a mess—New Orleans was under the military rule of the man they called Beast Butler, and relations between the occupying soldiers and the residents were not good. The Civil War gave way to Reconstruction. Locals were of the belief that a Yankee soldier was the killer, but in my mind, it's more likely that it was someone who knew the area very well, and traveled frequently, a merchant or other." He paused, unhappily reflecting on the past he remembered too well. "There's an old cemetery between New Iberia and Lafayette, just outside a little place called Broussard, that started out as a family plantation. The first owner, Gerard Justine, arrived in 1765 along with the first two hundred Acadians to settle the area. As the years rolled along, more and more people were interred there. It's still owned and operated by the Justine family, but they operate the cemetery as a business for the public and burials are—and have always been—nondenominational. The old plantation house, where many funerals and viewings are held, is reputed to be one of the most haunted locations in the state, if not in the country."

"Yes," Jackson said. "The Justine Plantation Mortuary Home and Cemetery are famous—or infamous—for being haunted. One of the suspects in the Rougarou case from the 1800s was the owner at the time, an Emil Justine. But Keri's book outlined several possible suspects. She didn't presume to name the killer, she just compared the Rougarou to the Artiste, or rather, the Artiste to him." He was quiet a minute. "So, Keri is still good friends with her old roommate, who now happens to be with the Bureau, too. Special Agent Cheyenne Donegal had been assigned to the Miami office until she was pulled back to NOLA, special assignment on a current case, not because she was involved before, but because she's from the area. It's starting over. Someone is taking women and killing them in a way that echoes the Artiste."

"And that's how the Krewe came in?" Andre asked. "Special Agent Donegal called her old friend Keri Wolf who, in turn, called us?"

"Exactly. You are more than familiar with the Artiste case, right?"

"Yeah," Andre said quietly.

He'd been there for part of it—well, at least at the last funeral.

Out of high school, Andre had enlisted in the navy. But right before he'd gone off to training, his old friend Jimmy Mercury had called him—his guitar player had become ill and they were supposed to play for the funeral of a local girl who'd just been murdered.

Of course, he'd said yes. He hadn't known the dead girl himself, though he had known several of her friends.

And when a girl had accused a man at the graveside, Andre had tackled Ryan Lassiter along with Jimmy. Held him until the cops had come.

Soon after, he'd headed to the United States Naval Recruit Training Center just north of Chicago, graduated and been sent to California to board his first ship, heading toward the Pacific. News from home had contained the details as they became known. His mother had kept up with him to tell him how wor-

ried she was about his sister, even if the Artiste had
been caught, tried and given his sentence—his sister
had kept in touch to let him know that their mother
was driving her crazy.

"So, this is him," Jackson said, pointing to an
eight-by-ten glossy photograph on a large board he
kept in his office, "Ryan Lassiter. He was responsible
for the deaths of six young women...that we know of.
His crimes might have entailed much more, but his
attempts to commute or forestall his death penalty—
which did take nearly a decade to implement—meant
that he teased prosecutors and judges and the police,
telling them that he could lead them to more bodies,
if he was simply allowed to live. However, since he
had failed at three escape attempts, and killed two
men in the process of the last, he was duly executed
just a year ago by lethal injection at the Louisiana
State Penitentiary."

Jackson was quiet a minute. "As you know, if a
single juror is opposed to the death penalty, the sentence becomes life. There wasn't a soul who opposed
this man's execution, except for Lassiter himself.
By all reports, he came across as a charming and
personable man, which is why a nurse and a guard
wound up dead during his last escape attempt. He
was active a long time—over a year—with no one
suspecting him. He was the handsome man every
woman adored, every man wanted to be."

"But he *was* executed," Andre said.

"Yes. Getting back to the Krewe and in more detail why we're determined to take on this case. We

know that Ryan Lassiter, the Artiste, was copycatting the unsolved crimes that took place during and just after the Civil War. And now we have a copycat in action again," Jackson said, holding up a picture, this one of an attractive young woman.

"This is Alicia Holden—in life. And this…" He added another picture, saying, "This is Alicia Holden after death. A second woman was kidnapped and killed, Anna Gunn."

Alicia's pictures were hung up—one of her alive, and another of her corpse. Then Anna's.

Another picture went up. "Cindy Metcalf, newly famous from a TV show, went missing from Biloxi and then her picture was delivered to a news station, and then another. Her prominence—and the crossing of state lines, since her body was discovered in Lafayette—called for the federal government to come in."

Then, Jackson added just one picture, that of a twentysomething brunette woman.

"A fourth young woman has been taken from New Orleans—Lacey Murton. Local police and a team member from the bureau, Special Agent Cheyenne Donegal, have been pursuing a suspect, a man who vacated a table in a Bourbon Street restaurant where the first photo was found this time, not far from the bed-and-breakfast where the girl had been staying."

The pictures were disturbing—the pictures of the women in death. Naturally, knowing that they were dead made the pictures upsetting. But not in the way such images could sometimes chill the blood of the most hardened agent. They were not images of murder victims covered in blood or brain matter, burned to ash, skeletal or gruesome in a more customary way.

They were chilling because they were so pristine. In death, they were left as beautifully as any mother could hope a child might appear in a coffin for one last viewing.

And for Andre, they were all too familiar.

Jackson stopped speaking for a moment and put another picture on the board. Then he continued, "That's Braxton Trudeau, known to be handsome and charming, as well. So handsome and charming that he started by fleecing a number of older women out of their retirement incomes. He did a two-year stint for armed robbery. How he got out so quickly on that one, I don't know, except that no one was injured in the attempted heist. He is being pursued now."

"The man has a record and he may be good-looking, but that doesn't make him guilty of murder. And—I'm looking at this from a legal standpoint the fact that a picture was found on a table after he left an establishment wouldn't stand for much of anything," Andre said. "I'm not saying that the man is not guilty, but I'd think we'd need a hell of a lot more evidence than what we're seeing so far. If law enforcement hopes to see him convicted."

Jackson nodded. "You're right. This man was, however, born in Houma, Louisiana, and has worked in Lafayette, Houma and New Orleans. He works most frequently as a musician, allowing him flexibility with his time, and it allows him to travel from place to place for reasons which might also be easily explained and accepted. At any rate, Agent Donegal isn't quite so convinced. They're pursuing Braxton Trudeau for questioning at least, though they've had some trouble locating him since declaring him a person of interest. Local police had tried to keep the manhunt quiet, but eventually had to show his picture on the news and ask the population for help. They received an anonymous lead that he was going to be in the French Quarter tonight. And as I said, a waitress had found a picture of one of the missing girls on a table right after he vacated it, as if he'd left a calling card. We have other agents from NOLA and we're not unfamiliar with the city ourselves. If necessary, we'll join you on the case, Andre. But for now, I'd like to get you down there tonight, working with the lead detective on the case and getting up to speed with Special Agent Donegal." He hesitated. "Naturally, this string of deaths has led to the media giving the new killer a name—he's become known in the press as the Mortician."

"He leaves them picture-perfect—as if ready for burial," Andre murmured. "And I'm ready to go whenever. I'm always packed."

Angela stood, looking down at him. "I'll have all the files prepared for you, hard copy and email, and your driver will have them when he picks you up for the airport." She turned to Jackson. "A driver is picking him up for the airport, right?"

"Yes, and the Krewe plane will be waiting. I'll see

to it that you have the full files. As with Lassiter's victims, these women have been taken in one place and left in another, covering a lot of the Gulf area from Biloxi out to Lafayette—a distance of about two hundred miles. You'll have all the particulars," Jackson said.

"I'll see to it," Angela promised him.

Andre thanked her, nodded to Jackson and followed Angela out of the office.

"Rougarou," she murmured. She paused and looked at him a long moment. "You know a lot more about the old cases than you were saying."

"I really don't," he told her. "Sure, growing up in that area, everyone heard about the Civil War killer everyone called the Rougarou. Thing is, at the time, so many people were dying constantly—in battle, due to disease—that finding a murderer wasn't necessarily the priority that it would be today. And he was traveling around the Gulf, so…he became more legend than reality. I'm sure Keri Wolf knows way more than I do. And as for the Artiste, yeah, I remember it all well enough. Mothers were terrified for their daughters, no one went anywhere alone, but I'd gotten past the age when we played in the old cemetery." He paused, shrugging. "That area isn't like, say, St. Louis No. 1—or 2 or 3, for that matter. Justine Plantation Mortuary Home and Cemetery lies in an area between Lafayette and New Iberia that is sparsely inhabited. A lot of old houses are out on spits of land in bayou country. There's a stone fence surrounding the property, falling apart in places, and the gates were seldom closed. People came and went all the time. The family didn't live on the property and they didn't employ guards. Anyway, like I said, by the time the Artiste got busy, I was out of high school and heading into the navy. But I did happen to be there when the Artiste was brought down. I was playing guitar for a jazz band accompaniment of a coffin to a tomb. And the young woman being interred was the final victim of the Artiste."

"Maybe you shouldn't be on this case," Angela said.

"And maybe I'm exactly the one who does belong on the case," Andre said.

Angela nodded. "Maybe," she said slowly.

She started to walk again and then turned back to him.

"So, do you know Cheyenne Donegal already?"

He shook his head. "No, why?"

"You were at the funeral of the killer's last victim— that would have been her cousin's funeral."

Andre paused, remembering.

No, he'd never met Cheyenne Donegal. But he did remember her. She had been the tall, red-haired young woman who had pointed at Lassiter and started screaming. He could recall—despite the chaos after—because she had stood so determined, a vision in a black-jacketed skirt-suit, conviction in her eyes. Of course, she'd been a young teenager back then. He might not know her now.

"I don't know her," he said softly.

"But at least you will have history and a lot more in common," Angela said.

Yes, history, and a lot more.

The Rougarou and the Artiste.

And now, the Mortician.

The man half lay and half sat against one of the oldest buildings in the French Quarter, eyes open, glazed and staring eerily ahead. There was no sense, Cheyenne knew, in searching for his pulse.

Blood stained his shirt, running down from a gaping wound at his throat. It was drying, coagulating and growing cold, staining the sidewalk and the old historic building, as well.

A bloody knife remained beneath his hand—as if he had savagely struck the blow himself.

The way he seemed to be looking, staring out at the world, suggested he'd been stunned, amazed by his demise.

"It's Braxton Trudeau," Cheyenne murmured, recognizing the man they'd been investigating for the last several weeks. Their key suspect in the so-called Mortician murders that had been plaguing New Orleans and environs for months now.

A copycat killer, replicating the crimes of the Artiste, the man who had been active years ago, taking so many young lives.

Trudeau had been thirty-seven years old, with rich curly dark hair all about his face, lean features and dark eyes—dark eyes that seemed oddly haunting now with their strange, blank stare. A handsome man, and in Cheyenne's mind, the most dangerous of all killers, the kind who could charm a young woman and keep her smiling and laughing…almost until death. And yet…

Even now, she just wasn't certain.

"Interesting place to kill himself," Detective Pierre Fournier said.

He stood a distance from Cheyenne. He looked at her and grimaced. "Obviously dead. We'll have to call the medical examiner in right away, then await his determinations. Nothing else for us to do here tonight."

Yes, they needed to call in the medical examiner as he or she would be the first to touch the body— no digging around it by them before that, according to the law.

When a suspect was obviously dead, no, they weren't supposed to touch the body, dig into the pockets for clues or disturb it in any way.

But they sure as hell needed to control the situation.

While this man—perhaps the killer they'd been seeking, as Fournier seemed to assume—had apparently been killed by his own hand or another in a true wee hour of the morning, it was no longer that rare in-between time when the area wasn't exactly quiet, but quieter than usual.

They were a few blocks north of Bourbon and in a slightly more residential area of the Quarter than Bourbon Street itself, but the entire Quarter was a tourist mecca, and pedestrian traffic was going to be picking up soon. One of the city's larger hotels was near, along with a few commercial establishments, not to mention the dog walkers, or the locals who worked 7:00 a.m. shifts in restaurants, hospitals, schools and more. It was, yes, a late-night city. Or, truly, a city that never slept, or barely slept.

And it was going to come to full wakeful life very soon.

Fournier, naturally, wanted all this over and done with. And she understood; he had been working the case a long time. He'd been the one to suggest that there might have been victims before the killer had solidified his signature—or truly learned his copycat expertise.

Cheyenne eyed Detective Fournier, her look clearly stating that he was negligent to leave this sight to be picked up on dozens of cell phones—and perhaps witnessed by the young and innocent, sure to be traumatized for years to come.

"Yeah, okay, okay, let's get the tape up, and block off this part of the street," Fournier said.

He was a heavyset man, sweating in the humidity, even if the sun had yet to really begin to rise. It was almost fall in some parts of the country, but a cooling trend came slowly to southern Louisiana, even if they had witnessed a bit of snow in the sky their last few winters.

"Hey!" he called out to the patrol officers who hovered nearby. "Let's get moving, *mes amis*, Special Agent Donegal wants discretion!"

The patrol officers were two of the best cops

Cheyenne had ever met. She'd seen these men in action since she'd been here, out on the streets at night, seeking the man they'd been calling the Mortician—a killer who had probably been at work much longer than had been suspected. He'd likely killed several girls around the Gulf area, but only come into prominence three weeks ago with the murder of a tourist from LA—a young singer who had recently come in first on one of the very popular network competitions.

Cindy Metcalf's body had been found just outside the city in a small parish town known as Broussard. The fact that Cindy had been a rising star had led to a media frenzy, and it brought to light the previously overlooked story regarding the bodies of two "junkie" prostitutes who had been found in the city and surrounding area in the preceding months.

Cindy Metcalf had come from LA and disappeared out of Biloxi, Mississippi, and then been found in Louisiana, and that had brought in the FBI.

Cheyenne had been born in the town of Broussard, so her supervising field director had decided that she should be the first one to test the waters with the local police—and hopefully bring down a highly dangerous serial killer as quickly as possible.

If it ever came up at work, Cheyenne had always downplayed her own involvement with the Artiste. Oddly enough, it hadn't been difficult. She had been the first to identify Lassiter, but after that, there had been such a frenzy that few people remembered who had first screamed out his name when he'd been standing in the cemetery, watching the agonizing finale of her cousin's life.

On the street, the patrol officers quickly had the area cordoned off; Fournier finished calling it in and walked over to Cheyenne, a broad smile on his face as he set a brotherly arm around her shoulder. "Special Agent Donegal, you are a good luck charm. Hell, you come on the case, and the next thing we know, the killer does himself in. Must have been afraid of you. No trial, nothing—we got him. Well, he got himself."

She smiled and politely extricated herself from his grasp. "Pierre, we don't have any proof that he was the murderer. And until the medical examiner says so, we don't know for certain that he killed himself."

"Oh, come on. What, did you turn into a defense attorney on me? We were chasing him. The picture was found where he'd been sitting. The guy had a record. And we may never know where he started, and just how many women he killed. He got himself good. He must have been sure that we were onto him and that things were going to get a lot worse. This is him, Cheyenne. And he's dead. And you can try to figure it from here to eternity, but you're never going to have all the answers. As for me, I'm doing the paperwork as fast as I can. And then, you know what? I'm hopping on a cruise ship with my wife and going to a beautiful tropic isle with a great beach. I think you should be doing the same."

As they stood there, the wagon from the coroner's office drove up—and right behind it was a van from a local news channel. As a small crowd was already beginning to grow, the officers held the media and onlookers at bay.

The ME on duty was Dr. Kevin Morley; he shook hands with Cheyenne and Pierre and asked a few cursory questions before gloving his hands and hunkering down over the body. He produced a wallet and a pad and pen from the dead man's pocket, causing Fournier to say, "See? It's him."

"He's been dead less than an hour," Dr. Morely told them, speaking over his shoulder. "One solid swipe to the throat. Caught the artery."

"Pretty cut-and-dried," Fournier murmured.

"He must have been in one hell of a panic and been one determined man," Dr. Morley said. "Of course, the blade is very sharp, but...wow, taking a knife to your own throat. Then again..."

"Then again, what?" Cheyenne asked.

"Well, the knife was in his hand just so—you didn't try to touch him when you found him, right?" Morley asked.

"No, we did not," Cheyenne assured him.

"Yes, it's possible that he did it himself," Morley said.

"And possible that he did not? That the knife was placed by his hand?" Cheyenne asked.

"Possibly. I don't know if I'll be able to give you more on that or not," Morley said. "But autopsy on this man will be tomorrow morning."

"Thank you," Cheyenne told him. "We'll be there."

"Detective—Special Agent!" one of the patrol officers called, ducking below the tape to reach them. He appeared distressed and disgusted. "Can one of you do something, say something... I really don't want to have a push-and-shove with the media."

"I'll take it," Fournier said.

Cheyenne had tried to keep civil the entire time she had worked with the man—and he was a good detective, following up clues and ready to hit the streets.

But he also held to his certainty that he was right.

And she...she just wasn't sure.

"No," she said. The FBI had been given lead; right now, she was taking it.

She stepped forward, heading to the edge of the crime scene tape, and lifted a hand to the gathered waiting reporters. "Please, in the interest of sharing nothing but facts, I can only tell you right now that we were pursuing a suspect in the Mortician murders, and in our search, found a man dead. At this moment, we cannot confirm foul play. Please allow us all to do our work. As soon as we know more facts regarding the situation, they will be shared with you."

"But women can go out safely at night again, right?" someone shouted at her.

Are the unwary—be they men or women ever truly safe by night?

Or day?

"The deceased was a person of interest. We do not know if he was the killer we were seeking or not. Please, give us time. That's all for now."

Her voice was firm. Most of the reporters milling around knew that they'd gotten all they were going to get. They were moving back to position themselves in front of their cameramen or were pulling out their cell phones to call the story in.

One man kept coming toward Cheyenne. He was tall with dark hair and a lean, sharp face. He had a breadth of shoulders that indicated a man who worked at his physical fitness, and he moved through the crowd easily and with authority—people gave way before him.

There was something oddly familiar about him.

"Special Agent Donegal?" he asked, reaching into his jacket pocket to pull out a billfold.

"Yes?" she said, frowning as she looked at his credentials.

"Andre Rousseau," he told her.

"You're from the Krewe of Hunters?" she asked softly, not wanting Fournier to hear her use that term.

Had she been foolish—should she have begged off this case? And had she overreacted, calling Keri, telling her what was going on...?

"I am from the Krewe," Andre said. He looked over at the dead man and the medical examiner for a long moment, and then back to her. "And I know you," he told her.

"You know me?" she asked, frowning. And then she gasped.

He had been there; he was the dark-haired young guitarist who had run down Lassiter with Jimmy Mercury. He had seen her scream and point...

He looked at her with steady dark eyes. Clearly sensing that Fournier was about to come join them, he asked quickly, "Am I late to the party? Or is the party just beginning? And I'm curious, but do your superiors know exactly how intimately involved you may be with this case? I think they'd want to know how pleased you might be with the death of a man who was imitating the Artiste."

What was he saying? He couldn't possibly be suggesting that she had killed this suspect rather than take a chance that a killer copying her cousin's murderer might get away?

Well, she had talked to Keri Wolf.

She had suggested that she might need a different variety of help.

Now she had gotten it.

And she was tempted to slug that help hard—with a well-placed right hook to the jaw!

2

There was all kinds of wisdom about going back home. Some sayings were about the fact that you could never go back—others suggested that there was no place like it.

For Andre, *home* meant much of the southern coast of the state. His parents had been artists— good ones—and they had traveled a great deal, and kept houses in several places, the last of which had been the place on Bourbon down close to Esplanade.

He did love the old house. He loved New Orleans and had spent a great deal of time in the city—even when he had lived in Lafayette. New Orleans had played host to different cultures; it had gone through war, storms and floods. Andrew Jackson and the pirate Lafitte had managed to put aside their differences, and beat back one of the world's mightiest navies of the time after a war had officially been over. This city on the river had grown to become one of the most unique and diverse cities in the country.

The city was anything you wanted it to be since it had so much to offer.

He walked the Quarter for a while. He'd attend the autopsy on their dead suspect tomorrow morning, but he hadn't been in on the chase, and he wasn't required to take part in the massive paperwork, which was going to occupy most of the morning for Agent Donegal and Detective Fournier.

Agent Donegal didn't seem particularly fond of him, though he was judging that on a brief acquaintance.

He headed down Bourbon, past the many tourist stops—the bars, the strip joints, the clubs and restaurants. Like much of New Orleans, the street was a study in contrasts, with elegant hotels and eateries set amid neon and tawdry signs for "cheapest beer" and a new one he hadn't seen before: Best-Looking Human Beings Mostly Naked!

But there was more to Bourbon Street.

Galatoire's, one of the city's most renowned restaurants, sat at 209 Bourbon, while the Cat's Meow, a wild karaoke venue, was at 701, and Lafitte's Blacksmith Shop—built in approximately 1770 during the Spanish colonial period and reputed to have once been a smithy owned by the famed pirate—stood at 941. Lafitte's was now an extremely popular bar/restaurant, visited by locals and tourists by the gazillions, but the sense of history remained strong around it.

Then, as he kept going, he reached his family's home—what was called an "American town house," and an odd one, since most such homes were Uptown in the Garden District and beyond. Nomenclature was a little mismatched, but that was because of the way the city had grown from day one, being French, Spanish, French again and American. *Most* of the architecture in the French Quarter had been built during the Spanish colonial period, since two fires had all but destroyed the city in the late 1700s. When the original mostly English Americans had come, they had started building in the areas of the Garden District, Uptown, the Irish Channel and beyond. The Rousseaus' home had been built around 1827 on a site that still had some foundations left, along with a sea of old ash. It had granite Greek revival columns, and while narrow and built almost wall to wall with its Creole-style neighbors, it had beautiful double galleries with cast-iron railings on the ground and second levels.

He pulled out his keys at the entrance. He'd dropped his travel bag off that morning first thing, but now he meant to spend some time here. He needed to lay out his files and review, just in case the situation wasn't as pat as it had appeared. It had been a while since he'd been home—even though it stood empty most of the time, his parents refused to rent the space out. They'd basically turned the residence over to him—other than for their flash visits for Jazz Fest and a few other occasions.

He paused for a moment at the doorway, thinking that it resembled a mini plantation house—or, at least, what most people considered a plantation house to be. The word actually referred to a large farm and could also refer to all kinds of building styles as well, but his home did, in a small way, resemble the homes construed as the elegant plantations most often seen in literature.

"Andre! Andre Rousseau, as I live and breathe!"

He turned. Their neighbor Rita Colin, silver-haired, slim and still elegant at about eighty, had stepped out onto the small porch of her more typical Creole style house. She beamed at him. "You home for a bit, son? I do say, I miss your dear mother and father being close, but I get those emails from them all the time, filled with fantastic beach pictures, so I do not blame them in the least for having moved on. They are doing beautiful work down there, too, enjoying those golden years they're coming into! But it will be good to have you around the next few days—or hours! Son, I have a big pot of jambalaya going, hotter than the surface of the sun, but I do have sweet cheese grits, too, in case your palette has toned down."

"Miss Rita, fine to see you. I have a bit of work right now, but I'll take you up on that food later."

It was barely ten o'clock.

"What am I saying? Got some homemade beignets going, too, if you like?"

"I'd love, but I'm going to get a few things done first, if you don't mind."

"Of course, you're an FBI man now. Oh!" she said, gasping suddenly. "You're here because of the dreadful killings, which makes it doubly nice that you've come. Though, I was watching the news. Seemed the fellow was caught or killed himself this morning, or something like that. Anyway, I've had my Ajax to protect me. There he is now, my great little man!"

Ajax was a terrier mix with an underbite and scruffy black fur. He resembled something out of the comics and he was about the size of a small pot.

Seeing Andre, he let out a vicious bark…while wagging his tail.

The dog ran quickly across the sidewalk from porch to porch and Andre stooped to pet him.

Dogs, he thought, never forgot people.

"He does love you so. He's getting on now, though. What will I do without him?" Rita wondered aloud.

Rita was a charming and generous woman, and she had loved her husband, Harvey, deeply. He'd been gone just two years. Harvey had been an amazing man, too—from his desk, he'd dealt in stocks, and done it well. After Katrina, he'd set out in his boat to help with rescue efforts in the flooded areas of the city—saving people and never protesting once when they refused to be saved without their pets. On her own, Rita had turned her efforts to various charities.

She was still lonely, Andre knew. He would make sure to spend some time with her.

"Right now…" he said, and then paused.

He could see Special Agent Cheyenne Donegal heading down Bourbon on foot—and right toward him. He found her to be a very attractive woman, bright hair gleaming in the sunlight, dark glasses shading her eyes, and her stride long and purpose-ful. She had the look of an important executive, and yet there was nothing that gave into vanity about her apparel—her shoes were practical, black with low block heels, and her pantsuit was pure business.

"Oh, you have a lady caller," Rita said. "Ajax, you get back here! The good Lord knows—Andy's parents sure would love some grandchildren!"

"She's a business associate, Rita," he explained quickly.

Cheyenne Donegal had just reached the sidewalk in front of Rita's porch.

"Why, honey, you are just too pretty to be a law officer!" Rita said, and being Rita, she stepped off the porch to offer her a handshake. "Rita, Rita Colin, miss, and you call on me for anything you need, from an emery board to a decent meal."

He was momentarily concerned that Cheyenne would brush off the old woman; but he was foolish to have thought she would take out her frustration with him on someone else. He knew where she came from—manners were just about inbred.

"How do you do, ma'am. Cheyenne, Cheyenne Donegal. And thank you so much," she said.

Ajax made his way over to the newcomer, barking a terrier bark, but still waving his funny-fur flag of a tail.

Cheyenne stooped to pet the dog. Then she rose and looked at Andre. "If you'll excuse us both now, Mrs. Colin, I have some business to discuss with…" She'd clearly been about to say *Special Agent Rous-*

seau, but she apparently decided that was too formal in front of this woman. "With Andre," she finished.

"Of course," Rita said. "Ajax, you come on in with me. And don't you forget, you young people, that I'm right here for whatever you may need." She started to open her door but paused. "I heard they got him. I heard they got the guy they're calling the Mortician. You'd know, right, if that was true?"

"A person of interest was found dead this morning, yes," Cheyenne said. "There's so much to sort through—we're not sure."

"Rita, I promise you, I'll let you know how things are going," Andre said. He looked at Cheyenne. "Shall we?"

He opened his door and motioned for Cheyenne to walk in before him. The house offered a narrow entry and hallway, with stairs almost immediately leading to the second floor. His small suitcase was still sitting near the door. At one time, the ground floor had been a dressmaker's shop. That had long ago changed.

"Please," he murmured, indicating the parlor inside on the right.

"You were already setting up, I see." She sounded surprised to note that he already had a corkboard there.

"Nope, that's from an old case. I had to come home for a funeral a while back and I was working via phone with some people who were out in Oregon. I like boards—cell phones are great but looking at a big picture, or a bunch of big pictures, works for me. Have a seat. I did plan on getting started, but it appears that I might have gotten here after the fact."

"Detective Fournier seems to think so," she said.

She didn't take a seat. She paced the small parlor, noting the artwork on the walls, the period sofa and chairs, and the entertainment center to the left of the fireplace—pretty much blocked by his large board.

"You don't think so," he said.

She sighed, picking up one of the decorative pillows and hugging it to herself as she plopped down on the sofa. "Too convenient, too easy. I mean, sometimes if it looks, sounds and acts like a duck, it is a duck. But do you really think this kind of a killer would suddenly run through the streets and slash his own throat? I don't. His ego has to be as big as a house—a very large house. The killer's ego, not Fournier's. I didn't mean to imply that. Fournier is a good cop. He's just tired, and the only evidence or plausible suspect we've had is the dead man, Braxton Trudeau."

"But?"

"Okay, so all the usual things were done—credit card checks on people, hotels, travel…and yes, Trudeau could have been in each of the locations when a woman was kidnapped. We don't know where they were murdered, just where their bodies were discovered." She hesitated. "I was working in Miami. I didn't hear about it until the second victim… I was and wasn't surprised when they called me up here on assignment. I knew right away someone was imitating the Artiste." She sighed.

Andre took the armchair by the sofa facing her, and she set aside the toss pillow to lean forward, making sure she had his full attention. "I know that many people questioned whether Lassiter was the killer, decrying the death penalty," she continued. "But he confessed, and from what I heard, he tried to bargain his way out of the death penalty, telling authorities that he would let them know where they could find more victims, women he had killed before becoming adept as an 'artist.' Lassiter *was* the killer. What's odd to me is how this new man knows his methods so damned exactly. The new name came, from what I understand, because one of the cops who found the first victim said that it was heart-wrenching, that she was so pretty and perfect, it was just like she'd already been laid out by a mortician for a viewing or a wake."

Andre hesitated a moment, thinking over what she'd said. "I've gone over the files," he said quietly. "There is evidence that this man may have been the killer. But he's dead—so there's no questioning him about the woman who is still missing."

"He didn't kill himself," she said.

"You're here, so you've done your paperwork. Fournier?"

"Like I said, he's a good man, and a good cop. But he wants to be done with this case." She stared at him hard. "I know that you know that my cousin was murdered by the Artiste. Let me be very clear that I didn't seek my own vengeance. I *did* major in criminology and become an FBI agent because of what happened. And though it's flawed, I believe in the system. So maybe you thought that I was convinced that we had the right man, trapped and at our mercy, and that either I or Fournier tripped and killed the suspect, but it didn't happen that way."

"I never suggested that."

"You looked at me as though I was a perp!"

He shook his head, annoyed. "I did not. I don't know what you read in my look, but honestly, that wasn't my intention. It was startling to be sent down here and immediately stumble on you and Detective Fournier over a body. That's all. I haven't been working this case, following your leads. There was no reason for me to step in at the time and so I didn't. I do intend to be at the autopsy. Once again, I'm not thinking that you're a vigilante agent on a vendetta, but it will be important to find out if it was suicide."

"The autopsy. Yes, of course," she murmured. "The thing is…there's still a victim out there. We don't know if she's dead or alive. A picture of her was found in a restaurant on Bourbon Street. No pictures of her in death have been found, so…"

"So, she may still be alive. And if Trudeau was the killer, she's imprisoned…somewhere…and we have no idea where. And if he wasn't the killer…"

"She may still be enduring torture as we speak," she said softly. Then she lifted her hands and let them fall. "Either way means she'll die. And we have nothing else. Nothing at all, except…"

"Except?"

She didn't answer, and he smiled. "I see. We have

nothing except your instinct. You don't believe that Trudeau killed himself or that he was the killer."

"I don't know. If we hadn't found him dead, I'd have been far more convinced. But in my mind, there's no way the Mortician would do that to himself, and therefore…"

"The actual killer killed him."

"You think I'm grasping at straws."

"No, I don't."

She gazed at him steadily. "I know that you were there the day in Broussard when we interred Janine in the family tomb…and the police took down Lassiter. I had to try to pin down why you were so familiar, but you were playing in the band with Jimmy."

He nodded. "Jimmy is an old friend."

She sat in silence, and he asked, "Do you have any other suspects?"

She grimaced and shook her head. "There are possibilities that we haven't explored, and I admit, we didn't expand our search at first." She leaned forward, looking at him warily. "You're not sitting there thinking that I'm way off base, are you? Do you think that Fournier is right and Braxton Trudeau knew he was going to get caught and stuck his blade in his own throat?"

"I'm open to all possibilities," he said.

"All right, then," she said, and took a deep breath before plunging in. "I think it has to be someone who knew Ryan Lassiter. Maybe even someone who was in on it—as if Lassiter had a protégé, someone who was maybe even aiding and abetting him."

"Cheyenne, that was a long time ago."

"Yes, I know. But we have no idea if this person hasn't…practiced before. Here's the thing, and it's sad and tragic, but people disappear all the time. No one notices when it's someone who is on the outer edges of society—say addicts who wind up on the streets, the homeless who have no one. Even with these recent killings—the killer started off with people on the fringes. Women who were prostitutes. We both know that police are overworked and overburdened. When families and/or the press get involved, the pressure is on. I was at a symposium last year and we learned that there are over two hundred thousand unsolved murders in the country, just since 1980. We don't know the true extent of any killer. So… Andre, I think our killer could have been practicing for years to get the basics down before really becoming an imitator of the Artiste. And Lassiter was just executed last year." She hesitated, grimacing. "Right now, I wish he was alive, and that we could question him. Oh, and as far as the death penalty, I don't know how I feel. On the one hand, as a family member of a victim, for a while I thought that Lassiter shouldn't just be executed—he should have been boiled in oil and slashed to ribbons. But on the other hand Lassiter might have helped us now, and maybe knowing that there is nothing left for a person in life but prison walls may be a punishment worse than death. I don't know. It's not my job to be judge and jury. I just want killers off the streets, unable to take that most precious gift of life from anyone again."

She stopped speaking and looked a bit embarrassed.

"We're both Feds," he said, trying to make it easier for her. He was somewhat surprised that she'd been sent here. She was clearly too close to the original Artiste case. Then again, this killer needed to be caught—and fast. She might have insight that others did not.

As she was suggesting now.

"Yeah," she muttered. Again, she took a deep breath. "Not to be horribly repetitious—Fournier is a good cop. We both know that New Orleans isn't easy, especially for the poor patrol cops. When do you let people have fun, and when do you have to step in because a situation is getting dangerous? Anyway, my point is this—Fournier finished his paperwork, he was just about euphoric, and everyone was congratulating him, congratulating us both, even though I was saying that we can't be sure that the right man is dead. I had to finish and get out as quickly as possible and…" She looked away. "Okay, so, you were the only one I thought might listen to me. My friend Keri Wolf called your boss, right?"

He nodded. "She's living with one of our agents and their home is near our offices now."

"I know. I called her the other day. I was frustrated, trying to do the right things, but not feeling as if I was making any headway. I asked her if she had any insight, and she said that she'd talk to a man named Jackson Crow."

"Our field director," Andre said.

"So, you're here because of me—and because you're from the area, too?"

He nodded. "I spent time living in a number of cities—Lafayette, Houma and obviously here, too."

"Cool house," she noted.

"Thanks. My parents own it. They live down in Florida now, but they're still locals here at heart—they wouldn't miss a Jazz Fest for anything. For Mardi Gras they prefer Lafayette—not as many people getting out of control. I was out by you during middle school, here in New Orleans for high school. And anyway, I'm here now. And they didn't even know until I told Jackson that I'd actually been there the day Lassiter was brought in."

He stood, thinking that it was great that she had come to him, that they were talking, and creating a good working relationship. Of course, maybe somehow something the next day would prove that they were done—that the dead man, Braxton Trudeau, was their killer.

But like her, he was afraid that wasn't going to be the case.

It was a little distracting to feel as close to her as he suddenly did. She'd poured her heart out to him, showing him a vulnerability he was certain few people saw. It was almost as if he'd known her for years.

Well, in a way he had. But then again, not at all.

She was exhausted, he was sure.

"You've been working this 24/7, like Fournier?" he asked.

She nodded.

"Well, at the moment, we have nowhere to go," he told her. "All we can do is think back, see what each of us can remember about everyone. Maybe we'll head out to see Jimmy—he's working with a band on Frenchman Street right now. For now, I'm going to get our board going."

"It's a plan," she murmured. She settled back into the sofa.

"Hang on," he said, then he went back to the hallway for his travel bag, opening the side with his computer and all the physical files Angela had gotten him.

He returned; she was just sitting, staring at the empty board.

"All right. The Rougarou."

He pinned a sketch of the monster—much like the one he'd seen at the museum—on the top left corner of the board.

"That's a picture of a legendary bayou monster, like a werewolf," she noted.

"Right, because the killer referred to as the Rougarou, back in the 1800s, was never caught. Here we now have Emil Justine, owner of the plantation and cemetery at the time, suspected to be the killer."

He put up a facsimile of Emil Justine, copied from a very old photograph of the man done sometime right before or after the Civil War. He looked extremely grim, but then, that was pretty much how most of the photographs from the time looked.

He had four more likenesses to put up—victims from the time: Ann Marie Matthews, Victoria Dupree, Melissa Carrier, and Alice DeMille. Two were also copies of old photographs. Two were sketches.

"There were probably more—many more," Cheyenne murmured. "No internet at the time, news traveling slowly and a war going on."

"Exactly. Okay, so, now, back in his day, he left sketches of his victims—except he had original photographs of Anne Marie Matthews and Melissa Carrier, as you see on the board. He was an expert with a knife, inflicting damage that he could hide once he 'prepared' them, but slicing them up all over, and thus his moniker back then—the Rougarou. When Lassiter decided that he liked the killing method, he was called the Nouveau Rougarou at first, but the press labeled him the Artiste, which stuck, and of course, made it clear which killer was being discussed." He hesitated. "I guess you went through all this with Keri Wolf when she wrote her book?"

Cheyenne nodded. "It was one of her first books. She didn't want to question me at first—she thought it would bring up bad memories. But..." She shrugged. "It was all right. I could tell her things about Janino, at least, that she couldn't get anywhere else. And by college, I was just determined to do what I could to catch killers."

He nodded, fascinated by her. She had taken a very bad situation and moved forward in life, rather than letting it bring her down.

Then again, maybe she had become a little obsessive...

"But I am not obsessed!" she snapped, as if she had read his mind.

"All right, so we both remember Lassiter's crimes all too well," he said then, going to the far right of the board. He put up a picture of Lassiter, and then pictures of his known victims—including a picture of Janine.

Cheyenne didn't blink.

"And now the matter at hand," he said, putting up a picture of the one real suspect they'd had—Braxton Trudeau, now deceased, and then pictures of his known victims: Alicia Holden, Anna Gunn, Cindy Metcalf—and the girl who was still missing, Lacey Murton.

Cheyenne Donegal stood, walking over to the board. "See?" she said, pointing to the arrangement of the girls' hair over their foreheads. "Lassiter's victims—and the new victims. See the way bangs are arranged, and when the girls had no bangs, the hair was brought over their foreheads in a slant. None of these pictures—those of the victims in death—were ever let out to the media. I've even checked online, in case someone had managed to leak an image. It may be a little thing, but it gets me back to thinking that whoever is doing this had to have studied Lassiter—maybe he even somehow aided or abetted Lassiter and knows exactly how he left his victims. There's something more—something that's so similar in the way the photos appear. I can't place it yet, but's it's there. I can't help but have this wrenching feeling that this killer was… I don't know, and maybe not quite so dramatic, but an understudy."

Andre studied the pictures; she was right about the strange slant on the hair—but did it mean anything?

And what else was it about the pictures that bothered her?

"All right, so who was close to Lassiter? I mean, that we know about?"

She walked back to the sofa and sat again, obviously drained.

"Can I get you something?" he asked her.

"You have any coffee in here? Oh, that's right—you just got here. I'm fine."

"I have coffee. My mother always leaves me coffee, and she keeps powdered creamer for herself, sugar and fake sugar in the cupboards."

She grinned. "I'm an FBI agent. Just about as stereotypical law enforcement as you can get—black coffee would be delicious."

"I'll be right back," he told her. He headed across the hallway to what his parents had called the music room, and which was actually a second parlor, identical to the other side, right down to having a hearth and mantel that doubled into the next room, the dining room on this side.

The music room, however, did have a fine grand piano, which his mother played exceptionally well, along with a few of his old guitars. The dining room had hutches full of dishes and crystal and a long table that would easily seat eight—twelve, if necessary.

Behind the dining room was the kitchen, and as he had known it would be, the cupboard offered several pounds of Community Coffee.

He put a pot on to brew and headed back over to the parlor.

Cheyenne Donegal was sound asleep; she'd crashed over and was half sitting with her head resting on the occasional pillow she'd held earlier.

Andre found one of his mother's old knit throws and set it carefully around her. She didn't wake. He left her, went to his travel bag and dug out his computer, and headed to the room behind the parlor—his father's office and library. Once there, he went over everything they had just discussed, considering her belief that the killer had to be someone who had known Lassiter.

That made him think back to the day of the funeral.

He hadn't known Janine Dumas, though his family had known her family, and he had seen her about, but not often. His parents had lived in NOLA by then, and he'd gone back now and then for friends' birthdays or the like.

Jimmy Mercury had been a longtime friend—they'd played ball together in high school. Lafayette was a fairly large city; New Iberia was small. The Dumas family had asked Jimmy about creating a jazz band for the funeral—jazz funerals being something Janine had always thought were terrific. Death, if they believed, was not the end, but a new beginning.

When it came to music, Andre couldn't come near

to Jimmy's talent. But his mother had been almost as fine a piano player as she was an artist, and valued musical instruction, so he'd had lessons ever since he was a young boy.

If he thought back, he could remember the day—and a young Cheyenne Donegal.

She had stood near her parents, but her mother had been consoling her own brother, Janine's father. And so, Cheyenne had seemed a bit apart—even from her school friends. She had been a few years younger than Janine.

Not far from her, there had been some of Janine's classmates. Nelson Ridgeway and Katie Anson had stood near her—high school lovers from the get-go. He'd heard that they'd gotten married and—miracle of all miracles—they were still married. Mike Holiday, an extremely good-looking quarterback on the football team, had been there, too, tall and blond and somber, just about next to Mr. Beaufort, or Rocky Beaufort, then coach and gym instructor at the high school. Jimmy Mercury had told Andre that Rocky Beaufort was now the owner of a fitness studio in the French Quarter, though he hadn't been there yet himself, and in fact, hadn't seen him since that day.

Andre closed his eyes, trying to clearly picture the scene again: the plantation sat up on a very small hillock, and a stone path led down to the cemetery. The entire estate was walled with stone, but in places, the stones were broken. The wall was—tops—three feet high. Anyone could hop over it at night—and did.

The Dumas tomb was in the middle of one of

about ten rows of family tombs, and the mourners had all followed the coffin down from the plantation to the site and stood angled around wherever they could as the priest gave the final service.

He could remember seeing Jacques, the church organist and an excellent musician himself, standing near the Dumas family.

Jacques had said that he didn't think he could play that day; he'd had Janine in his chorus for years, and the emotion might be too much. The man had been about thirty then, thin and sour in appearance, with long sandy hair and light, green-gray eyes.

Emil Justine III—the contemporary Emil Justine—had been maybe forty back then, balding, serious, with large almond-shaped brown eyes that seemed as grave as the services his family provided. He had stood politely at just a bit of a distance.

Ryan Lassiter had been on the trail back up to the plantation—a very small slant, not even a hill by most standards, and still, it had seemed he stood up a bit distant on that trail, as if he was a polite observer and not someone who really needed to be there.

The man had been stunned when Cheyenne Donegal had pointed a finger at him, screaming out her accusations.

We got to get him! Jimmy had said without hesitation, and so he had run, hard on his heels as Jimmy shot toward Lassiter, then tackling him down.

He remembered other faces besides Janine's family, he just didn't really know everyone.

Jimmy might remember others—he'd lived in

New Iberia until he'd graduated high school and come into the city for college.

But he knew, it wasn't just who had been there—the question was, who might have been close to Lassiter, so close that they might have been in on the man's kills?

"You're brooding," a voice, deep and masculine, said flatly. "Wasting time."

He looked up quickly; his visitor was not unexpected.

Nor was he among the living.

Louis Marquette—a member of Lafitte's band of merry men who had gone straight, changing his ways to become a tailor after the Battle of New Orleans—stood in the house, which had once been his. One foot forward, one hand on a hip.

While he'd died near the age of sixty, his spectral appearance seemed to be that of a man ten or fifteen years younger. That might have been because, according to the history of the man, he had lived determined on moving forward at all times, with energy and enthusiasm for life. He retained many of his dashing ways, with impeccable manners and a somewhat annoying habit of switching into French when he became annoyed or excited about something. His English was perfect, barely accented, but he knew that Andre's French was weak, and that he could often irritate him into action—or into leaving—by going on in French.

He made a striking appearance, dressed in breeches and a fine waistcoat and brocade jacket.

Most of the time Louis was a good "imaginary" friend, a man who devoured any talk shows about modern politics, eager to keep abreast with the news of the day.

His television habits were often troubling to the neighbors, since television sets would go on and off constantly when no one had been in the house for months on end.

Louis was an extremely talented spirit.

Andre's parents did not see Louis—but his mother had never doubted him, and his father tended to believe whatever his mother told him. Lily Rousseau had come from a family steeped in traditions and beliefs, so the fact that Andre might "see" a pirate who had lived in the house over two hundred years ago seemed perfectly normal. While his dad was more practical, he'd often told Andre that it was almost scary how Lily knew when someone was coming or that something was going to happen.

Louis had not been the first dead man to speak to Andre. When he'd been a small child, he'd thought that everyone saw the people walking about who appeared and disappeared, who often wore funny clothes, and seemed to drift through walls when they chose. He'd been so young when it had all started that when he'd finally figured out that he saw the dead, he wasn't afraid—just saddened that others couldn't talk to them. He became quickly aware that he shouldn't share information about his "friends" with others.

His dad had considered that, like many children, he was just seeing his imaginary friends. His mother had watched him more closely—it seemed that her own mother had often spoken with the dead. Lily had once done an incredible series of paintings called *The Ghosts of New Orleans*, which had sold for an exorbitant amount of money. She was more than open to the thought of sharing her home with a pirate, and though she didn't see Louis, she often chided him for leaving the televisions on.

"Qui est la belle femme?" Louis inquired.

Andre stood and walked to the door, looking out; thankfully, Cheyenne Donegal was still peacefully sleeping on the sofa. Though they'd had a rough initial meeting, things seemed to have changed.

He preferred the new side of Cheyenne. Still, she was FBI—but she *wasn't* Krewe.

"That is Cheyenne Donegal, an FBI agent."

"Ah, *mais oui*! The nastiness about these dreadful murders. And you, but of course, are here because of them also?"

"Do you know anything?" Andre asked him.

The look Louis gave him was scathing. "You know that if I did, I'd have appeared first thing—with or without *la belle femme* in the room! I watch the news, as you well know. Speaking of which, the latest broadcast suggests that this Mortician has been found. I have been eavesdropping, so what do you think?"

"*La belle femme*—or Special Agent Donegal—has been on the case the past few weeks. She has a bad feeling about it."

"There is still a woman out there somewhere. She may be dead already—she may not."

"Louis, I should be looking for her, yes. But there's a problem. We have no idea where she might be—I mean, none. The women that the newest killer has taken have been found in three different cities. Not areas—cities. Tomorrow, I'm going to the autopsy. I'm hoping to read everything and get up to speed, and work with Cheyenne *and* Detective Fournier. Sadly, the world isn't going to stop for me to catch up."

"Ah, my dear friend, you are still wasting time. The murderer must keep them at the same place—until he kills them. I believe that he must have a comfort zone where he knows he can hold on to the women and not be discovered. It's too risky for him otherwise. He is careful about making sure his victims cannot be found—until he wants them found."

"And if I had a clue as to where to start, Louis, I'd be out there now." He frowned as he spoke. "Louis, you might have just given me something."

"I remain to serve!" Louis informed him.

Andre ignored him.

He'd been thinking about the past. And while there had been those in the 1860s who had believed the Rougarou to be Emil Justine—original owner of what was now the Justine Plantation Mortuary Home and Cemetery—the current owner was now an Emil Justine, as well.

He had been there on that day.

It didn't make the Emil Justine living today a killer.

But he didn't have to be a killer for *someone* to be making use of the plantation house, or any of the outbuildings that were scattered on the property.

Andre strode back into the parlor. There was a map of southern Louisiana on the case board. Dots on the map showed the places where bodies had been found. He quickly marked the cities where the women had been taken. It wasn't completely obvious, but the locations made a rough circle around the cemetery.

3

"Yes?" Cheyenne opened her eyes slowly, blinking, trying to dispel the fog that seemed to have claimed her mind and instead wake up instantly alert and aware.

She usually woke in a blink, completely cognizant the minute the alarm went off—or by any other sound, even a creaking floorboard.

But not now. She'd slept like…

The dead.

When she opened her eyes, *he* was there, Andre Rousseau, hunkered down by her side, trying to wake her gently. "Cheyenne, I'm so sorry. But I'd like to try an idea. It's a long drive out and back, and I want to make it in daylight. I know you haven't had any sleep, and you can sleep in the car if you like. It's a drive I've made far more times than I could begin to count."

She had no idea what he was talking about; it seemed that her mind was clouded. But she figured out that she had fallen asleep on his sofa and that she hadn't wakened at the drop of a dime.

"Oh, no, I'm so sorry… I never do this… I'm sorry!"

She was embarrassed and so she jerked up.

And clunked him on his chin with her head.

"Oh!" she cried again. "I'm sorry again!"

But he was just laughing softy and rubbing his jaw.

"It's all right, it's all right—my fault. I should have used a squirt gun."

"Really! I didn't sleep all night, and I should have gone home and let others worry about the right or wrong of it, but I didn't think I'd fall sleep…"

She winced, shutting up and standing quickly, straightening her jacket.

"I'm so sorry," she said simply.

"No, I'm sorry," he said. "I should have let you sleep, but I want to get out to the Lafayette–New Iberia area right away. I think the Justine Cemetery is central to what's going on. Look at the locations." He pointed to the dotted map on the board.

"The cemetery?" she asked, frowning. "We checked on Emil Justine. Fournier had his doubts, but because of the history, I did check on Justine's whereabouts when the women were taken. He was in Philadelphia for a daughter's wedding during the abduction of Cindy Metcalf, and he was there a week before and a week after, so even if you play with the exact date she disappeared, he couldn't have been the one to kidnap her. And trust me, I confirmed with multiple witnesses."

"I do trust you. And still, the original Rougarou might have been the Civil War Emil Justine. There's the house itself. It could possibly be a connection."

"It's still a working mortuary. So many people pass through it."

"Argue with me while we drive," he said.

He was impatient with her. And he might have good reason to be. The plantation house wasn't all that remained. During the war, the house had been taken over by a Union general, and thus it had been spared any damage. The house and the outbuildings dated from the early 1800s. The smokehouse, carriage house, the original kitchen and seven small houses that had once been slave quarters still remained.

For the most part, they were abandoned. But she supposed it was possible that the property was somehow involved. It was there, in a way, that it had all begun—for her, at least.

"Let's go," she said. "It's going to take forever if you try to take I-10. Going through Baton Rouge, we'd hit traffic, and we might get stuck at the bridge—"

"I'm taking 90, not I-10. I know where I'm going."

He was waiting for her at the front door. He locked it as soon as she was out and started down the sidewalk.

She had to move quickly to keep up with him; his strides were very long.

Andre opened the passenger-side door of a small

SUV for her as they reached it. She slipped in, murmuring a thank-you.

"Broussard is small," she said, "and a lot of the population in the surrounding towns have been there forever—it's not one of those places people flock to when it's time to retire, but…"

"Your point?" he asked, sliding into French Quarter traffic and maneuvering around the tourists and the road closures.

"There could be a funeral going on," she said.

"Well, the family hasn't lived on the property in about eighty years, from what I understand. They're in a new ranch house somewhere in town. In fact, Mrs. Justine died several years ago and the kids are grown, so I'm assuming that it's just Emil. His children didn't want to manage the place, and at the moment it's run by a man who took over a few years back, after your cousin's funeral." He glanced her way. "They bring in an embalmer who works at other establishments, too. A lot of people in the surrounding areas have family tombs there, but these days, people do other things, too. I don't think that there's a daily funeral at the cemetery."

"Probably not," she said.

He glanced her way briefly again. "You're not going to give me an argument about a search warrant and all that, are you?"

"I'm just along for the ride."

"Hey, you're the one who doesn't believe you've found the killer."

"We're out of other leads, anyway," she said.

Her reservations about going back to Broussard were at least in part because she was never sure about going home. Naturally, she still had friends in the area—and there was much she loved about her hometown.

Still, it would always hurt.

"I haven't been out there in a long time," she said.

"Only child—and your parents moved to a beach climate?" he asked her.

She smiled and nodded. "You?"

"Only child—and my parents moved to a beach," he said.

She lowered her head, her smile deepening.

He did know the area, she saw. He'd made his way out of the Quarter and to the highway. Soon, they were moving out of the city, and then he could drive at a good pace. They'd gotten out of the house by about 1:00—no rush hour, and he knew exactly what route he wanted to take.

She was silent for a few minutes, then said, "Everyone is convinced that Braxton Trudeau was the killer, that my case is basically closed. I'm not expected anywhere until the autopsy. By everyone, I mean our local FBI office and the police. They're doing press conferences, asking for help in finding Lacey Murton. Do you think that we could be right—or, rather, you could be right—and she's out here somewhere? Wouldn't that be a twist—using the Justine place. I mean, after everything…"

"Ryan Lassiter really had nothing to do with the Justine Plantation, other than imitating the original

Rougarou. No one ever proved that the old Emil Justine was the Rougarou, but it's an educated guess, as evidenced by Keri Wolf's research," he said. "Seems like a logical place to start looking, doesn't it? Alicia Holden was taken from New Orleans, but according to all the information I was given, she was found in Lake Charles."

"She was the first victim. I wasn't on the case yet when she was found," Cheyenne reminded him. She thought about the investigation that had led them to their chase of Trudeau. "I have to admit that what we had did lead to Trudeau. Timeline, credit cards, and of course, most damning, the fact that he vacated a table and a picture was found just as soon as he left it. We could have held him. We had warrants for his DNA. But even then, all we had on him was circumstantial. The greatest distance covered was with Cindy Metcalf. She was kidnapped in Biloxi, and then taken over the state line. But there was a week between her being taken and the discovery of her body. She could have been found just about anywhere in the country with that kind of time."

She watched his profile as he drove. She was still so tired, and yet was increasingly aware that, at the very least, she needed to be grateful that they had sent her someone with an open mind. He could have played it the way everyone else *wanted* to play it, sure that they already had their man.

To be fair, everyone—meaning everyone in law enforcement, the police from Mississippi through every parish in Louisiana, the bureau and every other agency—were focused on locating the woman who was still missing. The problem was finding a place where the killer held his victims, which could be *anywhere* along that Mississippi/Louisiana line. Investigators had searched bars and cemeteries, hotels, gas stations and any properties that Braxton Trudeau was associated with. There had been no sign of the Mortician's victims—until they had been discovered. Dead,

Local police in all the towns and cities continued to search.

"Janine," she murmured. "My cousin… I'm thinking back to Lassiter. She went with him because she was charmed by him and flattered by his attention. He was so good-looking. All the young women in her class had a crush on him, and she was so excited that he'd chosen her. She knew who he was when she went with him."

He glanced her way, surely wondering how she could know that with such certainty.

"Kids talk," she added quickly. "No one wanted to believe it was Lassiter at first. He was such an amazing teacher when he was at the school, well liked, and I suppose it was easy for a girl her age to have a massive crush on such a man."

"Here's the thing—the man is imitating the Artiste who was imitating the Rougarou. A killer who has become more legend than fact, and the legend traces back to Justine Plantation," Andre said.

"It does," she said. "And still, would a killer chance such a thing?"

"Whatever he chanced, he has gotten away with it—whether it proves that the killer was Trudeau or not."

"It's strange," Cheyenne said. "If I remember right, when I was younger, there was talk of the parish buying the plantation as a historical site because it's so complete. We certainly don't want to romanticize slavery, but it's important that we do remember the history. There are… I think ten structures remaining outside the main house to the rear." She turned to him. "I've never been in any of them. When I was twelve, about a year before Janine was killed, some classmates wanted to slip out at night and break into some of the buildings, spend the night somewhere in the field of tombs. Kids love cemeteries, and Billy, one of the older boys, wanted to tell tall tales. I couldn't go—my mother got wind of the plan. And as it happened, my parents told the other parents, and all the kids were dragged home before it got very late. The odd thing was that it seemed all my friends who did go were thrilled that they'd got caught. Billy started telling them all that there was a real rougarou, a werewolf-like monster, and that he prowled the cemetery at night, hiding out, looking for people to eat. He'd cry out in his hunger, and he preferred young people because they were so tender. Everyone was totally terrified. I think they were happy they got rescued before the rougarou got them."

"Billy sounds like an interesting guy. Would I have known him or his family?"

"He wasn't here long. His dad was working for

one of the oil companies. I think they came from Ohio, and his father was transferred somewhere else in just a few years. I believe I saw somewhere that he's working in Seattle now."

"So, he's not likely our monster today," Andre said. She wasn't entirely sure if he was joking or not.

The drive from the heart of the city out to New Iberia and up to the plantation and cemetery just outside of Broussard took almost two and a half hours.

Maybe a little less—with Andre driving.

But when they arrived, it was still afternoon. Sun flowed over the landscape: the great trees dripping moss waved in the breeze, the crumbling stone wall, the house shimmering up on its little hill—and the cemetery, haunting, even by sunlight.

"Where to begin?" she wondered. Then she looked over at him. "I could just call Mr. Justine, you know. Get keys and permission to look around."

He looked at her. "You know him that well? And what if he refuses?"

"I don't know him well, but my parents did," Cheyenne told him. "I grew up on the edge of New Iberia, almost up here by the plantation. Small-town atmosphere all-around. I think he'd be willing to help, especially if he's innocent. I don't see any funerals going on. Arrangements are by appointment only, so…"

"You have a number?"

Cheyenne laughed softly. "He still owns the place, so he's listed!"

They got out of the car. She watched as Andre

leaped up easily on the stone wall by the road where he'd parked. He was looking out over the property.

Emil Justine answered Cheyenne's call with, "Justine Plantation Mortuary Home and Cemetery. How may I help you?"

"Mr. Justine, this is Cheyenne Donegal. I don't know if you remember me, but you know my mom and dad, Genevieve and Robert Donegal."

"Of course, dear, I knew your old English dad well—a fine bowler!"

Technically, her father's lineage was Irish, but if you weren't of Cajun descent out here, you were pretty much always "English." Her mother's family had been from the area as long as anyone could remember—and as long as any records showed.

"Oh," he said softly on the other end. "I hope you're not calling to ask about an interment?"

"No, nothing like that…" She plunged in. Of course, he remembered the terrible incidences involving Ryan Lassiter—how could any of them forget?

She went on as quickly and *sweetly* as she could about her job now.

And about the new murders.

He was immediately ready to help. "I've heard—the nation has heard about what's happened. You know, I've been hanging up on a lot of people, all wanting to know if my great-great-grandfather had been the Rougarou! You get in there and search all you like, young lady. Haven't been out to the property myself in ages… Got a man, Guy Mason, keeping up the place for me now. Not getting any younger, you know."

"May I get keys to all the buildings?" Cheyenne asked.

He chuckled and told her, "Broussard."

"You're…living in Broussard?" she asked.

"The Broussard tomb—you know it. Finest in the place. We have some of the long-ago Broussard family in there, and not so long ago, too. The gate won't look open, but it is. Twist the handle three times. There's a little altar in the middle, family all around. The keys are under the altar, beneath a box of votive candles. You let me know right away if you find anything, of course?"

"We will," she promised. "Thank you so much."

She came around the car. Andre was still standing on the stone wall. He looked down, and she thought that he would reach out a hand to help her up. But after the way she had fallen asleep on his sofa, she was determined to prove herself independently competent. She leaped up easily. Then she hopped down the other side and started walking toward the cemetery. She did know exactly where to find the Broussard tomb.

He followed. "Hey, did you have a problem? Are we breaking into tombs?" he asked.

She smiled and kept walking, turning down one of the cemetery paths.

She reached out with a gentle touch to acknowledge as they passed by the tomb with the name *Dumas* prominent atop the archway.

The Broussard tomb didn't date all the way back
to the 1700s, as some in the graveyard did. While
Broussard family members had been living and
dying in the area since the first Cajuns had arrived,
the tomb itself had been built about 1826, following
the manner of many created in New Orleans when St.
Louis No. 1 became busy with yellow fever burials
and the Our Lady of Guadalupe—the Chapel of St.
Anthony of Padua, back then—had been built as a
mortuary chapel to accommodate the dead who were
bound there just a street over. It was definitely the
most spectacular in the plantation cemetery, built to
accommodate the dead of generations, with a massive statue of St. Anthony over the ironwork door and
large plaque stating the name "Broussard."

The gate appeared to be locked, but by twisting the handle three times—as Emil Justine had
instructed—she opened it.

Many tombs didn't actually have mausoleum-like
interiors. They were simply large enough to accommodate coffins on shelves, with chambers at the rear
to collect the ashes and bones. In the intense heat, "a
year and a day" was the required time for a body to
naturally cremate and be pushed back to allow for
the newly dead.

But the Broussard tomb was a massive structure,
and the gate gave way to a small area and the altar
Justine had mentioned. She ducked down—with
Andre still watching her, bemused—and found the
box of votive candles.

The bottom was hollow, and there was a set of

keys beneath it, just as she'd been told. She turned around and dangled them before Andre.

"Beats leaving them under the doormat, I guess," he said. He looked around the tomb. "Well, there's nothing for us in here, at any rate. You've got the keys, so you call the direction."

"Start at the house and move onward?" As she spoke, she noted from the corner of her eye that they weren't alone; her cousin Janine was peeking in from the iron gate.

Christian was right behind her.

In school, she might have been the überpopular chick and he might have been the nerd, pining away as he looked upon others.

In death, they had become inseparable.

Once, Janine had told Cheyenne that she didn't really like "haunting" the graveyard; there were plenty of other places to be, places that recalled happiness, rather than the sorrow of death.

But Janine somehow managed to be at the cemetery anytime Cheyenne was there.

Cheyenne narrowed her eyes at the ghost of her cousin. She was just beginning to gain some credibility with this man. Now, being haunted could ruin it all.

"What did I say?" Andre asked her.

"Pardon?"

"You are fiercely frowning."

"Sorry—just my thoughts on the whole thing," Cheyenne said.

He smiled, turned and headed out.

She went after him.

And Janine, grinning, followed her, with Christian at her side.

"Well, well, well, what is going on here?" Janine teased. "The man gives a whole new meaning to 'tall, dark and handsome.'" She made a growling sound, like a she-tiger.

Christian had obviously been learning some of Janine's sass. "Butter my butt and call me a biscuit!" he declared. "Now, he is hot. If I weren't straight, I'd want to be all over that boy like bees to honey."

Cheyenne lengthened her stride, heading for the house. She could do without being ribbed by a pair of teenagers at that moment.

They still followed. Janine should know better; she knew what Cheyenne did for a living. She'd told Cheyenne she was often almost saddened by it, thinking her cousin might have done happier work if it hadn't been for what had happened to her.

"I know him!" Christian said suddenly. "He was around here when he was younger—went off to high school in New Orleans. He was here the day..."

"The day I entered my dear family tomb," Janine finished. "He was the one who went after Ryan Lassiter along with Jimmy Mercury. Is he a cop, too? Sorry, an agent?"

Cheyenne kept walking.

"And you're out here...now," Janine said. "What's going on?"

"We haven't seen anything...other than the usual," Christian told her. "People coming and going, bringing flowers…and bodies coming. They go around back. There's a drive that goes to the basement—it really is a basement. Guess the house is high enough on that little hill."

"But when he took me…" Janine said, but didn't seem able to continue. "But Lassiter is dead. I went to the execution. Call me vengeful."

Cheyenne wanted to stop. She wanted to ask the two of them to think, and think hard. Had people been coming and going from any of the support buildings? Had anyone come with a body, not arriving by hearse or ambulance?

But she knew them both, especially her cousin. If Janine could help stop a killer, she would. Not that Christian wouldn't do the same, but Janine had had all the hopes and dreams of a promising young woman stolen by such a man; she'd been tortured and killed by one.

And she stayed behind because life had been so viciously stolen from her, and she would want to stop it from happening to others.

When they reached the house, Cheyenne keyed the door open and then paused, looking at Andre.

"Perhaps we'd be better served if we split up. I have the keys. I can go to the outbuildings and start going through them methodically."

And if she left him, she could talk to her dead cousin.

"Wait. Let's do the house together. Once we're done here, we can split up for the outbuildings."

He was already walking past her. She winced and

turned and frowned fiercely at Janine and Christian again.

The ground floor of the house had been split into three viewing chambers. Cheyenne didn't think that there had ever been three viewings at the mortuary at one time—ever. But since the family had chosen not to live in the house anymore—maybe they weren't all that happy about living in a "city of the dead"— the whole of the old mansion had been turned over to the business.

The entry was grand with a curving staircase leading up to a gallery hallway and the second floor. The viewing rooms had names—not particularly imaginative ones: the White Room, the Silver Room and the Gold Room. Two were to the right of the grand entry, and one to the left. Cheyenne knew that behind the White Room—the one to the left— the kitchen remained; the mortuary was quick to provide water and coffee for guests.

Andre was headed into the Silver Room on the right. Cheyenne walked briskly toward the opposite side, a stern glance warning her cousin's ghost to follow her there. There were chairs arranged around a bier where a coffin would lie; a kneeling pew was before it. The room was beautifully draped with white curtains, peaceful and lovely. There were no cupboards in the room and it was easy to see that it was empty.

She quickly spun around to accost Janine and Christian. "I'm working!" she whispered tensely. "Please, this man seems to finally be taking me semiseriously, and I was so tired I babbled nonstop when we were first alone. Please, please, don't make him question my sanity now!"

"I'm sorry," Janine said, instantly contrite. "So, we've heard about what's going on, and if I hadn't attended Lassiter's execution myself, I would be thinking it was him again. But I thought you were working in Miami."

"I was, but I'm here now. And since you're here and have obviously been here—"

"We haven't been here that much," Christian said quickly. "Old Mr. Marcel has his horse farm just down the road, and you know Janine loves horses."

"We've been riding a lot," Janine said. "It's amazing. The horse knows us, and it's so much fun. People driving by must think he's just the most playful horse ever. He's like a dog—he knows we're there, but instead of being spooked, he loves us!"

"Okay, but have you seen anything other than official hearses or ambulances here—bringing bodies?" she asked.

They both shook their heads, solemn and serious.

"What about the outbuildings?" Cheyenne asked.

"No, but we really haven't been here all that much. I saw the car pass the farm, and I was curious, and then we saw you," Janine said.

"We did come for a funeral last week," Christian reminded her. "Old Mrs. Ruby. She was a teacher once. Great lady."

"Oh?"

"Katie Anson was here. You remember my friend

Katie, right? I guess she's Katie Ridgeway now—she and Nelson were married. They were here, oh, and even Jimmy Mercury was here. They had a jazz band accompaniment from the house to the grave, too. That was… I lose track of time. Last week, I think. Maybe last Wednesday or so," Janine said. "But you know, they were here for the funeral."

"Anyone else we know?" Cheyenne asked.

The two looked at each other. Janine shrugged. "I don't really remember who you know— you were a few years behind me. Back then. Now I'm younger. Hmm. Dying's not worth it. Anyway, let me think… oh, Mr. Derringer! You remember him. We were all in the church choir. He was playing piano, not the organ. There is no organ here, just a piano that can be rolled from room to room. They keep it on the other side, back in the Gold Room." She looked at Christian. "Can you think of anyone else?"

"That Cheyenne knew…hmm. Oh, yeah, Mike Holiday, remember him? Janine dated him for a while—he was cool. Captain of the football team out here." He grinned at her. "Heard he's just not a hot commodity anymore. He kept getting benched in college, wound up dropping out. He's a bouncer now at some bar or strip joint in NOLA. You remember them all, right?"

Cheyenne did; she could picture, all too easily, the day her cousin had been interred.

"Did you see Mr. Justine that day?"

"No, he wasn't here. I think he was supposed to

be out of town. It's hard to eavesdrop and learn everything," Janine said.

Cheyenne glanced toward the door, and then beckoned them to follow her into the kitchen. She hurriedly went through all of the cupboards and closets—finding nothing but dishes, cups and cleaning supplies.

"Okay, I need you to stick around here, okay? Keep an eye out for anything unusual that might happen."

They looked at each other. "Sure," Janine murmured slowly. "For—for how long?"

"However long it takes," Cheyenne told her.

"And I just got the horses not to be spooked by me!" Janine said. "I'm sorry, that's terrible. Of course, we'll watch here. But seriously, do you think that a killer would do something back here? Imitating the Rougarou—where the Rougarou was at work?"

Cheyenne looked nervously at the doorway again; there was still no sign of Andre, but she believed if he'd found anything he would have called her.

"I'm begging you guys, behave for me, please. Let me work as a competent and intelligent agent with all my faculties," Cheyenne told them.

"You are a brilliant agent," Janine declared.

"And we'll behave," Christian added.

Cheyenne hurried back out into the White Room. She called out to Andre. "I'm heading down to the basement. The embalming room is down there."

"I'll be right behind you," Andre shouted back.

Cheyenne hurried down the stairs.

The lower level had been outfitted as a state-of-the-art embalming room. In spotless, tiled rooms, the old foundation housed stainless steel gurneys, sterilizers, instruments, cupboards for gloves, makeup and more. IV stands, rows of jugs of embalming fluid and plastic bins for biohazard waste were strategically set around the room.

Cheyenne wished that her cousin hadn't followed her; she hoped that Janine didn't remember her time down here.

There seemed to be nothing at all out of place.

And while she opened every cabinet and looked under every gurney, there was no one hidden there, no sign of anyone having been kept there.

She had just ducked under one of the gurneys when Andre came down the stairs.

"Anything?" he asked her.

She shook her head. "Nothing."

"What's upstairs now?" he wondered aloud.

"Offices…a lounge area for families. Oh, and there's also one room kept as a bedroom, in case Mr. Justine or one of his employees needs to sleep here. I mean…" She paused. "I doubt that he rents it out."

"You never know," Andre said. "People love ghosts. A friend told me that no respectable house in the French Quarter was without a resident ghost."

"But here, above an embalming room? Hey, I'm accustomed to autopsies, and even I wouldn't want to sleep here. Ghosts are one thing," she said lightly, trying not to look at Janine and Christian, who were standing near her. "Really creepy stuff is another."

He smiled. "Guess we should all head up."

He turned.

"We're behaving!" Janine whispered behind Cheyenne as they followed him up the stairs, all the way to the second floor.

Andre and Cheyenne parted ways in the hall, Andre heading for the office and lounge, Cheyenne checking out the bedroom that had been kept. It was massive. As a family home, the plantation had grown to a good six thousand feet or so; that allowed for comfortable space now.

The bedroom was as fastidiously clean as the rest of the main house. She looked under the bed, into the walk-in closet and the bathroom—which had probably been a room of its own at one time.

"If I'd seen anyone who shouldn't have been here, I like to think I'd have noticed," Janine said. "But I guess I wouldn't always know who was and wasn't supposed to be here. Nobody has slept here in some time, it seems."

"But they keep it clean and freshen the sheets all the time, anyway," Cheyenne muttered.

"Talking to yourself?" Andre asked politely from the doorway.

"Office? Family lounge?" she asked him, wincing inwardly.

"Clear. But to be honest, I think that if anyone has been using this place, they would have used the outbuildings."

"I need to make sure to lock up," Cheyenne said, hurrying to leave the room.

She shouldn't have been in such a rush. She brushed past him in the doorway. He was rock solid, and she couldn't help but be keenly aware of him as a man, of his physical structure.

It was a moment that gave her pause.

She was used to working with all types of men. Many of her coworkers in Miami were in great physical shape—it was a beach city, after all. But she hadn't ever felt this kind of sudden sexual attraction for a man just by brushing past him in a doorway!

This was not to be tolerated. She didn't need any awkward, distracting feelings. She was working, she hadn't had any sleep and she was being accompanied by her personal ghosts.

Do they ever haunt anyone else? she wondered. She was going to have to ask.

They left by the front door. Cheyenne checked to make sure it was locked. Though, if other people knew where the keys were kept, there wasn't much reason to worry.

She and Andre, however, would know they had done things right.

"This place really should have been a museum instead of a mortuary," she stated. "I can't help but think that there are so many ways people can be horrible, it's good to remember—and hopefully make sure that we leave lessons for those to come after that we are capable of tremendous cruelty."

"Good point," Andre said, except she thought that he wasn't really paying attention to her. He was looking beyond her, out at the slave quarters, as they walked.

But he had heard her, and he continued with a smile and a shrug. "My grandmother would agree with you, and her mother was Haitian. She lived as a very rich man's mistress. He kept her quite comfortably—it was what was done in the day. She even liked his wife, and his wife liked her. She was often the babysitter for their children. It was very common in New Orleans. My grandparents went to New York to be married—no laws against marriage because of color there, ever. But some states had laws against interracial marriage that weren't repealed until the latter half of the twentieth century. I recently read a report, though, that worldwide, there are more slaves today than at any time in human history, especially in many underdeveloped countries despite efforts to create laws to put a stop to it—forced labor, child brides, prostitution. Slavery started just about with the dawning of man—and still exists. There will always be hateful people. That's one of the reasons we have this job."

"I'm well aware that we need to worry about national security, but the greatest promise of our country is that we are the land of the free—opportunity for all. Let enough generations go by and we're an impressive mix of all backgrounds."

He grinned. "So that's how a Cajun girl wound up being Cheyenne Donegal!"

"My family is a bit of everything," she told him. She heard Janine sigh behind her. Cheyenne ignored her.

"So, I'll take the smokehouse, the carriage house and the old kitchen. You can start with the slave quarters. How's that?" she asked Andre.

"Keys?" he asked her.

"Oh!"

They were clearly marked; she took a minute to separate them, handing him the ones he'd need.

As her hand brushed his, she looked up and saw that Andre was staring at her inquisitively. She took a quick step back and looked out at the yard.

"I'll do that one first," she said and headed immediately toward the closest buildings. He walked off farther down the dirt path that led out behind the house.

"I really like him," Janine told Cheyenne.

"I haven't even known him twenty-four hours."

"But you could do much worse. What am I saying? You have done much worse!"

"Janine, I'm trying to work here!"

The old kitchen hadn't been used as one since the beginning of the twentieth century. The kitchen had originally not been a part of the house—there would have been little available help in case of a fire back then. The giant hearth remained, cold now, no cooking utensils anywhere near it. Whatever cupboards had existed were long gone. Now the building contained nothing but piles of tools for the upkeep of the plantation—and cemetery.

"I wish so badly that I did know something," Janine whispered. "To think of what these young women suffer…"

"Nothing here. Let's move on," Cheyenne murmured.

She was starting toward the old carriage house when she saw Andre coming out of the small structure that was the farthest away.

"Cheyenne!" He shouted her name. The sound of his voice was harsh, and he was already pulling out his phone.

She went running toward him as fast as she could. His features were tense.

"I found her," he said.

4

Lacey Murton was still alive.

Andre had found her chained to the walls. Her abductor had made use of shackles that were over a hundred and fifty years old. Andre had ripped out a structural rod to break the chains that held her— thankfully, the boards were weak. He assumed that she'd been given some kind of sedative, but she was also very close to death.

She'd been left with nothing. Naked, no blankets, no water —nothing.

She'd even come to for seconds here or there as they waited for help to arrive, Cheyenne checking her pulse while speaking on the phone with the doctor at the hospital in Lafayette.

But Lacey hadn't said anything. Her eyes had opened wide a few times, and she'd tried to fight Cheyenne, who had soothed her, assuring her that she was all right. Everything would be all right.

Andre noticed that Cheyenne had a way with her, getting her to cooperate as the EMTs worked.

Cheyenne rode with the girl in the ambulance, while Andre followed closely behind in his car, making a call to Jackson Crow.

Jackson would inform the other agencies that the missing woman had been found alive.

Once they got to Lafayette, he paced in the waiting room. Eventually Cheyenne came out. She looked at him incredulously.

"How did you know?" she whispered. "Thank God you did, but how did you know?"

She looked exhausted and shell-shocked.

"The Rougarou," he told her, and shook his head. "But if it weren't for you, I wouldn't have thought to come here."

She sank into a chair, then leaped back to her feet as the doctor came out.

"Dr. Keaton," he told them, and in turn, Andre introduced himself and Cheyenne formally. Keaton was a serious man in his early fifties, gray streaking through his dark hair, the lines on his face showing a lifetime of concern for others.

"I believe she's going to make it fine," Keaton said. "She's been through a lot of trauma, but..." He paused for a moment, studying them. "I understand that her picture had been taken— the word has been out that she was missing and possibly still alive. I also understand that the killer, this Mortician or whatever, was found dead by his own hand this morning. It's a miracle that you found her. Dehydration would have taken her soon. But thankfully, he hadn't wounded her. He hadn't gotten to that, so what we're looking at is the trauma, a cocktail of drugs in her and severe dehydration. I believe, however, that she will pull through."

"Thank God," Andre murmured, and then he had to ask, "Is she lucid at all? Will we be able to speak with her?"

"Just a few minutes," Keaton said. "I understand how critical it is that you know the truth of what happened, but if her abductor is dead, there is no reason to cause her further stress until she's stronger."

Andre thanked him. Not thinking, he took Cheyenne by the elbow, and they followed the doctor. Lacey had been transferred up to an intensive care unit. Her room was private—and directly in front of the nurses' station with glass windows that allowed the staff to see her at all times.

Dr. Keaton went to her bedside first. Lacey's eyes opened.

"It's Dr. Keaton, Lacey. The FBI agents who found you are here. Can you talk for a few minutes?"

Lacey Murton's sandy hair had been pulled back. There were dark smudges under her eyes, and her cheeks were hollow and gaunt-looking. She nodded, though, looking past the doctor to Andre and Cheyenne. "Thank you, " she said. Her voice was barely a whisper.

"Lacey, we're so grateful to have found you," Cheyenne said, stepping forward and taking the girl's hand. "And you're going to be all right."

Moisture dampened Lacey's eyes and then tears trickled down her cheeks.

"I'm alive!" she said hoarsely.

Dr. Keaton would make them leave any second, and Andre understood why. He pulled his phone out quickly, bringing up a picture of Braxton Trudeau. He walked toward the bed and showed Lacey the picture.

"Lacey, I'm so sorry," he said, "but we need to know—is this the man who kidnapped you?"

She was grasping Cheyenne's hand. Lacey looked at the picture, frowning and shaking her head.

"No, no, that wasn't him."

Andre glanced quickly at Cheyenne.

"Do you know who did take you?" he asked Lacey.

She swallowed hard, her eyes closing.

"Lacey?" he pushed gently.

"It was a rougarou," she said. "It was a rougarou!"

Andre was silent for a minute.

Yeah, he should have known. The damned rougarou at the museum had *meant something.*

He wanted to be careful when he spoke again.

"She's been through a great deal," Dr. Keaton said firmly.

"Lacey," Cheyenne said softly, "do you mean that—"

Andre didn't have to speak at all. Lacey was ready to tell them.

"I went out back of the bar. I'd had a few drinks, and when I do, I get the urge for a cigarette. And there was this…wolf-man. I was laughing… I thought he was off-date for a Mardi Gras thing or Halloween.

He had a wolf's head. And his arms…they were in fur, and there was fur at his legs… He hopped around and danced, and I was enjoying his little show, and then…then he was on me and I thought he meant to smother me… I blacked out, and then… I woke up in that shed, and I screamed and screamed, and then he came back, and he had a knife, and he said that I had to be pretty for my picture. That knife… Oh, my God, there was dried blood on it. I was terrified, and he said not to worry, yet, not if I just smiled pretty… he had a man's voice, but, but…he was a monster!"

"She's getting upset," Dr. Keaton said. "And I'd rather not give her any more sedatives, given that we don't yet know what's been in her system. I'm going to have to ask you to leave now—for Lacey's well-being."

"Of course," Andre murmured.

"Lacey, just get well. Rest, and get well," Cheyenne said.

But Lacey clutched Cheyenne's arm. "Don't leave me. I'm so afraid. He'll come back. He's a monster, and he'll come back."

Cheyenne looked at Andre for help.

"Lacey, you're in the hospital now, you're going to be fine. We'll let your family know, and someone can come and be with you," she said.

Andre was already on the phone, calling Jackson—who had the power to see to it that the woman was protected, even if the general opinion was that the Mortician had died that morning.

He could tell that Cheyenne knew exactly what he was doing.

"Lacey, Andre is talking to his boss—they'll get an officer out here to watch over you," she said.

"I thought that the man who took her was dead?" Keaton asked quietly.

Andre spoke briefly with Jackson and it didn't take long. That was one of the best things about being Krewe. Every member was trusted without lengthy explanations.

He looked at Dr. Keaton when he hung up. "There's no proof yet that the man who died this morning was the killer. Until we do know, it's prudent to see that Miss Murton is protected. An officer will come, but he'll stay out of the way of your medical staff."

"It's okay, I know the drill. And Lacey, if that will help you, then I'm all for it," Dr. Keaton said. "But now, young lady, you must try to get some rest, some natural sleep. See that IV—saline and just the right mix to get bad things out of your system and good things in."

"You'll come back?" Lacey begged the agents.

"Absolutely," Cheyenne promised her.

They left the hospital room. Andre thanked Dr. Keaton for his help, and the doctor assured them that all the staff would watch over the young woman, and that she was in good hands.

"We're not leaving until the cop gets here, right, or whomever Jackson is sending?" Cheyenne asked.

"Right," he replied.

And so they waited.

The man who arrived was a young officer who introduced himself as Brian Wilmette. Andre was glad to see, he didn't seem to think of this as a sleep-in-the-chair or play-on-his phone kind of detail. Cheyenne and Andre both explained that—no matter what the media was saying—they didn't know for certain that the Mortician was dead, and if the man they had found dead in the French Quarter early that morning wasn't the killer, Lacey Murton could still be in danger.

"I've been following the case," the officer assured them. "We're all just grateful that the young lady is alive. I promise you, I will not take this responsibility lightly. I will guard her, alert and wary to all and any danger."

They both passed him their cards, and finally, left the hospital.

It was nearly midnight.

"I'd have stayed overnight, if it wasn't for the autopsy," Andre said.

"And I'd have been glad to do so, but we've got to be there in the morning," Cheyenne told him, leaning back. "Frankly, I'm glad it's your car and that you're driving. Is it okay if I try to sleep?"

"I did destroy your nap, didn't I?"

She smiled at him briefly, settling as comfortably as she could into the passenger's seat. "Andre, you really couldn't ask for a better day, with what we do. I don't know how your mind came around to searching the old plantation and cemetery, but if we hadn't gotten there when we did..."

"A good day," he agreed. "I can't take all the credit. You were convinced that you might not have caught the killer. If you hadn't shown up and talked about the past, the way things had been so close to what Lassiter did—"

He broke off, thoughtful, then shrugged.

"You made me think, so it turns out that the people in charge made a good decision, sending in agents close to the case. Your instincts were right, and that prompted my instinct. So...it was a good day, and for you a long one. You started out finding a dead man, but finished the day saving a life."

"She still has you to thank," Cheyenne said.

He glanced her way again; she was pleased, of course. They both were. And it was all right for them to be both surprised and grateful.

But he knew that they both believed it was far from over.

Her eyes were closing. She had to be exhausted.

"Hey," he asked softly. "Before you drift off... Where am I taking you?"

"Monteleone. Royal Street," she murmured.

"I know where it is," he said. "You know, there are four bedrooms in my folks' place. Maybe you should move on over. We have the board up, and it'll be convenient if we need to move quickly on things."

He would have put out the invitation to any agent. But he realized, she wasn't any agent, she was an extremely attractive woman.

It might be misconstrued. Actually, it sounded like the worst pickup line in history. He started to apologize or try to explain. He didn't need to. She was sound asleep.

He shook his head and forced his attention to the road. They had at least two hours to go, and the autopsy on Braxton Trudeau was going to be painfully early.

And he had a lot to think about. Cheyenne saw the dead. He'd seen the two ghost teenagers following her around the plantation house. She hadn't said anything; she'd acted as if nothing was out of the ordinary.

Should he just confront her?

Or wait and let it all come out on its own?

Dr. Kevin Morley was one of the newest MEs for New Orleans Parish.

Cheyenne wondered if Andre thought that Trudeau should have been assigned to their oldest and best, but she liked Morley. She'd met him briefly the day before, when he'd come to the site after they'd found Trudeau dead.

Detective Fournier met them at the morgue. He was a good guy, Cheyenne thought. He seemed happy to meet Andre—just as he had been okay with the bureau sending her to work with him.

Shaking Andre's hand as they suited up and headed in, he'd said, "This thing is crazy. Happy to have any and all help on this one, and glad that it's really in your lap now."

Cheyenne loathed autopsies. They were incredibly important, she knew. An autopsy could be the most crucial aspect of an investigation. Cause and method of death were key, but also the other information to be gleaned from a dead body: stomach contents could provide clues to be followed that might lead to an arrest; marks on the corpse could be instrumental— one case she'd been on in Miami had been solved because the medical examiner had found a tiny tattoo on the murder victim, and that had led them to the tattoo parlor where they'd found the murderer.

She knew the importance…

Still.

There was—by necessity—something cold and chemical about the way the body was treated. No matter how compassionate a man or woman might be while conducting the procedure. By nature of their profession, they had to set certain feelings aside.

She, Fournier and Andre stood by while the basics were completed. Trudeau had been thirty-seven, five-eleven, approximately two hundred pounds. Law enforcement had his records, so those simple facts were known. His last meal, the doctor said knowingly, had been gumbo, consumed three or four hours before death. Tests, of course, would confirm that, but Cheyenne had the feeling that this young ME would know.

Gumbo, of course, could be found in just about any restaurant in New Orleans, but when media went out asking for help with information, it might become important. Cheyenne and Detective Fournier had been on Trudeau's trail through the night, but if they found where he'd eaten dinner, that information could lead to people with whom he'd had contact. Since Lacey Murton's photograph had been found in a restaurant, they might find the second deathly photo at the last place Trudeau had eaten. Though Cheyenne hoped that wouldn't be the case.

"Well, I mean, the *cause* of death is obvious—in simple terms, a knife to the throat. He bled to death. As to *method* of death…"

Maybe, despite his youthful passion for the job, the good doctor had also wanted to be an entertainer: he let his words draw out dramatically.

Fournier interjected, "He killed himself! Fiercely going for his throat rather than face law enforcement!"

"Ah, no," Dr. Morley said, frowning.

"No?" Fournier's disappointment was palpable.

"I don't think so. Our dead man was obviously right-handed, which would have meant that he would have taken the knife across his throat thus."

Dr. Morley demonstrated on himself with a pretend knife.

"The slash wound across the throat goes from his right to left—something that a person intending suicide would, in my humble opinion, not do. It appears to me that his attacker was left-handed and caught up with him from behind, clutching Trudeau's back against his own body and swiping right to left."

Fournier still appeared disbelieving. "No," he said simply.

"I will be ruling it a homicide," Morley said. "You're welcome to question my findings and demand a second opinion."

He turned on Cheyenne, almost as if it were her fault the autopsy hadn't confirmed what he'd believed.

"So, who the hell killed the suspect?" he demanded.

Cheyenne glanced at Andre and then said, "This is just a theory. But I believe the real Mortician might have seen Trudeau getting all of what he sees as glory and attention—obviously, a man who leaves pictures of his victims to be found, and then his victims exposed as if prepared for a wake, wants attention. Even if he was setting Trudeau up for a fall, if he then felt that Trudeau was stealing his thunder, that the ruse had worked too well, he wouldn't hesitate to kill the man."

"There's also the possibility that he was waiting on killing Lacey Murton because he wanted to make sure that her time of death proved that Trudeau hadn't killed her," Andre said. "Lucky for us—and for Lacey," he added quietly.

Fournier looked at the young ME. "You're certain, kid, you're really certain?"

Kevin Morley arched a brow. "That's *Doctor* kid, Detective," he said, and smiled.

Fournier had the grace to wince. "Sorry, sorry... just..."

He turned around, starting for the door.

"Where are you going?"

"To cancel my cruise—before I lose it all!" Fournier called over his shoulder, and then he stopped and turned back, looking at Cheyenne and Andre. "Guys, keep me up to speed, okay? I didn't know anything about your trip out to Broussard. I'm happy to have you all be lead, but hey, make an old man look good, huh? Keep me in the loop!"

"Sure," Cheyenne said.

"Of course," Andre told him.

"Guess he didn't mean right now, this second," Dr. Morley said. "You can tell, you know, when someone was right-handed or left-handed. And I doubt this guy was ambidextrous. I mean, if you're going to slice your own throat, you make it good, right?"

"Hey, I believe you," Cheyenne told him. "I don't believe that the Mortician would commit suicide, anyway."

"Fournier is a good guy—he's been the detective on several of the cases when I've been the ME," Dr. Morley said. "He does give it his all, but I think he just really wanted that vacation."

"Probably needs it," Andre said "Anyway, thank you."

"Naturally, you'll receive the full report," Morley told them.

"Great," Andre said. "Will you do us a favor, though? If you *think* something, but it's not a fact to put on paper, will you call us?"

Morley appeared pleased with the question. "You bet."

Out on the street, Andre said, "Okay, we found Lacey Murton out at the Justine place. And you thought from the beginning that someone from the old case had to be involved. Let's head back to the board at my house and then check on all our contacts out in Broussard."

"All right. I'm going to call the hospital while we're on the way, make sure Lacey is doing okay. I'm sure they would have contacted us, but…"

"It never hurts. I'm going to make a few calls, too, once we reach my place."

It didn't take long. And in a city where parking was at a premium, Andre once again managed to find street parking.

"No courtyard or garage at your place, huh?" Cheyenne asked him.

"No, sadly. The houses are just about wall to wall here and my parents didn't even keep a car when we were living in the Quarter. They'd rent one when they wanted to go out of town somewhere. Anyway, I'm almost surprised that they keep this place, but as much as she loves warm water and the beach, my mom loves Louisiana best."

As they walked toward the house, Cheyenne glanced his way. "Maybe I should just move my things over here."

"Pardon?"

"Well, I know I was half-asleep and the idea of answering you last night seemed like an impossible task. While I do love the Monteleone, truly an exceptional hotel, it might make more sense to set up here. If the invitation was real."

He was startled, and she knew that he hadn't realized that she'd heard him the night before.

"No, no, the invitation was real—I just didn't repeat it because, seriously, I heard myself, and it sounded like an absolutely horrible line. But I believe Jackson is going to come into town, possibly with another agent who used to be in the offices here. We're not going to be able to be everywhere we may need to be, with the distances we're covering." He paused. "We could need an army for that, but another few agents who really know the territory will be better than trying to cover all that ground on our own. My place can be home base."

"We can stop by later for my things," she said. "Let's do some brainstorming now. Thinking about someone who knew Lassiter well—and might have become his disciple. I feel like we're looking for a stack of needles...in a stack of needles. But at least we can determine who might have been in the French Quarter in the wee hours yesterday—and who might have had the opportunity to kill Trudeau."

"Because you believe that the killer killed him because he wound up being jealous of the misplaced attention Trudeau was getting." He used his key and opened the two locks on his front door, stepping back for her to enter.

"And so do you," she said as she stepped in, heading immediately for the parlor to the right side of the entry.

"Well, more or less," Andre agreed. "Here's the thing—it's been a lot of years since the day Janine was buried."

"But Lassiter was in prison, unless he made friends inside who came out to imitate him, which I suppose is possible. But he was kept with max-sentence prisoners. I don't think any of his buddies are back out on the streets."

"True. But I will ask that Angela look into all of Lassiter's visitors. Knowing her, she's already done a ton of research on the man, looking for anything that might help now. I'm shooting her a text to see if she can help." He took a second on his phone and then refocused on the case board. "Okay, so...looking at what we've got. You do realize that half of the suspects here were about seventeen when Janine was killed?"

"I do." She walked up to the board and studied it. "Okay, so. Janine was really beautiful—I'm not being prejudiced because she was my cousin. She was the girl who everyone else wanted to be. Popular, and with really good grades, as well. I think she was a true prize to Lassiter, and that he worked up to her." She paused. The next bit was painful. "When he killed her, he was especially vicious. He never slashed anyone in the face—that would have ruined things when he set his victims up for his second picture. But she had wounds that went beyond what he'd done to the previous women."

Andre's phone rang. "That's Angela," he said, looking slightly apologetic, and he picked up the call.

"Angela, it's Andre, here with Special Agent Cheyenne Donegal. We're on speakerphone."

"Great. Nice to meet you, Special Agent Donegal. That was great work you two did yesterday. A girl is alive."

"We're very grateful," Cheyenne said.

"What can I do for you that will help? By the way, Jackson is tying up some things, then he wants to head on down there. He was there not too long ago. A serial killer jumped a ship in NOLA."

"All help sincerely appreciated," Andre said.

"So. The girl said that she was taken by a rougarou," Angela's voice mused. "How eerie was it, thinking back, that we also saw a rougarou."

"You saw a rougarou?" Cheyenne asked skeptically.

"In a museum," Andre said quickly.

"Yes, but it's odd, don't you think?" Angela asked.

Andre lifted a hand. "I'll tell you later," he murmured to Cheyenne. "We just came from the autopsy. Braxton Trudeau didn't kill himself."

Cheyenne plunged in. "From the time we found him dead, I just didn't believe that the Mortician would have killed himself. We can't help but think that this killer is following in Lassiter's steps. But another theory is that it's a prison buddy—someone with whom he might have relived his murders, someone who would have enjoyed hearing about them."

"I contacted the state prison asking for any and all pertinent associations and contacts. The man's lawyer saw him, and a priest. The lawyer is J. K. Mc-

Connell of Baton Rouge, but I've already checked him out. His credit cards don't place him outside the city during the last three months. On the day Cindy Metcalf was taken, he was on a camping trip with his son—dozens of witnesses. The priest is a man named Father St. Anne. I'm trying to get video from the prison, and whatever they have. I can't find a Father Dumaine Toulouse St. Anne—not anywhere. I think that this priest might not be a priest."

"You're not going to find him," Andre said thoughtfully. "Those are names from here in New Orleans. You've got the names of three streets in the French Quarter. Whoever he is, he managed to get an identification for a fake priest."

"Of course. I should have recognized the street names," Angela said. "The name didn't sound real from the get-go, but still, I searched and searched and spoke with dozens of clerks and even an archbishop. Priests visit from other countries all the time, but so far, I haven't found anything. If this fellow used street names…well, that makes sense."

"And who would think anything of a death-row inmate having a heart-to-heart with his spiritual adviser?" Cheyenne asked her.

"I also checked out anyone he might have gotten close to in prison. His one buddy died of a heart attack a year ago. According to prison officials, there was only one other, and he's still waiting on appeals—he received the death sentence, too."

They both thanked her.

"Keep me posted. I may or may not come down

with Jackson, depending on the workload here. Take care."

Andre ended the call and looked at Cheyenne. "So, which one of our suspects might best dress up as a priest?"

"We need more—or new—pictures for our board," she said. "Let me try to remember. Nelson Ridgeway and Katie Anson—whoops, sorry, Nelson and Katie Ridgeway now—were both friends of Janine's. Jacques Derringer was the organist at the church. He might well be able to imitate a priest by now. Oh, he could play just about any instrument, I think. He didn't play at Janine's funeral, though. It was too emotional for him. We've looked into Emil Justine, and because it's his property where we found Lacey Murton, he looks suspicious—but he was away when several of the kidnappings took place, up north, with solid alibis. Then we have Jimmy Mercury, your old friend. He helped catch Lassiter with you. You'd have thought that if they were buddies, Lassiter might have given it away somehow. The two of you are still friends, right?"

"Yes, I'd say we're still friends. Not that I've seen much of him in years. We try to get together when I'm in town."

"And you think it couldn't possibly be Jimmy?"

"I don't think so, but hell—I don't think it could be any of these people, and yet, I agree that the killer must have known Lassiter. There were tons of people at the funeral and tons more in town who might have known Lassiter. But this is a group we know to have been in the area at the time of the original killings."

Cheyenne was thoughtful again.

"Mike Holiday, he was really popular, too. He was in Janine's class, a beloved football star."

"And he's now a bouncer at a new place in the heart of Bourbon Street. Bourbon and Gin. Jimmy told me. The new owner had called Jimmy about playing, but Jimmy said it's not his scene—he said it was worse than a titty bar. Mike comes on at six. Jimmy doesn't start playing until eight—a few blocks over."

"Okay, we can hit the titty bar right after six," Cheyenne said.

He gave her a grin. "Women do go in."

"I know. I have been to strip bars—male, female, gay, straight. Whatever," Cheyenne assured him.

He shrugged. "I'm not making any assumptions," he told her. "Other business, Detective Vine in Lafayette agreed to a meeting. They're going to give us reports on everything that the crime scene people found out at the Justine place. Having a talk with him will be good."

"Sure. You could talk over the phone, and he could email you reports. You have another reason for going out there."

"Of course I do. Where else are we going to find the church organist—other than at the church?"

"What about our married duo?" Cheyenne asked. "We need to see them."

"We do," he agreed.

"Oh, one more guy, Rocky Beaufort. He quit teaching and coaching and opened a gym here in New Orleans, right in the French Quarter. He certainly has physical capability—I guess he'd make a great rougarou. Then, so would Mike Holiday…or Jimmy. Then, again, maybe the rougarou wasn't even big or particularly athletic. You can get away with a lot by catching people off guard."

"Let's go ahead and get your suitcases or whatever from the hotel. Let's grab lunch somewhere first—sorry, I haven't done any grocery shopping. And we'll work on these files until it's time to hit Bourbon and Gin."

"That's definitely a plan," she said. "And if we have extra time…"

"You can show me the path you were taking with Fournier the day when you were hunting down Braxton Trudeau—and found him dead."

"Wait—what about Katie and Nelson?" Cheyenne asked.

"Let's call our guru," Andre said, and pulled his phone out again.

He called Angela, not putting it on speakerphone this time because he'd called with one simple question.

Angela said that she'd get right back to them.

"Where do want to get lunch? I don't know about you, but I skipped breakfast," Andre said.

She hadn't had breakfast; she was accustomed to

the morgue, but the concept of breakfast just hadn't been appealing that morning.

And breakfast took time. She'd slept as late as possible, but she'd been in the lobby waiting for him when he arrived. There was no way she wasn't going to be punctual.

"Let's just go to the Monteleone. Their food is great. Then, we'll be right there," she suggested.

"Logical. I like it."

"I just have my computer bag and one roller bag. We can walk."

"I like that, too," he told her.

He hesitated strangely before closing the door to his house, glancing back over his shoulder, though she couldn't see what he was looking at. "Just a minute," he told her, stepping back in.

She thought that he was talking to someone, but she knew there was no one else in the house.

Maybe he was one of those people who talked to themselves. Rationed things out aloud.

Maybe she'd imagined the sound of his voice.

He reappeared shortly, a smile on his face.

"Do you have an imaginary friend?" she asked him.

"What?" he asked, frowning.

"Sorry! Just teasing."

"Oh, yeah, sorry—I didn't mean to bark like that. It's uh…nothing. Let's get going. Every day has to count in this." His expression was suddenly grim.

"What is it?"

"I was just thinking how much every day counted.

We found Lacey. News will go out that law enforcement most probably did *not* find the killer dead. That means, if I'm following the mind of this Mortician at all, another young woman will be taken—soon."

5

Andre felt the strangest assortment of emotions regarding Cheyenne Donegal.

They shared a lot, as Angela had pointed out. Places, people, legends—history.

She made a great partner. He'd be thrilled if she was a full-time partner for him.

That was as far as work was concerned.

Then there was his reaction to her as a human being.

She had, apparently, gotten over hating him—or believing that he had *thought* her capable of killing a suspect in cold blood.

Maybe he shouldn't have asked her to stay; Louis was highly encouraged by the fact that he had asked her to do so.

The old ghost was acting like the candlestick in *Beauty and the Beast*.

He was fascinated by Cheyenne, and had suddenly appeared to Andre, stopping him from leaving the house, just to let him know that she was the one—no, The One   with whom he might find some kind of lasting happiness. He was a busy man, and certainly—Louis had stood back to assess him—enough of a man for many an affair, but what was an affair in life?

Louis hadn't really considered himself to be a pirate—he had been a buccaneer, and the operations he had engaged in had been necessary smuggling because of all the embargos that had been set up, and then enforced during the War of 1812. He'd been arrested with the brothers Lafitte, but with the help of the local population had easily escaped, and when Andrew Jackson had come to Jean Lafitte for help, Louis had gone to war.

When it was over, he had wed a local girl and set up as a merchant, bought the house on Bourbon and turned the first floor over to his tailor/dressmaking shop.

"Trust me, I know! I sailed the high seas, I knew adventure and danger, I knew the incredible rush of victory—but I never knew happiness until I met my Lisette, and woke up with her beautiful face beside mine each morning."

Andre's reply had been a groan. "Louis, we're working! There's a killer out there!" he had admonished before shutting the door.

And Cheyenne had heard him. But she hadn't yet seen Louis. Well, there wasn't much he could do about that. It wasn't as though he was going to stop seeing the dead anytime soon. But soon enough he'd have to talk to her about it.

They started off down Bourbon toward Canal, but then they dropped down to Royal Street at the first corner. Cheyenne stopped walking for a minute, looking at one of the shop facades. She gave him an odd smile.

"One of my favorite places in the world," she told him.

"Fifi Mahony's?"

"You know it?"

"My mom shopped there for all her Mardi Gras wigs," he told her.

They passed several well-known destinations along Royal, antique shops, a Community Coffee café, the Andrew Jackson Hotel and the famed "Cornstalk House," both of the latter being charming bed-and-breakfast establishments now. They commented on things they had done as children and young people; Cheyenne had never lived in the City of New Orleans, but she had come often with family and friends.

"I used to love coming to Jackson Square and seeing the fortune-tellers and the artists—visual artists, and the human statues, and everything that went on!" Cheyenne said.

He laughed. "Well, I didn't always love it so much. My parents are, seriously, very good artists and they wound up in galleries around the world. But in high school, I used to be one of the people sitting in a little travel chair—hawking the art at Jackson Square."

"I'd love to see some of their work!" she said eagerly.

"You may have seen some. My mom loved the artist Rodrigue, and his *Blue Dog* images. Someone else was already doing cats, so she created a line of mythical beasts and set them in New Orleans, having beignets, out on the river, touring the cemeteries—"

"I have seen her work! It's fantastic!" Cheyenne told him.

He liked the way her face lit up with her honest enthusiasm.

In truth, I simply like her face. Hmm. In truth, I like a great deal more.

She paused and shook her head. "I do wish I'd come back to visit more often. I'd love to be here, just as a semi-local kind of tourist. Go to the zoo and the aquarium and the New Orleans collection and the museums on Jackson Square and—"

"You never know. We may have this finished soon."

"They'll call me back to Miami. And you…" She studied him and quickened her pace a bit at the same time. "I've heard things about the Krewe of Hunters. You're an 'elite' unit?"

"We have a good number of agents now, but we're still small—and directly responsible to Adam Harrison, who is something of a magician when it comes to breaking down procedure and red tape."

"I've heard your team referred to as the 'ghost busters.' What's that about?" she asked him.

Was she mocking him? Or looking at him seriously?

It was an interesting question because he knew

damned well she saw and talked to the dead. She had chosen not to tell him about it. And while he could have challenged her yesterday, he had chosen not to.

Her question was one that often came up when they worked with other law enforcement. And all the Krewe members had a pat answer.

"We are just willing to go the extra mile in any direction," he said. "And we consider options that might seem...unconventional to other agencies."

Like an actual rougarou.

Well, he didn't believe in monsters of that variety, and he didn't need to. People could be monsters.

And they could be amazing, too—sometimes even when dead.

"Trust me," he said, smiling. "We don't 'bust' ghosts."

He started walking again; he figured when she chose to trust him, she would tell him about her own ghosts.

They reached the Monteleone and headed to the restaurant. He chose a shrimp and grits dish; Cheyenne started to choose the gumbo but changed her mind and went with chicken.

She'd probably remembered that the corpse they'd seen dissected earlier had consumed a last meal of gumbo.

"You were there. I wasn't. I mean, I wasn't living out by you when Janine was murdered. Tell me what you remember about her friends," he said as they ate.

She was reflective for a minute. "I remember that Nelson and Katie were coupled up early on. They were both shy—the nerdy kids, I guess. I liked them both okay. You have to remember that I was three and a half years younger, and at that stage of life, that can be a lot. I wasn't anyone's pick for a movie on Saturday night—not by my cousin's crowd. I know that Mike Holiday was considered a hunk—all the girls said that he was a hunk, but I think his teachers actually helped him through some of his classes because he was a hotshot on the football field. A few of Janine's close friends—Nelly Simmons, Blair Winn and Gretchen Brule—moved away. Far away. Nelly went to Seattle for college, Blair to UCLA, and Gretchen somewhere out in San Diego. Of the people we remember well who are still in the area, you knew Jimmy Mercury a lot better than I did. He was—at that time—way older than me."

Andre couldn't help but ask, "What about the kid who committed suicide? Christian, I believe his name was?"

She looked down, pretending interest in a bottle of hot sauce.

"Well, he's certainly not guilty of anything. He's dead."

"No, I meant, had she been friends with him?"

"He didn't really have any good friends then. Honestly, I don't think that any of the girls meant to be cruel. They teased him. Everyone teased him. And he took it to heart. He didn't fit in, and he did horribly in sports, but...he was a nice kid. Bright and kind. He might have gone somewhere."

The subject seemed to hurt her. He felt guilty and moved on.

"We'll be honest, if we're able. If we actually get a chance to really speak with Mike Holiday, we'll tell him why we're here. And it will be in the news tomorrow, if it's not already out there, so we'll make sure he knows that we don't believe Braxton Trudeau was the killer. If he is guilty of anything, I want him to know we're still tracking him down."

"You don't think that will be feeding into what he wants?"

He shook his head. "Not at this point. Everyone knows that Lacey has been found. It's amazing that the news didn't come out until this morning and it's more amazing that our names were kept out of it. We're 'two FBI agents.' That's a good thing."

"So, we don't let on that we found her."

He shook his head. "We're here on the case. We're in New Orleans. That's one good thing about the cemetery and plantation being so far out of the way— no news cameras could get there very quickly."

"Thankfully. But if people have watched the news, they know I was there when Trudeau was found. I spoke to the press."

"I think that's fine."

His phone rang; it was Angela, he saw, and he answered it quickly.

"I found your friends—Nelson and Katie Ridgeway," she said.

"Where are they?"

Cheyenne was watching him, and he gave her a nod and listened to Angela.

"Very near you, I imagine. They opened a shop on Conti, not far from the wax museum."

"Ah, interesting. Do you have a name?"

"Miracle Music. The hours are 11:00 a.m. to 10:00 p.m. I guess they're far enough off Bourbon to close fairly early—considering."

"Considering," Andre said. He looked at Cheyenne and repeated the information Angela had given him. "Hey, anything else at the moment?" Angela asked.

"No, thanks. We're on the move," he told her.

"I'm here when you need me," she said, and they ended the call.

Andre saw their waitress and asked for the check; Cheyenne left him in the beautiful old lobby, and he thought that he rather wished they were local tourists, too. He had the urge to take a picture of her by the handsome grandfather clock.

She was down in a matter of minutes—quick and efficient.

They walked back briskly, without taking the time to comment on shops and places they loved.

He showed her a choice of bedrooms—she chose one of the two guest rooms, even though his parents' empty room was the nicest.

"That's their room," she said, smiling. "They come back here. I'd feel like I was trespassing."

"As you wish," he said.

"You're in your old room?"

"Hey, I leave things here. Not many things. But it's…it's home, my stuff will be here—my folks will never sell it. We'd better get a move on. Conti is way toward Canal."

"Can't take the heat, huh? Am I walking you too much?" she asked.

"Nothing like a challenge," he told her.

He couldn't help it; when they started out again, he used his longest strides. She had to break into a little trot now and then to keep up.

He paused once along the way. Old Vinnie Ballou had set up his one-man band in a portion of Bourbon that had been closed to vehicular traffic.

Vinnie was talented. Amazingly so. He often played his harmonica and guitar at the same time; when he wasn't playing the harmonica, he was singing, and could set his keyboard to do percussion, so it always sounded as if there were more players.

He could perform Broadway tunes, popular music and gospel. His voice was deep, rich, husky and unique.

And he'd been playing on Bourbon as long as Andre could remember.

He was doing "Ol' Man River" as they walked down the street.

Andre stopped abruptly. Cheyenne crashed into him.

"Sorry," he apologized quickly. "Gotta do this."

He walked up to Vinnie and set a bill in the hat laid out for donations. When he turned around, Cheyenne was smiling.

"He's amazing," she said. "So many great musicians are just on the street here—better than concerts in most cities!"

"He is incredible," Andre agreed. "And he may be of some help—he sees everything. I won't stop him right now since he has a crowd. I'll try to catch him later."

They hurried on, reaching Conti and making a right.

A few blocks down, they found Miracle Music.

There was a young man behind the counter. He had long hair, a scruffy almost-beard and wore a T-shirt that advertised the deceased musician Leonard Cohen.

A bell had tinkled over the door as they entered, and he looked up.

"Hey, welcome," he told them.

A couple was in the store, studying a row of guitars. A single young woman was searching through a rack that held sheet music.

Andre and Cheyenne approached the counter.

"Hello," Cheyenne said. "We're actually looking for the owners—we're old friends. Is Katie here, or Nelson?"

"Oh, yeah, man, cool. Katie is in back. I'll go get her," he said. "I'm Simon, by the way." He produced his hand.

They each took it in turn. "Andre and Cheyenne," he repeated after they'd introduced themselves, as if to firm up their names in his memory.

"Cool man, cool," Simon said. "Give me a sec."

Simon disappeared. Cheyenne started wandering the shop; Andre did the same, heading over to the guitars on the wall. Some were new; some were used.

The young couple there was arguing over the expense of a guitar. It was a used Gibson, and appeared to be in excellent condition—the price was definitely good.

"Maybe they'll give you a discount," he couldn't help but say. "This is nice, though." He picked it up and strummed a few chords. "Really nice!"

"See," the young man said.

"If we could just get it a few dollars cheaper, we could eat next week," the young woman with him said.

"Ask. It never hurts, but I'd say it was a good buy."

"You like guitars, sir?" the girl asked.

"Love them," he said.

He turned to glance at the doorway between the counter area and the back of the shop.

Katie Ridgeway was on her way out.

The years had been good to her. She had slimmed down since high school. She was never going to be considered conventionally beautiful; her features were an odd assortment of things too narrow and things too broad—her cheeks remained chipmunk cheeks and her eyes and lips were small. But she had managed a mass of thick dark hair into a smooth cut that slanted against her cheeks, making her face more attractive, and she'd learned how to wear makeup that accented her eyes.

"Oh, I am so glad you're here!" she said enthusiastically.

Katie wasn't referring to him. She had her arms opened wide and was heading toward Cheyenne.

"Katie!" Cheyenne said, greeting her with a hug. "I love this place—it's wonderful! And congratulations to you and Nelson. Of course, it was meant to be, and I'm way late, but congratulations!"

"I knew you were here. I'd been hoping you'd have time to look us up," Katie said. "I saw you on the news. Everyone was so relieved, thinking you'd found that horrible Mortician dead. People were getting less afraid, they were going out again. But I just saw another report that it's probably not the guy… Business was just picking up again. Oh, it's NOLA, and Bourbon is still somewhat insane at night, but not as insane as it should be. For tourist dollars, of course. But you are going to catch him…right? You will catch him?"

She glanced up, suddenly seeing Andre where he stood by the couple who were now determining how to ask for a discount. "Oh!" Katie said, and she frowned, clearly recognizing him and trying to remember from where.

"Katie, this is Andre Rousseau. He and I are working together on this, but you—"

"I remember Andre, of course. Andre, how are you?" Katie walked toward him. He thought she was going to shake his hand, but she hugged him, as well.

He hugged her back.

"You're working the case, too?" she asked. "You're an agent?"

"Yes, ma'am."

"Gave up the guitar?" she asked him. "Wow—that's too bad. Especially since we sell them."

"Oh, I didn't give it up. I just play for my own entertainment. That's good enough, in my mind," he told her.

The couple was standing behind him then, with the young man hugging the Gibson.

"Young kids," he said softly. "Think you can give them a break?"

"That's a fine Gibson!" Katie said. "It's already priced low."

"Yeah, but I see a young musician in love with a guitar," Andre said quietly. "He may be great, and one day, he can say, 'Thanks to Miracle Music, I got a break!'"

Katie stepped back from him and looked at the young man. "All right, let's see what I can do for you, sir. Ten percent off is the best I can offer. You know your guitars, so you know it's a steal!"

"Thank you, thank you," the girl said, "ten percent is food for us!"

"Fine, then, fifteen—you're skinny as can be," Katie said, and she turned back to Cheyenne and Andre. "Give me a minute. Simon is accepting a delivery of strings."

Katie went to the counter. The young couple thanked her effusively as he counted out the money. No credit cards for them; they paid cash.

The girl with the sheet music muttered something

about being back, and then they were in the store alone.

"Well, I'm certainly pleased enough that you found this place and came by," Katie said. "But this isn't just for old times, eh?"

"Katie, we're worried," Cheyenne told her. "We think that the Mortician is still out there. And because of certain similarities to the murders Lassiter committed, we keep thinking it had to be someone we knew back when Janine was murdered. We're asking all our old friends to see if they can think of anything—anything at all that might help."

"Oh!" Katie said, looking at her wide-eyed. "Wow. Lassiter was that substitute teacher everyone loved—he was so good-looking. And I mean, high school girls do get crushes on older men. And the guys...he was all-around Mr. Male, you know, so the guys thought he was cool and wanted to be like him."

"Was there anyone you thought to be especially close to him?" Andre asked her.

Katie grimaced, lowering her head. "Janine," she said softly.

"Anyone else?" Cheyenne asked, a hardness in her voice.

"I know that Mike Holiday was jealous of him. We see Mike now and then. But not a lot. He's got a chip on his shoulder a mile wide. He was Mr. Hero, you know, and then...well, he's a bouncer. Let me see... Oh, I know who! The organist. We all kind of grew up with him. I mean," she added dryly, "we were all in the choir, including you, Cheyenne. What's his name? I haven't seen him in years. The dude always reminded me of Ichabod Crane. Derringer—Jacques Derringer. Oh, yeah, and remember the gym teacher—Rocky Beaufort? He's here now, and we see him more often. He has a gym down near Rampart…trying to remember which street. But I'm sure you can find him. I don't remember him being especially close to Lassiter, but I would see them talking when Lassiter was subbing—they were hanging together at one of the football games." She shook her head suddenly. "Oh, but it's all too horrible. No one we know could have done these things!"

"We knew Lassiter," Cheyenne reminded her.

"We did," Katie said. "But still… Nelson and I… we weren't the in crowd, really. The only reason we were invited to events was Janine being kind. It may be sophomoric, but sometimes I can't help but be glad that Mike Holiday is barely making it as a bouncer! He was such a dick to us—a total dick!" Her expression became one of concern. "But the fact that he behaved that way as a teen, well, I still don't believe that he could…"

She broke off.

"We're going to see everyone we can remember—and reach," Andre told her. "How's Nelson? Is he around, too?"

"Nelson is deliriously happy. We're doing well here. Before, he was working as a number cruncher for the IRS. He loves, loves, loves the shop! We've had it going a few years now and we're doing great with it. Don't ever tell him I said this—I will call you two the nastiest liars in history—he plays horribly, but he does love his keyboard. And not reporting nine to five."

"Is he here?" Katie asked.

"He'll be back. We eat in sometimes, and then, somedays, we take different lunch times. If I know him, he's down at Napoleon House—they make his favorite muffuletta. Live together, work together—sometimes it's good to take little breaks, you know?"

"I'm sure everyone needs some private time," Cheyenne said. Then she added, "Well, we're just going to have to get together. I know that our schedules are kind of packed, but coffee, a drink, dinner—something somewhere," she said. "Talk to Nelson, see if you two can make some time."

"Oh, I will, I will. It's so good to see you!" Katie said enthusiastically.

"Call, please," Cheyenne said, giving her a card.

"And if you don't get her…" Andre handed over a card, as well.

"This will be great!" Katie said.

"Do you two ever get out together?" Andre asked.

"Yep—we have Simon to cover," Katie said.

"Okay, well, talk to Nelson and give us a call," Cheyenne said. "We'll get out of your hair now, but hopefully, hear from you soon."

They headed out of the shop.

"What did you get from that?" Andre asked Cheyenne.

"The fact that Katie really, really didn't like Mike

Holiday and that she'd love to rub his nose in the fact that he's nothing but a bouncer and she and Nelson are running a very successful business."

"But as Katie said herself, that doesn't make Mike Holiday a killer."

"No," Cheyenne agreed.

She fumbled in her pocket; he realized her phone was ringing. She answered it quickly, giving just her last name. Then her expression changed.

"Lacey, some of your officers are going to be nicer than others, but they're all there to watch over you. Yes, yes..." she said. She looked at Andre. "Yes, we'll get back out there tomorrow. I promise."

She hung up, looked at him and sighed. "I did tell Lacey to call me for anything," she said.

"What was the anything?"

"One of the cops physically searched Lacey's mother. It's not really worthy of note—the cop sent to watch her for the early-morning shift was a young woman. I think she took her assignment with gusto."

"We will go—" he said, but then he stopped suddenly.

They were passing an electronics store. He could see the news on one of the TVs on display and hear it dimly.

A picture of Emil Justine flashed on the screen.

"What?" he said.

Though he could barely hear the words through the storefront glass, the images had captions.

He turned to Cheyenne, frowning. "The local police brought Emil Justine in for questioning—they're labeling him as a person of interest in the case."

"How can they? He wasn't even there. He helped us."

Andre shook his head. "Who knows, but I'll bet he's not feeling fond of us. We're the ones who found Lacey held captive on his property. But we should have all been informed. We're supposed to be lead on this case. I have to find out what the hell is going on."

They weren't quite on Bourbon Street, and the neon lights and loud music weren't what they would be at night, but there was still a bustle of activity around them.

"Let's duck into that clothing store—I'll engage the clerk. You make the calls in peace and quiet."

She all but dragged him into a little boutique. This one didn't sell the same T-shirts and souvenirs that could be found in dozens of stores. It was obviously upscale, and he thought that some of the pieces were one of a kind.

Cheyenne walked enthusiastically up to the clerk, smiling and telling her that she was looking for a friend, but she was specifically looking for a dress in between business and formal, and would she mind showing her what she had.

The clerk came out from behind the counter to help her.

Cheyenne glanced over at Andre, waving a hand in the air. "Oh, please, don't worry, my husband will just make business calls. We have time!"

Andre smiled, took his phone into a corner and started calling.

He spoke to Jackson; he'd been informed that Detective Bill Vine, with the state police department, was determined to hold Emil Justine as a suspect until Andre and Cheyenne had time to go over everything that had happened with him.

"He thought you two would be sticking around the Lafayette New Iberia area for a few days. I informed him that it was imperative you two be back in NOLA for the autopsy. I also promised that you'd be out there tomorrow."

"Yep, we were heading back. Thing is, the news the police are giving out make people think that they're safe. First with Trudeau, and now, if they have Emil Justine's picture plastered everywhere, people will believe that he was the Mortician and that his ancestor was the original rougarou."

"I'm trying," Jackson told him, "but I'm having a hard time controlling the press. Oh, by the way, Angela and I will be out there sometime tonight. We'll join you at the Justine place, and see where we go from there."

"Lacey Murton just called Cheyenne—she isn't happy with her overseers. She's understandably nervous."

"One of us will stay with her," Jackson said. "We'll figure it out when we get there, but Angela, as you know, is especially good with people. She might even be able to get Lacey to remember more. And even if, as time, space and logic imply, Emil

Justine is completely innocent, the killer *was* making use of his property. I know how your mind is moving on this, but logic also dictates we talk to his manager and the embalmer there. Gut instinct is bizarre. I feel that you two are on the right path, but any possible lead or obvious suspect must be pursued."

"I agree," Andre said.

"See the people you need to see this afternoon and evening. I don't know when exactly we'll be arriving, but sometime around ten this evening. We'll be in touch as soon as we're there."

"Great. See you around ten." Andre hung up. Cheyenne was writing down styles and prices, chatting away with the boutique owner.

He had just pocketed his phone when the woman suddenly said suspiciously, "I know you! You're an FBI agent. I saw you on the news the other morning when the man was found who was supposed to be the Mortician but then wasn't, or they don't know, but they've arrested another man now and... Why are you in my shop?"

"I am an agent," Cheyenne assured her. "But," she added, smiling, "even agents have friends, you know. And I really am a fan of your shop."

"Oh, good, I thought... Oh, my God! For a moment, I was afraid that—that he might be in my shop! That you— " she pointed at Andre "—might be a killer! And that she was trying to distract you, or..."

"No, ma'am," he said politely. "I swear to you, I am not the killer."

"Anyway," Cheyenne redirected the girl, "thank you! I'll let my friend know about your dresses. We'll be back," Cheyenne promised.

The shopgirl gave her a half-hearted smile.

It was clear that she didn't care if they came back or not.

Preferably not.

Back out on the street, Andre told her about his discussion with Jackson. "We won't be stretched so thin. And if we're pursuing those who are in NOLA now, we'll have someone out with Lacey and dealing with the state and local police."

"Sounds good. I'm intrigued to meet them. Jackson Crow has a reputation."

"He does, doesn't he? Ghost buster, eh?"

"Ah, but many of my coworkers have been in awe of him," she said. "So…off to the strip club?"

Bourbon and Gin was adorned with the customary neon—beneath the words in lights that advertised its name, there was a neon image of a very well-endowed female with a minuscule waist, lassoing in a cowboy.

Mike Holiday was sitting on a stool next to the door, asking for ID from a group of young men. He noticed Cheyenne and Andre as he returned a wallet. He waved the group in. "So, you're here, too, huh?" he said. He rose; he'd put on some weight since Andre had seen him, but he didn't appear to be too badly out of shape. There were premature lines etching his face, but there was still something of the good-looking young football player to him.

"Sorry, bad greeting. Cheyenne, great to see you—I saw you on TV. Andre, didn't know you were working the same gig." He grinned wryly and waved a hand indicating his thankless job. "See how the mighty have fallen, eh?"

"Hey, Mike—you're making a living. Nothing wrong with that," Andre said.

Mike grimaced. "Well, there were days when I thought I was going to grow up to be the next Tom Brady. Anyway, yeah, I'm making a living. An honest one—and I'm sure you know, it would be easy enough around here to make a not-so-honest living. So, this is a messed-up reunion. You guys are after a serial killer, huh?"

He was behaving more humbly than Andre remembered, but life did that to everyone.

"Cheyenne." Mike smiled at her like an older brother. "Well, you sure did grow up beautiful. You're doing okay on this?"

"I'm doing fine, thanks, Mike," she said.

"And this guy," Mike looked at Andre. "He was a few years above me in middle school. Cool dude then. Nice to see you two working together. How did you like high school in the big city after our little place out in Cajun Country?" he asked.

"Love the old homestead as much as the new," Andre told him.

Mike looked him dead in the eyes. "Man, looks like the cops are having trouble with this—first a dead guy was the killer. Now, they have old Emil Justine locked up. Well, he is kind of creepy. I mean, who turns their family home into a funeral home? I'd have turned that place back into a mansion to rival the best—at the very least, a museum home like Oak Alley or something like that." He frowned suddenly "Oh, no—seriously. Do you think I'm a suspect?"

"We're hoping you might help us," Andre said.

"Oh. How?"

"By thinking back. Someone was close to Lassiter, we believe. A disciple, if you will. Can you think of anyone who was close to Lassiter back then?"

"Wow. We were all a little in awe of him. Every girl had a crush on him, including Janine, who I had always figured was going to fall hard for me. Sorry, Cheyenne."

"It's all right," Cheyenne said.

"Did you hang around him sometimes?" Andre asked.

"He was a teacher, I was a student. Thing is, we were seventeen and eighteen when we were seniors. He was only about twenty-four at the time. That made him closer than most of the teachers—he was tech savvy, he liked the same music, he rooted big-time at the games." He looked at Cheyenne again.

"Go on. I've accepted Janine's death for a long time now," she said.

Is it easier for Cheyenne because she still sees her cousin as a ghost? Andre wondered.

Mike continued, "I'm sure he first set his sights on Janine when she was cheerleading. She was something. That's why everyone thought that we'd be the golden couple. And it would have happened—except for Lassiter. You know how those outfits look on girls, and Janine was…really beautiful. And I do remember Lassiter hanging around coach at the games. Hey, you know that Rocky Beaufort has a gym here in town? You might want to check in to him—I mean, he'd know more about whoever Lassiter might and might not have been hanging around with. I'd say you need to look at that weird organ guy—I think that he was close with Lassiter, though memory doesn't always serve perfectly. And all the kids seemed to be in the choir at some time or another. Well, mostly the girls. But some of the guys, too. All our parents were big on us being with the church somehow." He grinned suddenly. "Hey, I go up to Our Lady of Guadalupe now, just on Rampart. The old holding church for St. Louis No. 1. Jazz mass is like going to church—and a really fun concert!"

"Nice—I love jazz mass there, too," Cheyenne said.

He excused himself to take another few ID cards and let a giggling group of young men in.

It was getting later. Young women wearing bridal headbands were walking down the street, laughing and plowing into one another, their gaits unsteady. Couples were wandering by; a little cart advertising cheap beer rolled out near them.

The sound of music—heavy metal, jazz, pop

rock—was coming from about every doorway, every venue trying to be louder than the next.

Mike turned back to them. "You could check out Nelson and Katie. They were friggin' weird!"

"Yes, we've talked to them. We're going to everyone for help," Andre said. "We're on our way to see Jimmy Mercury."

Mike nodded. "He's great. Maybe he'll let you sit in with him." He shrugged. "You can find good bands on Bourbon, too, no matter what the locals tend to say, but in my mind, Frenchman Street is always the best. Hey, you guys are welcome to go on in if you want."

"I was thinking we'd hop on up to the gym and try to see Rocky Beaufort," Andre said. "But thanks."

Mike shrugged. "I know it's a topless bar, but some of the girls in there…they can really dance. I mean, they're talented and strong—they use those ribbon things and all. This one girl was with Cirque du Soleil for a while. The kid is good."

"I've seen great dancers in strip clubs," Cheyenne said. "I believe you. But I guess we'd best get moving on."

"Yeah. Well, I'm here most nights, if you want to see me—different days off every week. Anyway, good to see you both. And contrary to popular belief, I'm doing fine."

"Glad to hear it, Mike," Andre said. "Hopefully we'll see you again."

"Sure. I'm available. Days," Mike added with a

grin. Then he grew serious. "Mark my words!" he said. "You need to see that church organist—Mr. Derringer. Or really investigate Nelson Ridgeway. I'm telling you—the organist is downright creepy. And Nelson—man, that guy is just weird!"

6

Neon blazed, people laughed, music all but screamed around them. But there was something about the way Mike Holiday had spoken that seemed ominous to Cheyenne.

She forced a smile and thanked him, and she and Andre moved on.

"He was cheerful," Cheyenne said. "What was your take?"

"Yeah," Andre said. "He was cheerful—and just as charming as the *Crypt Keeper*," Andre said flatly.

"At least he was just trying to give advice, and he didn't finish it off with a diabolical laugh."

"Nice to know our old acquaintances are so willing to point fingers at one another. Of course, we haven't even seen Nelson yet. Maybe he walks around in a rougarou costume."

"I wonder who Rocky Beaufort will want to point us toward."

"Maybe he'll just confess, throw himself on our mercy."

Cheyenne looked at him.

"Sorry," he told her. "I'm still upset that they brought in Emil Justine without even a call to us. Everyone was so polite the other night. Most of the time, in my experience at any rate, there's sometimes a bit of jostling for position. The locals carefully watching the Feds, but all working together. They brought in Justine despite everything they had from the FBI, and surely, their own sources. Are we missing something? Could he have been at dinner in Philadelphia at midnight and back south to snatch a girl by 2:00 a.m.?"

"Not unless he has talents we can't imagine," Cheyenne said. "Maybe their theory is that he isn't the killer—but he is aiding and abetting him and allowing him access to Justine property to carry out his murders."

"Well, we'll get into all that tomorrow," Andre said. "For now, back toward Rampart Street."

It was a walk again, but really, there was nowhere in the French Quarter that was all that far. The oldest section of the city, it stretched from the Mississippi River to Rampart Street, and between Canal Street and Esplanade. It was an area of seventy-eight square blocks, making cars unnecessary for many people, such as Andre's parents. The French Quarter, or Vieux Carré, didn't begin to encompass all that was so unique and wonderful about the city, as far as Cheyenne was concerned, but the size of the old city center did make it easy to traverse.

Rocky Beaufort's gym was in an old building refurbished with glass windows to the street and lined with treadmills, exercise bikes and other machines. Through the window, as they approached the door, they could see that beyond the cardio equipment, there were all kinds of machines for muscle development, and beyond that a door that was marked Free Weights.

"Looks good. I guess our old gym teacher is doing okay," Andre noted.

"And I'll guess he's still in fairly amazing shape," she said, and shook her head. "If the killer made all the women pliable—through drugs or a crack on the head—massive muscle wouldn't have been necessary. But you'd still need to be in decent shape for moving bodies around. A person, living or deceased, is very heavy—dead weight, as they say, whether dead or alive."

"Let's see if old Rocky is in," Andre said, opening the door for her.

They entered the gym. A cheerful, very perfect-looking young woman at the large counter centered before the doors greeted them.

"Hello, and welcome! Newcomers, I see. Have you just moved to New Orleans? Are you looking to keep up with your regimen?" she asked.

"We're old friends of Rocky Beaufort," Cheyenne said. "Is he in?"

"Well, hello. Sure, Rocky is in his office. I'll just buzz him."

With her perfect smile in place, she picked up the desk phone and made a call. She looked at them as she spoke and asked, "Who shall I say is here?" she asked.

"Cheyenne Donegal and Andre Rousseau," Andre told her.

The girl smiled and repeated their names. There was something in her voice, something in her smile, that suggested she knew her boss very well. She couldn't have been more than twenty or twenty-one.

She hung up the phone. "Mr. Beaufort will be right out."

Rocky came from a door across the room, wearing gym shorts and a T-shirt that advertised his own business. In his early fifties, he was a mass of lean muscle. His gray hair was close-cropped to his head and his eyes seemed a very bright blue against the tanned contours of his face.

Cheyenne had to wonder if he'd had work done— he wasn't just fit; he hadn't seemed to have aged much at all in the decade-plus since she'd last seen him.

"Hello!" he said, coming forward, a hand outstretched to Cheyenne and then Andre. "Missy," he said, addressing the girl behind the desk. "Two of my old students. This one here is Andre Rousseau—he could have been a fine addition to the high school team, he could carry a ball down the field faster than any fellow out there. And this is Cheyenne Donegal, who—"

He broke off. She thought he'd been about to say that she'd have been an amazing cheerleader for his team; Janine had been a cheerleader, and everyone had expected that Cheyenne would have followed her cousin's example.

Rocky Beaufort simply said, "Who was one of the finest young ladies I ever had the privilege to teach."

"Well, thank you," Cheyenne said. Then, before they could get caught in a conversation that included Missy, she asked, "Coach, could we speak with you in private?"

"Come on into my office," he said. "I'm not a coach anymore. Well, I am a fitness coach, but hey—you two are all grown up now. Call me Rocky. Please."

He led the way.

Missy looked after them—obviously curious.

Maybe even a little afraid?

His office was nice, with a big dark wood desk. On the wall, pictures of himself showing off his muscles along with old photos of his winning teams, and one wall that featured professional head shots of his personal trainers. A large comfortable sofa sat in front of his desk. He indicated that Cheyenne and Andre should take the sofa and he rolled his desk chair to come around and face them, closer than they would have been had the desk been between them, and far more intimate.

"What can I do for you? Andre, heard you went

off into the military. I know your family... So. I know you're both on the case of the Mortician, and you must be facing incredible pressure. It is him, it isn't him—and a girl found out at the Justine Plantation Mortuary Home and Cemetery... Go figure, the one you get out alive is in a graveyard! Anyway, just what the hell is happening?"

"Emil Justine is being held as a possible accomplice," Andre said. "The debate continues on whether or not Braxton Trudeau was guilty of all or any of the murders. We've learned that he wasn't a suicide."

"Do you think an angry father might have gotten suspicious and stalked the man? Maybe not a father, but a brother, a friend, a lover?" Beaufort was thoughtful, his question held concern. "You have to understand that this entire area has been under pressure. Revenues are down—people have been afraid to go out. Women especially. All right, here, I admit...and trust me, I'm not happy regarding the reason, but our revenues have been up—we have a few martial arts and kickboxing classes that we offer each week. The sign-up sheets have been packed like never before. I had to add more classes."

"We're still actively investigating," Cheyenne told him. "We're asking all our old friends and acquaintances if they can remember anyone who might have been close to Lassiter."

"Lassiter—the Artiste?"

"Yes," Andre said. His eyes were steady on Beaufort. Cheyenne thought that she would not like to be interrogated by the man; Andre made a perfect agent. He could be unerringly polite, but his intensity could be chilling, and his eyes were also as dark as coal and seemed to have a real fire that burned within them when they settled on a person. Cheyenne doubted that there was a man or woman in the gym with tighter, leaner muscles.

At the moment, though, size had nothing to do with it.

It was all in the eyes.

Their old coach looked down—perhaps uncomfortable.

"Close to Lassiter?" Beaufort repeated.

"He used to hang out with you at games," Cheyenne said. "We were hoping you might be able to point us in the direction of someone he might have been friendly with—someone who was, perhaps, a protégé."

"The protégé of a murderer?" Beaufort asked.

"This new killer is obviously imitating him."

"Dear God," Beaufort said. "All of us… Cheyenne, it was all so horrible, and to this day…well, I'm so sorry about Janine. She was a true joy. Sassy. Lovely."

"Thank you," Cheyenne said.

"Sure, he, uh… Man, I get chilled just remembering!" Beaufort said. "Yeah, he stood next to me at games. He knew a lot about college football. I never realized he was ogling the cheerleaders. And to think about it now…"

He broke off, shaking his head, cringing.

Cheyenne didn't say anything, and Andre also

let them sit in the somewhat uncomfortable silence. Then Beaufort continued. "I haven't a clue who else he was buddies with. I saw him when he came in as a substitute teacher. He was there often that year... the year Janine...died. Miss Pritchett had a baby and she was out for months, so he was in for her. I'd see him in the teachers' lounge. He was big on reading—I'd see him with all kinds of history books. Oh, yeah, I remember kidding him about one he was reading—it was on Jack the Ripper. I can try—I can think back. But I can't think of anyone I saw him with regularly. Oh, yeah, well...he liked Mike Holiday! He would always congratulate him after a game. Who else, who else... Your friend!" he said, his eyes steady on Andre. "The musician, Jimmy Mercury. When he wasn't teaching, Lassiter picked up gigs, mostly on his own, playing coffeehouses and other little venues where they wanted a one-man band. He wasn't great—but he was an okay guitar player and singer. Oh, I forgot the music—he was friends with the church organist, too. I didn't know the guy well, but Lassiter said he was going to be playing with him at the church one Sunday, so I went to church—I'm not a big churchgoer, usually. But those two did play together. Derringer and Lassiter obviously knew one another. Now, that guy Derringer is...a little off. He's someone you might want to check out. I hear he's still at the church, going strong. Maybe...man, I don't know. Couldn't be. But then again, Lassiter—hell, if Lassiter was a crazy murderer, anyone might be."

"Thanks," Andre told him, smiling and standing. Cheyenne and Beaufort did the same.

Andre offered his hand. "Thank you, sincerely. And if by any chance you think of anything else— anything, no matter how small—please, call."

"My God, of course," Beaufort said. He pumped Andre's hand again. He was more gentle with Cheyenne. He gave her an odd look, and then said, "Hey, you two have obviously been hitting the gym. While you're here, you come in anytime. I'll let the girls who handle the desk know that you are just free to use these facilities anytime."

"Thanks," Cheyenne murmured. "We're…busy, and kind of running all around the area, but maybe we'll see you again."

"Great. You're always welcome," Beaufort said.

He walked them back out to the desk and leaned against it as he waved goodbye.

Just as they started to turn away, Cheyenne noted the way his hand landed on the counter—his fingers just touching Missy's.

"Everyone wants it to be the creepy organist," Andre muttered as they exited. "Because he might be a killer—or because he's a creepy organist?"

"Creepy organists tend to be high on anyone's list," she replied. "What did you think of Beaufort?"

"Nothing one way or the other," he said. "Except he likes young women."

"He's sleeping with Missy."

"Yeah, I thought so, too."

"But I think she is of legal age, and I've seen

plenty May-December affairs, both ways, and it doesn't mean that..."

"I don't know. He could be her father."

"Still. I believe she is legal."

"He suggested that we look at the organist and Jimmy Mercury. Have you seen any kind of a pattern here?" he asked her.

"Sure. Everyone has suggested someone else."

"Not just that," he said. "Everyone has suggested someone else—on our list."

His words chilled her.

No one ever wanted to believe that a friendly face, a well-known friend or acquaintance—even a relative—could be a killer.

"Yes," she said. "But," she added softly, "creepy organist did come up several times."

"And we'll see him tomorrow. Let's get to Jimmy's place on Frenchman, and then back to the house. Angela and Jackson will be in sometime before midnight, but before then, we need to study the Mortician's pictures again. I want to try to figure out what it is that bothers you."

Frenchman Street wasn't far, but still, it would have been a good walk from where they were—close to Canal and Rampart, while Frenchman was accessed from Esplanade on the opposite side of the Quarter. They hopped a taxi, and the cabbie swept them around quickly, staying on Rampart and off the heavy-laden pedestrian areas.

It was a quick ride, and soon they were in the restaurant/bar where Jimmy was going to be playing.

Jimmy was a striking man, tall, with ebony skin and a quick, charming smile. He was on the stage, setting up, but hopped down when he saw them enter. He greeted Cheyenne with an embrace and did the same with Andre.

"I don't go on for another ten minutes. Hey, by the way, let me introduce you to my guys. That's Sly Carter on percussion and Frank Nesmith on keyboards and we're all whatever else we need to be, but you know that. Sly, Frank—Cheyenne Donegal and Andre Rousseau. Old friends from way back when."

Sly and Frank greeted them, then Jimmy ushered them to a table. He reached into the denim jacket he was wearing and produced a packet and handed it to Andre.

"What's that?" Andre asked.

"Anything you could want on me for the last three months. Figured you might be investigating me. I've seen the news. We have the guy, we don't have the guy. We have a guy who might have helped the guy. Anyway, thought I'd save you some trouble. When that Cindy Metcalf was taken, I was off watching my favorite band, Trombone Shorty. Pics are there with a timeline to prove it. They were playing out in Denver and I went to three of their shows. There's more— credit card receipts, hotel receipts, airline tickets… you can verify it all, and you could have gotten all of it. I just thought that I'd make life easy on you."

"Well, thanks," Andre said.

"Anything," Jimmy said. He leaned back in his

chair, looking at Cheyenne. "I'm so sorry, kiddo. I will never forget Janine's funeral, as long as I live."

Cheyenne smiled. "And I will never forget you chasing the man down without hesitating. Believing in me—that we couldn't let him slip away. And don't worry, everyone stumbles over Janine's name. Her loss will always hurt, but it also means that I'm determined, in her memory, to make this stop."

Andre leaned forward. "Well, what do you think?"

"I think I'd have never pegged Lassiter as a killer, but remember, I was older—out of high school. Out of the choir, living in New Orleans, playing here. But I could hear the certainty in your voice when you pointed him out. So the news says the last victim was found alive, out at that same funeral home," he said, staring at them. "You two found her, am I right?"

"You should be with the FBI," Andre told him. "How did you get that from staring at us?"

Jimmy shrugged. "If anyone would know to look there, it would be the two of you. Or me, but I'm not a cop or anything. And weird old Mr. Justine was around back then, too. I heard they've taken him, but he hasn't been arrested?"

"He's got alibis for the abductions. He's being held for aiding and abetting—they're looking for something to charge him with. I don't think he was in on it."

"Who was managing the place?" Jimmy asked.

"We haven't interviewed him yet. His name is Guy Mason."

"Don't know him," Jimmy said.

"He's new to the area, I understand," Andre said. "But I'm sure we're going to find that the police out there have questioned him. We're heading back tomorrow."

"You've seen folks who were there for the Lassiter thing who are living in NOLA now?" Jimmy asked.

"We have—just came from Rocky Beaufort's gym," said Cheyenne.

Jimmy was thoughtful. "As for Mr. Beaufort..." He shook his head. "He does like them young," he said at last.

"Yep. We figure he's sleeping with his twenty-year-old receptionist," Cheyenne said.

"Yeah, there was almost a scandal just a bit back," Jimmy said. "Some of the old guard were talking about him—nothing libelous, but there was all kinds of chatter on social media. A mama was mad, and you know how mamas can be around here. I think one of his employees swore that she was eighteen— and she wasn't quite. Tall girl, and beautiful—tall can get away with a lot. Anyway, the mad mama was the kind who is nicely rich and truly old-school, and she let it drop rather than turn it into a scandal. I hear her daughter is now in some finishing school in Europe. Just what the hell is it that those places 'finish'?" he asked.

Andre's phone rang; he excused himself to answer it, standing to step outside where he could hear.

Jimmy smiled across the table at Cheyenne. "I swear, kiddo, it wasn't me. I— Everyone loved Janine."

Cheyenne returned the smile. She didn't think that she'd believe Jimmy could be a killer—even if she saw him with a knife in someone's back. He could charm. She hoped her instincts were right.

But that very talent was part of Ryan Lassiter...

"She was crazy about your music, Jimmy. Janine, I mean. I'm sure that's why my aunt asked specifically that you put together a jazz band for the funeral."

Andre stepped back inside, features tight. He reached for her hand.

"Jimmy, thanks, and I can call on you anytime, right?"

"You bet, *mon ami.* Anytime. And hey, you come back, you have to play with us. Mr. Authority, hot G-man—you've got to play."

Andre didn't reply; he just smiled, catching Cheyenne's hand and hurrying her out.

"What is it?" she demanded outside.

He turned to her. "That was Dr. Morley. He's in close contact with one of the crime scene technicians working the Braxton Trudeau case."

"Right, and?"

"You know they've been comparing everything— they found a hair matching a victim from almost a year ago, not even considered a victim of the Mortician. There were no pictures of her left anywhere— before or after her death."

"And Dr. Morley got this information first?"

"The crime scene tech who gave him the information is *Mrs.* Morley. He wanted me to know right away—no matter how tangled it all gets between jurisdictions, he considers us lead."

"We are supposed to be lead."

"Right, and here's the fear—if this info gets out, everyone will start believing that we're alarmists, and that Trudeau was the killer."

"And then law enforcement and the cops guarding Lacey Murton will be called off the case, and they'll be wanting to send me back to Miami and… Andre, Trudeau might well have been a killer. But he wasn't the Mortician."

"Yep, but heads up—tomorrow will be hell. Let's get back to my place. Jackson and Angela should be arriving soon."

"Right. We need to figure out our next move."

She was sure, to the depths of her soul, the Mortician was still out there.

Andre was in the kitchen, setting down paper plates and taking food from bags. He'd ordered in, figuring that no one had really eaten and while it might be eleven at night, that was the time, it seemed, when the body reminded one that fuel was needed.

Angela came into the kitchen first. Jackson— being Jackson—was studying the board Andre had created in the parlor. He was also adding to it, using pictures they'd scooped up from social media showing their new range of suspects.

Cheyenne was settling into the guest room, taking the fastest shower known to man; she'd sworn she'd be right down.

"He's charming—quite the ladies' man in his day, I imagine," Angela said.

For a moment, Andre frowned. "Ah," he murmured, "you're referring to Louis."

She grinned. "He knocked before coming in to say hello. He was delighted to speak with Jackson and me." The two of them had set up in Andre's parents' room—and of course, they were welcome to it. His mother was a true child of Southern hospitality—everything was always in readiness for guests, including her own seldom-used space. Angela continued, "He says you don't want him near our other guest."

"I never said that to him, but hey." He hesitated. "Angela, she speaks to the dead—Special Agent Cheyenne Donegal, that is. Her cousin—her murdered cousin—was at the cemetery with a friend, a kid named Christian. He committed suicide not long before Janine's murder. But I saw them, and I got to see Cheyenne trying to pretend that they weren't there."

"Really? Hmm, you'll have to tell Jackson." She sat down at the table and scooped up a chip and guacamole from the to-go containers on the table and then began to cough. "Wow! Forgot just how spicy food can be here."

Andre produced another container from the bag. "This one isn't spicy," he told her. "I always order two."

Angela laughed. "Mexican in New Orleans. Whatever."

"No, burgers, salad and fries—and guacamole and chips," he said.

"Whatever it is, it's great. We were rushing around all day." She paused. "It all began just a few blocks from here. A corner on Royal Street. The Krewe. Seems like a lifetime ago, and yet, not so many years. Our second case was near here, too. Out on one of the Lower River plantations. And we had another up in St. Francisville."

Andre nodded and smiled at her. "I know Krewe history," he assured her. He sat down across from her. "I had a friend here, a movie guy, who bought one of the decaying old mansions on Canal. He used it for a movie, and then a paranormal group bought it. I was with him when they were setting up one of their rooms, and the woman started telling me about their ghosts. I asked about their stories but she didn't know them. She basically told me that New Orleans was one of the most haunted cities in the world, and there were dozens of spirits here and…well, if you build it, they will come! I wasn't certain that she had any 'paranormal' ability at all, but in the interest of being as polite as my mama taught me, I kept my mouth shut."

"Silence is often valor," she said. "So…you're not going to say anything to Cheyenne about Louis—and others?"

"I'd like to let her speak first, but we'll see."

He fell silent; they could hear Cheyenne coming down the stairs. Her hair was still damp, appearing now as a beautiful, burnished, coppery red. She smiled at Angela—the two had seemed to like one another immediately—and then looked at Andre.

"Is there anything I can do?"

"Nope. Sodas are in cans, I'm afraid, right there, center of the table, and the burgers are not gourmet well, they could be, if it weren't so late. They will make you a peanut butter and jelly burger if you like or give you all kinds of combos in your bun. These are just burgers. Sit, please, eat."

She took a chair and reached into the bag for one of the wrapped burgers. He'd left condiments on the table. He was reaching for his own food when Jackson joined them.

Jackson sat, taking the bag from Andre and saying, "I have added our pictures and what information we have regarding Mike Holiday, Rocky Beaufort, Jacques Derringer, Katie and Nelson Ridgeway, and Jimmy Mercury. And Emil Justine. Tomorrow, we have to choose directions. The hair found on Braxton Trudeau matches a victim not on our lists— Fiona Kiley, of Pensacola. Her body was found in a hotel room in Metairie nine months ago. On initial search, we couldn't find anything that would connect Trudeau to her for any legitimate reason. Still, the hair does suggest he murdered her—if no one else. She wasn't displayed in a manner that matches the Mortician's victims. But we believe that the Mortician started out killing before he very obviously began to imitate Lassiter. Practicing murder, perhaps, horrible and sad as that may be."

"You really don't think that Trudeau was the killer?" Angela asked.

Cheyenne chewed thoughtfully. She shook her head and set down her burger. "No, there's just something else about the Mortician's photographs that remind me of the Rougarou's and the Artiste's. Something subtle. And while images of the kidnapped women from the older murders were shown publicly, police in both cases kept the death photos away from the press in the interest of not ripping up families and friends further."

She stood and headed out of the kitchen.

Andre, Angela and Jackson looked at one another, and then followed her.

Andre knew that she had headed straight out to the board, and she was studying it intensely—looking at the images of the women in death.

Andre stepped forward. "This bothered Cheyenne, and I see it," he said, pointing to the strange slant of the hair in each picture.

"I see. It's subtle, but something of a signature," Jackson said. "It is odd that bangs or no bangs, long hair or short, that same slash to the left is there."

Cheyenne gasped suddenly. "That's it!"

"What, what—I don't see!" Angela told her.

"So small, but…look, they're all wearing the same cross. Okay, not the same from the first, but look at those women, sketches. Each one is wearing a cross—almost hidden here, in this image from the 1860s. Then, look, we're up to Janine."

Cheyenne spun around, looking at the three of

them. "That exact same tiny cross Janine is wearing is around the necks of the other girls. You don't really see it there—on Cindy Metcalf—because it must have twisted when he took the picture. I'm sure he was utterly infuriated with himself when he realized it. Look at all of Lassiter's victims. There's the cross…covered a bit by hair there. And you wouldn't notice it because many, many people wear little crosses. Each young woman from way back must have had her own. When Lassiter started killing, it looks like he had one cross and placed it on all his victims, removing it after the photograph. That could mean a little remorse or it could mean he wanted them to go to heaven. It could also mean that he was just a sadistic killer playing with us, laughing his ass off because he'd left clues that we didn't discover."

Andre saw exactly what she meant. Yes, the girls wore the same cross.

"Janine was not wearing this cross when she was found?" Andre asked her.

"No, in fact…" Cheyenne's voice trailed, and her lips tightened to white with her memory. "Her mother was upset. Janine usually wore a tiny crucifix that her mom had bought her when they were in Italy on vacation. It was beautiful, real gold, and she should have been buried with it. Janine wasn't wearing it when she was found. So, Lassiter had the cross—he took it off each girl after he took her picture."

"And the Mortician has it now," Andre said, pointing to each of the pictures of their latest victims.

Strands of hair fell over the piece of jewelry, tufts of lace covered it slightly in one photo, but it was there—hidden, but there.

"Our killer knew Lassiter—well enough to take over when the time was right," Cheyenne said.

"Cheyenne, you've just nailed it," Andre told her.

She was staring at the pictures, a look of sadness in her eyes. No way out of that—you learned to live with a loss. You never forgot it.

She turned to them. "So, how do we proceed from here? It seems that other law enforcement agencies are convinced that they've got their man. How do we convince them that Trudeau might have been a murderer, but not the murderer playing games as the Mortician?"

"I'll take care of that," Jackson said. "We have the ME's report and the fact that they had a match with a victim who hadn't been grouped into the obvious Mortician killings."

"We've had people studying video from the prison, and sadly, there is no good capture of the fake priest. He wore a wide-brimmed black hat and appeared to have thick dark hair—a wig, probably. And anyone decent with makeup could have darkened the brows, twisted the nose, and sharpened the chin. Artists up at headquarters are working with the images we've been able to catch, but they were having a very hard time coming up with something definitive," Angela said.

"But tomorrow we'll head out to the Lafayette/Broussard/New Iberia area, check in at the police station with Emil Justine—and see Lacey Murton," Andre said.

"Settled," Angela murmured. "So, I'm finishing my burger."

She headed back to the kitchen. Jackson followed her.

Cheyenne was still studying the board. "Cheyenne?"

She smiled at him. "Trust me, I got my emotions regarding Janine under check years ago, but I think I'm done with my food. What time do you want to head out?"

"Early—before traffic."

"I'll be ready. I think I'll run up, then, if that's all right."

"Whatever makes you comfortable. Our plan is in motion and it is nearly midnight now. We'll get on the road at seven. Oh, bring a bag. If things heat up there, we might need to stay in that area overnight."

"Sounds good," she said. "I'll be down for coffee before."

"I'll set it on a timer," he promised.

She left the room and headed up the stairs; Andre returned to the kitchen.

Jackson and Angela were deep in conversation. They stopped speaking and looked up when he entered the room.

"So—you were talking about me, or Cheyenne?" he asked.

Angela laughed. "She's a good agent with a great record and a better eye. Jackson thinks she'd be an asset."

"All I'd need is an interagency transfer," Jackson said.

"What do you think?" Angela asked him.

He smiled grimly. "What I think doesn't matter. I'm been playing a wait-and-see game," he told them. "She hasn't told me that she's carrying on with the dead."

"And you haven't admitted that you do," Jackson reminded him.

"None of it's my call," Andre said. "If you're asking me about her as an agent—yeah, she's been great to work with. Strange circumstances here, of course."

"There really wasn't anyone out there better equipped to work this case, though, in all honestly, it would usually be the other way around," Jackson said. "Anyway, we'll keep in close contact tomorrow. We'll be waiting to hear about Emil Justine's position in all this, and about whatever you can learn regarding the choir master and organist, Jacques Derringer, and the manager and embalmer, *and* if Lacey Murton can remember anything else. Talk her through it—you know how. There may be some small detail that we can connect to a suspect."

"And we can switch places later," Angela told him. "If Lacey remains frightened and if we feel she shouldn't be alone, we—or I, at least—can head out there and watch out for her. It may be a smart plan, assuming our killer is still out there. He may be afraid that she will remember something."

"I think we'll start with the cemetery," Andre said.

7

Cheyenne wanted to sleep; it was necessary. It allowed for one to be alert and capable.

But sleep eluded her for a long time. When she was drifting, she heard voices. The room Angela and Jackson had taken was right next to the guest room where she was sleeping—or trying to sleep.

She kept hearing voices, male and female. Must be Angela, Jackson and Andre going over and over everything that had happened, perhaps plans for the investigation—perhaps just plans for the future because they were, after all, friends as well as coworkers.

She really wished, however, that they'd stayed downstairs to keep talking.

She didn't want to lie there awake. She kept thinking, her mind in a whirl. She kept running through it—she couldn't believe it was someone she had grown up with, or someone who had been around when she'd been young.

The coach—their coach! Praising the cheerleaders, urging the players on, a friend to them when they were feeling down. Mr. Beaufort. Big, fit and so reassuring.

Mike Holiday—sometimes a jerk, but still…the school hero.

A pair of nerds? Katie and Nelson—happy nerds, now.

Jimmy… Jimmy Mercury. The gentle musician who loved his instruments—all of them! He could play the sax, keyboards, guitar…the harmonica. Probably any instrument known to man. Her mind wandered to Andre. Sleeping—or talking— just down the hall. He walked with an air of confidence, but not arrogance. She liked the tone of his voice, commanding at times, easy and almost mesmerizing at others.

It was impossible not to think about him. This was the home where he'd spent his last formative years, his high school years. Even the house, the relationship he seemed to keep with his parents, made her like him.

There was much to admire.

She'd been angry when she'd first come here— angry that he could judge her without knowing her.

But he hadn't. And he had listened to her. He had believed in her *before* the autopsy had proven that there was some evidence Trudeau had not killed himself.

She liked the feel of him when he brushed by her, when he touched her.

In all honesty, she just liked him.

In all honesty, she had imagined him naked. She'd imagined...sex.

Not a useful train of thought—she needed to go back to ruminating about suspects, trying to determine if there had been anything in what they had said or done that might point to them being killers.

She needed not to think at all; she needed to sleep.

Finally, she drifted off, and then slept deeply.

It was painful, just for a minute, when her alarm rang.

At 6:45, she was downstairs. She didn't need to set coffee; it had been done. She poured herself a cup and found Andre in the parlor, studying the board again.

He looked at her and said, "That cross. You're good—you're really good."

"Lucky, more likely," she said. "And I stared at all those pictures for hours before noting the cross, so... yeah, lucky is more like it. But I'll take it."

"If you're ready, we'll head out."

"Ready," she said.

There was traffic already—but not that much. Parents were out getting their children to school and those who were early risers with early work shifts were heading in.

Many who worked night shifts were going home to bed.

And still, it was much easier to maneuver through traffic and get out of the city quickly at that hour than later in the day.

They were soon on the highway. "So, I thought

we'd start together and head to the cemetery first. The crime scene people have finished there. The police have Emil, though his family have rallied around with indignation and his lawyer is having a fit, so they won't have him much longer. We'll stop at the cemetery and then we'll see him. He'll be angry. It was his allowing us to search that sent him to jail as a suspect. But I think he'll help us. I'd just like to get in and—perhaps this makes no sense—get a feel again for the place," Andre said.

"Fine," she agreed. "We won't even need to climb over the wall."

"No?"

"It opens at nine, though, I admit, I don't know who would be in charge of opening it, unless, of course, no one has thought to accuse the mortuary manager of anything yet. I'm curious about that— Emil wasn't here during several of the kidnappings. That would mean that—funeral or no funeral—the manager should have been responsible for what was going on."

"I believe that the man was brought in for questioning, but they had nothing on him. He's only worked there a few months, and his duties only had to do with meeting family members and arranging for the opening of tombs. I don't think that clears him, but they haven't held him. He's also defended Emil, though, saying his boss is really too feeble to have done anything like what they're saying. And he's told them that he'll be available for questioning at any time—he hates that the place was used by a killer. But of course, we'll talk to him ourselves."

"You learned all that last night?" she asked him.

"I read everything that Jackson had in files from contact with other agencies," he said.

"Read? You guys talked forever last night!" she said.

He frowned. "No. With Angela working, we have constant reading material. She and Jackson are amazing at liaison skills." He smiled at her. "It's always best to have a good working relationship with people. And of course, most of the time, we're asked in, which helps. Though sometimes with Krewe work, we're asked in by other people, and then you have to play a diplomatic game. But for the most part, I believe all law enforcement is happy when a case like this is solved."

"You didn't talk in their room?"

He hesitated—too long, she thought.

"They were awake a while, I guess," he said with a shrug. "So how long were you in Miami?"

"Two years. I started in New York, spent time there, then Chicago, and then Miami," she said. He'd really neatly sidestepped the question. At the moment, she decided not to push it. It was that, or just accuse him of being a liar. "You?"

"Military, college, the academy, Houston, New York, and then the Krewe."

She had looked up the Krewe, as much as she was able; they were considered both an "elite" unit and a "weird" unit of the FBI. They were also known for being one of the most effective units in the agency.

There was no way to earn your way into the Krewe—Adam Harrison approved you or he did not, with Jackson's endorsement probably being the first step. But you could be a rookie, or a person with years of service, or not in the agency at all—and be a pick for the unit.

So, what was the criteria?

He glanced her way. "You came into this line of work because of your cousin," he said, and she wasn't sure if it was a question or a statement.

"And you?" she asked, taking his words as a statement.

"It was probably because of your cousin, too," he said. "And that makes me think that Jimmy Mercury has to be innocent. I remember that day. He just looked at me with an expression that said *Let's get him*. He knew that we just couldn't let Lassiter get away. He knew Janine —he was just a few years older than her in high school, though he was living in New Orleans by then. He believed you when you cried out."

"You acted with him, just as quickly," she reminded him.

He smiled at that. "I knew that day that taking down a man like Lassiter meant something." He chuckled ruefully. "Up until then, I'd thought maybe I'd follow Jimmy's footsteps, make music my life. Music, of course, is the best drug in the world to soothe people, but I'm not a genius like Jimmy. But I am good at what I do."

"A genius?" she asked him.

He glanced her way with an odd expression. "I have talents." He was thoughtful, and again changed the subject—subtly.

"It's true that I have a hard time thinking that Jimmy could be guilty of anything because he's my friend, but I've learned that you can never rule anyone out unless you can rule them out by solid evidence. I knew Jimmy. I knew Mike a bit—we played ball together when I was young. I knew Coach Beaufort because he was involved in community games. I didn't know Katie or Nelson well because we were never involved in the same activities. And the choir... I thought I was a jock. I never worked with the organist, Jacques Derringer."

Cheyenne thought about Derringer. "He's maybe a strange one. He made it obvious when he didn't think you should be in the choir. He had his favorites—but in our community, he couldn't throw anyone out, no matter how bad they were."

He glanced at her with a smile.

"Did he like you?"

"I was Janine's cousin. And I can carry a tune. Not like Janine, but he didn't want to kick me out."

"So, he had a thing on Janine."

"Maybe," she said. "I didn't know Katie and Nelson well—you were a few years older than them, but remember, I was a few years younger. They were gamers from a young age, and I was never as keen on video games. I mean, I was a kid, I played them like everyone else, but when they weren't playing games online, they were still quiet and into one another."

"Katie seems happy now."

"Isn't that the way it can often be? The jocks don't do so well later in life—and the nerds have the brains and the ability to take over the world?"

"They own a music shop—that's not exactly taking over the world."

"But they're doing well."

"True," he agreed.

Andre drove fast, but safely, and they arrived at the cemetery in good time. He parked on the grass by the stone wall, near the entrance.

The cemetery gates appeared to be closed.

"That's so unusual. Almost everyone living anywhere near here has a relative here in a family tomb or just their own small cement tomb…the gates are always open by this time," Cheyenne said.

"We might have stirred up a pot and made things different," Andre said, but as he spoke, he set his hand on the gate—and it gave. The gates had been closed but not locked.

"I wonder if the house is locked," Cheyenne said, heading down the path that led to the house, with the cemetery to the right near the entry.

She hadn't intended to go in toward the mausoleums and tombs. But as she walked, Janine popped out from between tombs, Christian right behind her.

"Cheyenne," Janine said in a stage whisper.

Cheyenne glared at her.

"Sorry! Okay, you can't answer me—G-man on your tail. So, just listen, there's a note on our tomb! You have to come see. Oh, my God, you need to leave, to get out of here. I'm afraid for you!"

Cheyenne was startled when Andre almost brushed her aside, frowning fiercely—and looking straight at Janine.

"A note?" he demanded. "On your family tomb?"

Cheyenne stared at Andre, disbelieving at first.

"You see… Janine?" she demanded.

"And her friend," he said impatiently. "The note is on the tomb?" he asked.

He was already walking. He knew the family tomb. Cheyenne stared at Janine and Christian, and then hurried after him.

"Hey!"

He wasn't paying attention; he was at the tomb. She didn't see a note on the gates because it had fallen to the ground, she thought—or there was another bit of trash on there—and Andre had pulled on a glove and stooped to retrieve it.

The note appeared to have been written on a cocktail napkin—from a bar/restaurant called The Last Cavalier on Frenchman Street in New Orleans.

Andre read it and then looked up at Cheyenne.

"We have to get this in immediately—see if our techs can get anything off it. Fingerprints, ink, anything."

"What does it say?" she demanded.

"'Tombs are lonely if no one enters after a decade,'" he read. He looked at Cheyenne with genuine concern. "We should get you out of here far, far away."

"You've got to be kidding me," Cheyenne said, angry. "That doesn't mean anything. And if it did, I'm an agent—trained. I can take care of myself. I also believe that our killer is a coward. He goes after defenseless women, not trained cops or agents. And what is the matter with you? You *see* Janine and Christian, and you saw them before, *and you didn't say a word*?"

"Frankly, I was wondering when you were going to introduce me," he said.

"You son of a bitch!" Cheyenne exclaimed.

"Hey…that's not the point here!" Janine said, turning to Andre. "I'm Janine Dumas, which, of course, you know. And I remember you. I didn't at first, but now…you were there. You helped Jimmy go after Lassiter. This is my friend Christian Mayhew, and…well, we're doing our best to help in some way. And you're right. I'm terrified for my cousin."

"Pretty scary," Christian murmured.

"Stop it!" Cheyenne exclaimed. "You found that note on the ground. It could have been for anyone and meant anything."

"No, originally, it was attached to the gate," Janine said. She stared at Andre. "Wow. You see us! I can't tell you how rare that is. I mean, we can make people *sense* us—shiver and look around and all and say that a place is haunted—but the only person to *see* us before was Cheyenne."

"It is rare," Andre assured her. "And nice to re-meet you. Christian, I'm not sure we ever met, so I thank you for being here, for helping."

"Where Janine goes, so go I!" Christian said.

They were all behaving as if they'd met over at coffee, or at a party.

Cheyenne could do nothing to control the anger sweeping through her. She stared at Andre. "You made a fool of me," she snapped furiously.

"I didn't. I merely waited until you were ready to tell me, but then, today…with this, I had no choice any longer." He turned to Janine. "When did you find the note?" he asked, raising it in his gloved hand.

"We just saw it this morning—maybe an hour ago. We kept checking to see if you two were coming back here—or, frankly, watching for anyone else who might have come," Janine said.

"But I'm sorry, we should have been, but we haven't just been hanging out here. I mean, under normal circumstances, it's just depressing," Christian said.

"We should have stayed on guard," Janine said.

"It's all right, you couldn't have known," Andre said. "But here's an important question—have you seen anyone visiting? Specifically, your old friends or acquaintances, who might have known Lassiter and secretly admired him."

Janine and Christian looked at one another. Janine answered for them both.

"We just…we haven't been here. We can be here, though, and we will be here."

"Why were the gates left unlocked, do you know?"

"We saw the guy Mr. Mason, the cemetery manager, here last night," Christian said.

"But he was just at the house. Some people came through. Old Mr. Tybalt died the other day—he was over a hundred, so it wasn't a tragedy. Anyway, his people met here to plan a funeral. It's going to take place Saturday."

Three days, Cheyenne thought.

"He was only at the house?" Andre asked.

"As far as we saw. We did hang around awhile when the police and the crime scene experts were here—they were everywhere. As of now, we just saw people at the house. Again, not sure what that means, since we weren't here the entire time."

"Do you have any friends who might have been here?" Andre asked.

Again, Christian and Janine looked at one another. "Anthony and Gerard, maybe," Christian suggested.

"And who are they?" Andre asked.

"Captain Gerard Bouche and Lieutenant Anthony Kendall," Janine said. "The first was Confederate calvary—his family tomb is over there. And the second was Union infantry. Anyway, he was interred in Gerard's family tomb at Gerard's request. Anthony tried to save Gerard in life, he was the medic who pulled him off the field, and in death…they hang around."

"Wait!" Christian said, his features knit in thought. "Janine, remember, it was some time ago,

and I don't remember the last time I saw her but..."
He broke off, looking from Cheyenne to Andre.
"Once, just once, we saw a young woman, so pretty...
just staring up at the house. I talked to her, and she
was polite and sweet, but she didn't want to be with
us. She said her name was Melissa. She was so sad."

"Melissa Carrier," Janine said softly. "She was
killed in the 1860s—by the Rougarou. At least, I
think that's who she was. Her dress was beautiful,
antebellum. Many people died and were buried here
in the Civil War, but she said she was Melissa, and
she was so sad, and she seemed to want to be alone,
and so we left her alone.

"Oh!" Janine said. "There's Mr. Macy, but he
was killed during Prohibition. He's cool—when
he's around. I don't quite get what they're all waiting for. Maybe we all have a reason. I do believe
that I know why I'm hanging around—I might well
be here as I am because my cousin is an idiot agent
who thinks she's untouchable," she finished, looking hard at Cheyenne.

None of this was improving Cheyenne's temper.

She had to get away from all of them. She felt
such a burning anger—irrational, wrong, *maybe*—
it didn't matter. "I'm going," she said. "I'm going to
the hospital to see Lacey Murton. You all can figure
things out here just as long as you like. If you need
me, if there's something important, you can call me."

She turned and left; she thought that someone
might pursue her, but they didn't.

As she headed out, she remembered that Andre

had driven since it was Andre's rental car they had used, and he had the keys.

That was okay; she had a phone. She could call a ride through an app.

Standing in front of the gates, she waited only a few minutes, and then the car and driver arrived.

In fifteen minutes, she was at the hospital. She hurried up to Lacey's room, trying not to think about her situation or argue herself out of being angry.

Andre had *seen* Janine and Christian before. He had heard every word that they'd said. She couldn't remember quite what they had talked about that day, but she was still…humiliated. Why, she wasn't sure—being seen just talking to oneself could have been more embarrassing.

She tried to refocus when she got to the hospital; Lacey should be much better now. They should be releasing her shortly. Now she could talk; now hopefully she could remember.

Lacey had been moved out of intensive care and was in a private room. Cheyenne headed right up and gave her credentials to the officer on duty. When she walked into Lacey's room, an attractive woman in her early fifties came quickly to the door, looking at her suspiciously, but Lacey twisted around in her bed and saw Cheyenne.

"Oh, thank you—you did come back!" Lacey said.

"I told you that I would," Cheyenne said. "I want to know how you're doing and how you're feeling."

"Hi, I'm Lacey's mom, Sheila," the older woman said, offering her a hand.

"Special Agent Cheyenne Dumas. Sheila, nice to meet you."

There was worry in the woman's eyes; they were light gray, enhancing the darkness of her hair and the paleness of her cheeks.

She must have been worried sick for her daughter, and then relieved beyond comprehension. And now frightened again.

A monster was still out there.

Sheila Murton looked at her daughter and gave her a weak smile. "If this agent is here now...this wonderful agent to whom we are so grateful," she said, her face showing the depth of her emotion, "I'm going to head down to the cafeteria for a bit. That's all right with everyone?"

"Perfect, Mom, you take a break," Lacey said.

Sheila still looked concerned. "I'll be here a bit," Cheyenne promised.

Sheila pursed her lips in a worried smile and started to exit. She paused, looking back. "Thank you. Thank you for...for everything."

"We're grateful, too," Cheyenne said.

Lacey's mother left the room. Cheyenne took her chair.

"They're going to let me go tomorrow or the next day," Lacey told her.

"Don't worry, we'll keep a guard on you, if it will make you feel better. I'm not actually with his unit, but I know the head of Special Agent Rousseau's unit, and I know he'll make sure that you have one of his people watching over you."

"I'll be okay. I'm going to my parents' place for a while. My mom has this incredible Belgian shepherd who will warn me… Then again, having an ace protector won't be a bad thing," Lacey said. She sounded far more cheerful than she had before, but then the last time Cheyenne had seen her, she had barely made it to the hospital.

"I think it will be a good thing," Cheyenne assured her.

Lacey shivered "You think that he hasn't been caught. You think that he might come after me again."

"I really don't know," Cheyenne said honestly. "They've arrested Mr. Justine, but I don't think he's guilty—just older, tired and oblivious. We're looking into others involved with the cemetery and mortuary, but—" she paused and grimaced " —as of yet, we don't know. We don't have a solid suspect. We have what are called 'people of interest.'"

"I wish I could help catch him," Lacey said. "Although, as I told you, I thought he was some kind of a performer, or someone just dressed up for a wild party. We both know that there can be a wild party in NOLA with or without a special holiday going on. Or I thought that maybe he was usually one of those human statues that you see sometimes on Jackson Square. I would never recognize him again if I were to see him. It's so frustrating. And scary."

"I know. You told me that, but I was hoping that maybe we could go back through it all—and you might remember something, a little detail."

"But—"

"Will you try it my way?"

"You saved my life," Lacey said softly, "I'll do anything you ask."

"Technically, Andre Rousseau saved your life," Cheyenne said, smiling gently to hide the war of emotions going on within her.

Andre was good; damned good. His instincts were right on, he could listen, he didn't accept what appeared on the surface to be truth, but was willing to question it. And she had been attracted to him, right or wrong, in the middle of all this, but she had found herself more than keenly attracted…physically attracted… She had liked him, really liked him, and he had made a fool of her.

"Is something wrong?" Lacey asked her.

"No, no. What I'd like you to do is close your eyes, and then we can go through the night that you were taken. You remember what was going on before, right?"

Lacey nodded, pulling up the sheets on her hospital bed. She was already almost seated, the bed raised to a high incline.

"Close your eyes."

She did.

"You were out with friends, just having a nice time. Tell me about it."

"My friend Amelia works at a restaurant on Magazine Street. She just got a raise—and became night manager. We were celebrating at a little bar off Decatur. No smoking in it, so… I think I told you, I smoke when I drink? I wasn't drunk— though I'd had a few. Maybe even one too many."

"What was the bar like?" Cheyenne asked.

"More for locals. No band but the music is great. They serve some wonderful appetizer foods, too, and we were all just enjoying bits of this and that."

"Did you feel that anyone was watching you? Did anyone approach you all?"

Lacey shook her head.

"No smoking inside. Do you remember any smells or anything like that?"

"Delicious smells. Their little riblets are like no others, and I could smell food—deliciously cooking."

"So, then you went outside alone, right?"

"Yeah, no other drinking smokers in my crowd. There's a tiny alleyway between the bar and the next building, and a back area with a big dumpster. I had only had a couple drags when I saw the…thing. The rougarou."

"And why do you think it was a rougarou?" Cheyenne asked softly.

She paused, shaking her head. "I grew up in Morgan City and moved to New Orleans after I graduated. We all heard legends of the rougarou— especially the so-called Rougarou killer back during the Civil War. I'd seen pictures…we told each other stories about the rougarou getting campers and hikers and hiding out in bayou country. They were legends, like stories about vampires… But there he was."

"Lacey, it wasn't a real rougarou."

"I know, of course. I knew it was someone dressed up—and that's why I wasn't disturbed in the least. I was in New Orleans!"

"And people might be wearing costumes for any number of reasons," Cheyenne said. "Don't be angry with yourself. I'm sure I would have thought that it was a performer on his way home from something, myself. We see those human statues all the time. Don't beat yourself up for not being afraid. Your reaction was certainly normal enough for anyone from here. For anyone who has walked Jackson Square at night and seen 'living statue' vampires, monsters— or robots or angels."

"Really? You wouldn't have been afraid?"

I'm wary—most of the time! Cheyenne thought. *But I lost a cousin to a serial killer.*

"You shouldn't blame yourself at all. We enjoy street performers all the time. And there's no way you could have guessed his intentions."

"Thanks," Lacey murmured.

"It's just the way it is," Cheyenne said gently.

"Okay. Um. I was leaning against the wall, inhaling, and he came around the corner. He was dancing, and I was watching and laughing."

"Did you see anything else at all? Anyone else, anything else?"

"No, I was watching him. I—"

Lacey broke off suddenly, frowning.

"You did see something else," Cheyenne said.

"Someone… I thought I saw someone coming around the corner, and I was going to say something like 'Hey, come enjoy this,' but…I must have imagined that someone was there. The rougarou was in my face, and then…"

"And then? Did you smell anything?"

Lacey wrinkled her nose. "Trash."

"And anything else at all?"

Again, Lacey was silent, and then she turned to look at Cheyenne, her face knit in consternation and surprise.

"A strange mix," Lacey said. "Trash… I was close to the dumpster. But then, he was near me. And I could smell more…garlic. Garlic, mixed with…cologne. Some kind of cologne or aftershave or…there was definitely a scent of it. Not very strong…but mixing with the trash and the garlic!"

"And then what happened?" Cheyenne pressed.

"Then I was knocked out."

8

"We're holding him and we're going to arraignment—accessory to kidnapping," Detective Vine told Andre. "Hell, Special Agent Rousseau, the girl was found on his property. There were shackles in there—looked like we went back over a hundred and fifty years."

Andre had driven to the police station right after bagging the note and mailing it overnight to the lab at headquarters—after photographing it and sending it to Jackson and Angela.

He didn't think that he would be making it back to NOLA that night.

Now he was at the station, meeting with Vine, the local detective who had handled the investigation at the Justine Plantation.

"You have his fingerprints on anything in there? Anything that proves that Emil Justine has been in that building—ever?" Andre asked.

The man was so certain. Andre had met so many police who questioned their findings—even with an abundance of evidence. He understood that suspicion would immediately fall on the owner of the property where Lacey had been found—and where the killer had possibly brought his other victims before determining where to display them.

Detective Vine shuffled papers on his desk. "He's part and parcel of the Mortician case—it's obvious. No, there are no prints. Well, there are dozens of prints, but most can't be matched to anyone. They're decades old. The crime scene people found plenty of blood spots—some too contaminated to do anything with, and others promising. The killer—the Mortician—was a clever man. He knows to use gloves. Looks like he learned everything he knew from Lassiter." He was quiet a minute. "Unless Lassiter isn't dead, but he was executed, and there was an audience. Lassiter was the killer we all fear most, from what I understand. He charmed his victims. Now, as far as the killer goes, it's my understanding that a man was found dead in the French Quarter— Braxton Trudeau—and that a hair from a victim of an unsolved murder was found on his body. I think we've solved this case, Special Agent Rousseau, and that the federal government just doesn't want to accept it."

Andre tried very hard to keep complete control of his temper.

He smiled. "You're wrong. The federal government—state, parish, here, Mississippi, anywhere else—would be delighted to know that the killing had stopped. What I'm not willing to do is accept what you seem to think of as obvious."

"We have excellent crime scene experts," Vine said, reshuffling the papers on his desk. "They went over the house and every outbuilding with fine-tooth combs. The only evidence was in that old shack, but it was damning. They believe some of the bloodstains were there for over a decade, suggesting that Lassiter used the place, and that Emil Justine knew Ryan Lassiter."

"So did half the countryside," Andre said. "Did you question the manager, who has had far more access to the property in recent months than Emil Justine?"

"Well, of course, we questioned him," Vine said, appearing to grow agitated. "He hasn't been there long enough to have left old bloodstains—"

"I believe we've established that they're from Lassiter days," Andre said.

"He's new. He's never been in the outbuildings, except for the old kitchen. Actually, those old buildings are in horrible shape. The only reason they're still standing is a historic board whose members claim they're some of the few left. That old shack is the farthest structure from the house, and it's a sizable property."

"One that is open through the day—and anyone might have used. Not to mention that you can hop over the wall with minimal effort."

"Here's what I think," Vine said, leaning forward. "All those years ago, Emil Justine knew exactly what

Ryan Lassiter was doing—he was abetting him. Somewhere along the line, he met Braxton Trudeau, another charming killer who was a musician working here, there and everywhere along the Gulf coast, and getting to know all about the art of murder. We've got our culprits. And thanks to you and Special Agent Donegal, the last girl taken has survived. We should be grateful and move on."

"Here's what I know," Andre said quietly, "there's no certainty on anything, except that Trudeau is dead, and the one girl he's linked to wasn't even considered a victim of the Mortician. And there is no proof that we have stopped this killer, and if we haven't found him, other women will die. As lead on the case—which crossed state lines with the kidnapping and murder of Cindy Metcalf—I intend to keep the case open."

Vine looked angry. He sat back in his chair. "Knock yourself out," he said.

"We'll expect your cooperation. Special Agent Donegal's family has known Emil Justine a long time. So long, in fact, that he freely handed over his set of keys, which he keeps in a crypt on the property. I'm sure he's assumed that only a few people knew where the keys were kept, but that knowledge might have become quite commonplace. We will, as I said, continue to investigate." He was standing by the time he finished speaking, ready to leave the precinct. He didn't wait for a reply from Detective Vine.

He'd thought about visiting Emil Justine, who was still being held in the jail, but had decided that Cheyenne did have more of a relationship with the man, however minor that might be. She might well have a way with the man that could help.

As Andre headed out and to his car, he was surprised when a young officer stealing a smoke outside the building called to him. He saw that it was the same man who had first arrived at the hospital to keep guard over Lacey Murton.

Wilmette—that was his name.

"Hello," Andre said, approaching him.

Wilmette smiled and looked a little nervously back at the building. "I guess you were just meeting with Detective Vine," he said.

"I was."

Wilmette looked hesitant. "You know that they're convinced that Emil Justine is guilty…of aiding and abetting, at least?"

"I do." Andre studied the man. He wanted to tell him something; the officer didn't want to be disloyal. "We're not dropping the investigation," he said.

Wilmette nodded, looking at the building again. To see him, though, Detective Vine would have to have X-ray vision.

"I intend to interview Mr. Mason, the manager, and anyone else who has worked at the plantation, mortuary and cemetery in the past year."

Wilmette lowered his head for a minute, then looked up at Andre and nodded. "Here's the thing— they let Mason go almost immediately. You see, he's a second cousin or something to the detective, and of course, Vine refuses to believe that it could be remotely possible that kin is involved. Me? I think all kinds of things could have gone on in that place with no one knowing anything. I think that Detective Vine was just too quick to believe what he heard. Or, not even that... I mean, he didn't keep Mason long enough to ask him who else might have been around, or anything else about the house, the grounds or the cemetery."

"Thank you, Officer, and not to worry. I intended to speak with Guy Mason. It has to be solved without question."

Wilmette nodded. "If I can help in any way..."

"We will call on you," Andre told him.

"Who would ever figure that you have to protect the dead?" Wilmette said. "Kids around here may sneak into the cemetery to drink or smoke some pot or just tell stories, but we've never had a problem with vandalism. Just about everyone has a loved one there, and you know how we can be—superstitious as all get-out."

"Yeah," Andre said. Wilmette must have figured out that Andre had grown up in the region, and that seemed to create a brotherhood. Not a bad thing, here. "Oh, and if you're looking for Guy Mason, he should be up at the plantation again, *and* meeting with the embalmer they use. Last preparation for old Mr. Tybalt."

"I'm heading right over," Andre said.

He left the station and walked toward his car, his steps fast at first, and then slowing. Wilmette had said something that was simmering in his mind. He couldn't pinpoint what it was.

He let it go, sliding into the driver's seat.

He'd learned that fixating on it wasn't going to help. It would come to him.

He put a call through to Cheyenne.

She would answer, no matter what her personal feelings at the moment.

She picked up almost immediately. He quickly filled her in on Vine's reluctance to keep the case open, and Wilmette's tip-off.

"I'm on my way to see Guy Mason now. I didn't speak with Emil Justine because I thought you might have a better rapport with him. Anything on your end?"

"Something, maybe nothing. Lacey thinks that someone else was there—peripheral vision, for just a second. And she remembered smelling garlic and cologne."

"It could prove to be something important. Anyway, I'm heading back to the cemetery and plantation now."

"I'll go and speak with Emil Justine," she told him.

"Lacey is okay?"

"Doing well. Talk later."

She hung up.

Andre drove back to the cemetery.

Detective Vine wasn't rude to Cheyenne; neither was he welcoming. He seemed to be shaking his head at a waste of time when he led her to speak with the man.

"He will go to trial. You know, that's one thing. We do still have states' rights in this country, and we will prosecute where we feel we have the evidence to prove a person's involvement. Yeah, he claims innocence—what lying, cheating bastard doesn't?" he asked her.

She didn't reply.

Emil Justine looked like hell.

Naturally, he'd been interrogated and locked in a jail cell.

When she joined him in the tiny cinder block–walled room he was perched miserably on the edge of the cot, frail and broken-looking, and she told herself that, in one way, the detective's words had been true. Once in a while, when caught, a killer, kidnapper, rapist or other vicious criminal was suddenly proud of his deeds—even aggrandizing them. Sometimes, confessions came because of a deal that might be made with the prosecuting attorney. But most of the time, criminals pleaded innocent.

Emil Justine looked at her with pale watery eyes—without even the strength to be angry.

"Well, there it is. Imagine. I try to help and here I am."

"You saved a life, sir. If we hadn't gotten to Lacey Murton when we did, she most probably would have died," Cheyenne told him.

He nodded. "For that, I am grateful. I am an old man. A few years left at best. She is a young woman,

and therefore, I am eternally glad that she's alive."
He almost smiled at her. "I'd never imagined that a
family inheritance could be such a curse. I didn't
help Lassiter when he was killing people, and I sure
as hell haven't helped anyone now. I don't know how
to prove it."

"I believe you, Mr. Justine," she said.

He seemed to brighten just a bit, frowning with
doubt as he looked at her. His face looked like an
unpaved road, streaked with lines and ruts, from the
passage of time and the misery in which he found
himself now.

"You do? My son came in from Baton Rouge with
an attorney. He's getting me out on bail until trial,
but...there's all kinds of red tape, it seems. Honestly,
I knew nothing about the process. I never so much as
stole a stick of gum in my life." He sighed softly. "I
even paid for the sealing of coffins into crypts when
my neighbors just didn't have the money. No good
deed goes unpunished, eh?"

"Mr. Justine, I'm here because I believe you, and
because I'm hoping that you can think back and tell
me if anyone was around at any time that you find
might have been unusual or suspicious in any way.
My partner and I are going to find the truth—no
matter how long it takes," she told him.

"Okay," he said slowly. "It's a cemetery. I always
thought it was ironic that I'd spend my life looking
after the dead... The first tombs went in before the
Civil War... The area is so small, there weren't any
city councils or other officials arranging for burial

grounds back then. The family had the property, they liked their neighbors, they started putting in graves. Pretty soon, there were crypts and graves and larger mausoleums all over, and in the late 1800s someone decided that hey, we have a family business here. But my father also made some good investments, so it wasn't a do-or-die operation...and still, we kept it as a business. My son didn't want to take over. My daughter married a military man and is on the other side of the country. And so, I just kept on, hiring managers because I got tired. Old."

"When is the last time you were in any of the outbuildings?" she asked him.

He shook his head. "I haven't even been in the storage area in years."

"Who else knew about the keys?"

He shrugged.

"I'm not sure. We didn't really keep it as a deep dark secret. You know that people around here still don't even bother much with locking their doors. They only started up when we had a serial killer up in Lafayette some years back. Guy knows, of course. He has a set of keys himself, but just in case there was some kind of emergency and someone else needed to get in, that set of keys was put in there. I mean, your average thief?...vandal?...wouldn't know to go into a family vault and look for keys under votive candles. Right?"

"I wouldn't think so," Cheyenne agreed.

"I... I wish I could tell you something. You can't imagine just how much I wish that I could help. But in all honesty, as far as I knew, that old building out back had been decaying for well over a decade. Preservationists wanted them kept… I thought they should have been torn down." He was quiet for a minute. "We've always been open and casual. I can't begin to guess who we might have spoken in front of who might know about the keys." He was quiet. "Thing is, they were there, so if someone had them, that someone maybe made a copy to have?"

He looked at her hopefully.

"We'll look into that possibility," she promised. "And I'm so sorry. I know you are suffering because you let me have free rein of the place—but you did save a life."

He smiled wanly, a trace of humor in his face. "You know where to find me. Oh, I think they will get me out on bail, but I promise you, I won't be going anywhere."

She thanked him and exited.

As she was leaving the station, Vine said, "See—he's got nothing. That creepy old dude has been up there all those years, killing, or getting his vicarious thrills through watching people die. Guess he felt he needed to fill up his cemetery, huh?"

She should not have stopped; she should have gone on.

She spun around. "Detective Vine, you are aware that I'm from this area—that my cousin was the victim of a vicious murderer? Somehow, that still hasn't made me certain of anything, unless I have a confession or indisputable evidence. You're so sure? Well, if another victim winds up dead, you just remember how positive you were, and how unwilling you were to look further. I'm very glad that we are lead on this investigation, and for your future, I suggest you quit being so damned sure of yourself!"

She didn't give him time to reply.

She walked out and only then remembered that she wasn't driving. Andre had the car; she'd taken a cab to the station and had meant to ask if a patrol-man or woman could drop her off at the cemetery.

Sighing, she walked down the street before call-ing a car service again.

The gates to the plantation and cemetery stood wide-open.

Andre drove straight in, finding three cars parked right in front of the house. One had Justine Plantation Mortuary Home and Cemetery written on the side.

He parked in back of it, blocking it in, and walked up the old steps of the Colonial porch. The door to the house stood open, just slightly ajar. The foyer was empty, but he heard voices and he moved on to the office and peeked in.

A woman he thought to be in her midfifties sat with a young man and a young woman who looked as if they might be twins.

He remembered the name Tybalt from his child-hood, but he wasn't sure that he knew any of them.

Behind the desk was the man he assumed to be Guy Mason. The man was in his late thirties or early forties, nicely dressed in a navy suit, with dark, slicked-back hair—and an appropriately serious expression.

The children were discussing the fact that their dearly departed grandparent would have been furious at the expense of a pricey coffin.

The woman was reminding them that there was going to be a viewing.

Andre slipped away; he could wait.

As he returned to the foyer, he paused, instinctively moving against the wall. There was someone else in the house.

But a moment later, he saw a man in a smock coming from the other side into the foyer. He stepped out.

The man was sixty or so, white-haired and wearing gold-rimmed reading glasses atop his head.

"May I help you, sir?" he asked as Andre stepped forward.

"Yes, thanks," Andre said, presenting his credentials.

"The FBI! Figured I'd see you sooner or later. The cops aren't happy, you know. They want to handle local stuff locally. Well, I'm a liar. We have a great police force usually willing to get down with anyone when we do have a local crime. Anyway, I'm Herman Peterson, out of Baton Rouge. I come out when I'm needed." He sighed. "Embalmer, mortician…best in most circumstances if you don't identify yourself. People automatically think that you have to be a creepy human being."

Andre shook his hand.

"For what it's worth, I think that Emil Justine is

a fine man who wouldn't have had anything to do
with anything evil whatsoever," Peterson offered.
"Then again, Guy Mason is a good man, too—and
I just don't see either of them accommodating a sick,
wacko killer. If they're guilty of anything, it's expecting the best out of people and being oblivious."

"Have you ever seen anything here that seemed
suspicious?" Andre asked.

He winced. "No. And I... I'd been here. I was
working on a fellow killed in a car accident and so
I was here..." His voice trailed.

"Here—when?" Andre asked.

"Years ago. I was up at the house when the police
came for Ryan Lassiter. I've worked for Emil Justine
for years and years. That's what I mean—I know the
guy. He isn't a murderer—or aider or abettor or whatever it is they want to charge him with." His eyes
narrowed suddenly. "I've seen you before—you were
younger. Way younger, like a teenager. You! You and
that band fellow— that Bill Mercury—"

"Jimmy," Andre said.

"Yeah, yeah, Jimmy. You were here!" Peterson
said. "You were at that funeral."

"Yes, I was."

"Well, then, you know. Emil Justine is a good
man."

"I'm afraid I'm going to have to find a way to
prove it. They can hold him since his property is involved, and then decide if they want to charge him,
whether that would stand up in court or not. Then

it's up to a judge as to whether he gets bail or not. That's why I'm looking for help."

Herman Peterson was silent for a minute. He sighed. "I'm not here that often—I'm on loan when I come out here. You don't really have enough residents around to need an embalmer every day, you know."

"But have you seen anything—anyone—behaving strangely around here, or overly interested in the place or hopping the wall? Oh," Andre added, "back on that day ten years ago—do you remember anyone acting strangely, distraught about Lassiter, or trying to see him, trying to speak to him, when he had been taken, when the cops showed up?"

The man squinted, pursed his lips and thought hard. "Trying to picture the day—it was so long ago," he said.

"Take your time."

"Yeah… I remember the priest being just dumbfounded. It was Father Mahoney back then—and he died a few years back. He was trying to continue the service, make sure that the religious stuff was covered, you know, so that the poor girl could rest in peace. People were in groups…the kids, her friends…they were together and…in groups, too. I remember one couple. They were just clinging together for dear life and whispering to one another. Some guy near the priest—something to do with the church—kept trying to help the priest…let there be an end to the service. A big guy— Oh, I know! The school football coach. He was trying to help the police, along with a big kid. And a lot of people just wanted the hell out—they didn't wait. They slunk away, not wanting to be part of it. Everyone was talking and whispering, of course. It was sad, it was good, it was..." He broke off, shrugging. "Sad and good—so sad for the poor girl. So good they caught the bastard."

Andre reached in his pocket for a card. "If you think of anything else—anything strange you've seen around here—call me?"

Herman nodded strenuously. "You bet. And I can promise you, if they bring Emil Justine to court, I will be there. I'll swear up and down he's the best human being I ever knew."

"Good to hear," Andre told him. He glanced toward the office door.

"He'll be a while longer, but if you wanted to pay respects to anyone out there, you go on ahead. I won't let Guy leave. He'll wait to talk to you. He's appalled by what's gone on, too."

"All right," Andre said. He was willing to wait right there, but he had also made sure that the man wouldn't leave—he'd blocked in his car.

"Thanks. I'll take a walk around," Andre said.

He headed down the hill toward the cemetery with its tombs and family mausoleums. He hoped that Janine and Christian were still there; they'd promised to keep watch. He didn't expect anything to happen here again, though.

The killer knew that his little hideout and torture chamber had been discovered. He wouldn't be going back…

Or would he?

Does this place mean something to him—the house or the cemetery?

"Hey! Special Agent Stud!"

He paused, lowering his head and smiling. He could hear Christian, whispering and chastising Janine for not calling him by name, and he heard Janine's reply.

"Hey! I don't have to be politically correct. I'm dead!"

He slipped into the small space between tombs where the two were hovering. "We've been watching, and we managed to talk to a few friends about you. Let's move back by my family's tomb, huh? They'll watch for us there."

"Sure," Andre said, striding back on the path toward the Dumas tomb.

"Cheyenne's really ticked off, isn't she?" Janine asked as they walked.

"So it seems," Andre said.

"I'm sorry—it's really our fault," Christian said. "I mean, we should have realized that you were seeing us. It's just that I didn't believe it when Cheyenne saw us. It's a good thing she did, of course."

"How would we know? Most people don't see us," Janine said. "Anyway…" She walked around the Dumas tomb. "They promised they'd keep watch," she said, returning. And then she cried out with pleasure, and Andre turned to see three people—three ghosts—were coming toward them.

They were all young. One man had a rich sandy beard and a full head of hair to match; he was dressed in a Confederate calvary officer's uniform. The second had dark hair and light eyes and was dressed in Union blue.

Partially between them and yet a step behind was a beautiful young woman. She had very dark hair that curled around her shoulders, and large green eyes framed by naturally thick, dark lashes. She couldn't have been more than sixteen or seventeen at her death.

Right about the same age as Janine.

"Special Agent Andre Rousseau," Janine said, "I give you Captain Gerard Bouche and Lieutenant Anthony Kendall, and this is the very lovely Melissa Carrier."

"Sir!" Captain Bouche said, saluting; Lieutenant Kendall saluted as well without speaking.

Andre returned the salute and thanked both men for seeing him, and inclined his head low to the young woman, greeting her by name. "Miss Carrier, my most sincere thanks."

She'd been shy in life, he thought. She appeared to blush and looked at her friends before answering him.

"I'd be pleased to help you, but I'm so sorry—I truly don't know if I can. I still don't know who murdered me," she told him.

"Miss Carrier is the epitome of grace and kindness and generosity. If we could have solved that for her, I assure you, sir," Lieutenant Kendall said, "we'd have done so."

Andre frowned. "I was under the impression that both of you…died here?"

"Ah, sir, yes, that we did!" Captain Bouche said. He smiled grimly. "You'd have to understand what was happening here. New Orleans fell in 1862, and the Union went up the Mississippi, they came after Baton Rouge, and the Bayou Teche battles were fought, but…mostly, Louisiana had little defense. General Lee was busy elsewhere, and the war here… well, a lot of guerilla warfare went on, and that segued into deserters and no-good men just waging war on anyone."

"I was with a small contingent of men out here, barely holding on—we had seized the plantation, but not to cause destruction, just to create a hospital," Lieutenant Kendall explained.

"He was a good man," Bouche said. "He saved my life on the field."

"I was trained as a medic," Kendall offered.

"He saved me—and died wretchedly of disease," Bouche said.

"And I am quite honored to rest in the Bouche tomb," Kendall said. "It was a strange war out here. What I've not explained is why we didn't know how Miss Melissa came to be so cruelly murdered."

"Well, in a way…as you see, it was rather a no-man's-land out here to the midsection and west of the state. No one had enough troops, and bless us, but no one had decent food. There were so many dead. So very many dead. But as I said—we had jayhawkers out here. You know, those fellows who would kill anyone at any time. Maybe they were tired of war. Maybe they were just no good from the start. They probably even started out as guerillas and wound up angry over conscription laws. But there were cutthroats, murderers, rapists and thieves aplenty, and many an ill was done here that went far beyond the law. Those in power tried, but...a war was being fought. The whole country was in turmoil."

"War is bitter, and in the midst of it, many sins may go unresolved," Andre said. He looked at Melissa, smiled gently and asked, "What do you remember of what...happened to you?"

She winced. "So long ago," she murmured. "And still I've seen it again and again, and in all that time, only once have I seen justice."

"You didn't see your killer?" Andre asked.

She grimaced, moving a little closer, as if she was coming to trust him.

"I grew up here and when I was young...ah, when I was a child, we loved the rivers and the vast expanses, and we played from plantation to plantation! My great-grandfather came with the first wave of Acadians and my father married an 'American' girl whose parents had emigrated from Ireland and Germany. I grew up just yonder on a small plantation where all those 'apartments' are now. We played in bayous and told one another stories that our parents probably brought through Canada and all the way from France, stories of the loup-garou or rougarou, and we laughed about them, and thought of them as legend. As I grew older, real life was far worse than legend. We were always told what the Union soldiers would do—tear us to pieces, murder us! But soldiers from both sides came and went in small numbers—none ever hurt anyone here. They didn't destroy the area, as they did others. Perhaps we were not important enough. I don't know. But I had gone out. I was walking down to visit one of our neighbors and suddenly...there he was."

She stopped speaking.

"Who?" Andre asked.

"The Rougarou," she said softly. Then she smiled again and shook her head. "Not a rougarou, of course, but a man dressed as a rougarou. And he was in front of me, dancing and postulating, and I almost escaped him, but..."

Andre waited patiently, and it was Captain Bouche who urged her on.

"I tripped." She looked at Andre and flushed again. "We've gotten around, you know. We slip into homes and watch TV."

"And head to the cinema!" Lieutenant Kendall interjected.

"And in horror movies it is always so ridiculous that *everyone* seems to trip and fall when they're being pursued. But...I tripped. I was looking back. He grabbed me and ripped my skirt, and when I tried to run again, I tripped over the ripped hem of my gown. And he was upon me, and I got up and I fought, and he hit me in the head with a piece of log from a fallen tree. I never saw his face, I saw something like a wolf's mask…as if he'd worked in a circus before the war, or…" She paused, shaking her head. "I never saw his face. And then I remember pain. And then waking up here…and I realized that no one saw me, or heard me, and that I was dead. And I wandered around sobbing, and sometimes it seemed as if someone heard me, and sometimes I knew that they did not." She smiled suddenly. "Then these two found me, and it was so amazing. They were friends, because there is no war in death, just… just, I think, trying to learn, maybe, to do the right thing."

"I'm so sorry," Andre said softly.

She smiled and slipped ghostly arms through those of Captain Bouche and Lieutenant Kendall. "It's all right. They found me. I was so terrified of course, but I was always a bit afraid of everything. I'm also learning not to be quite so afraid. And… I think I can help you."

"You do?" Andre said with surprise. "You saw… you saw who has been here, who has been doing these things—now?"

"No, no!" she said. "I am so sorry, sir. It's not that simple. But…" She hesitated, looking from Bouche to Kendall, and then to Janine and Christian. "They said that anything at all would help. I hadn't spoken to Janine then…she and Christian met Lieutenant Kendall first. I mean then, back when Janine…when she was being interred here. I watched when they—

you, you and your friend—accosted that monster Lassiter. It was different for her, she…knew who took her."

"*She*—as in me—was a complete ass," Janine said. "Sorry, language, I know," she told Bouche and Kendall, grimacing. Janine turned to Andre. "I don't know if this will matter or not, but I don't think that Lassiter knew that the Rougarou was called that because he dressed up as the creature."

"Interesting—so the new killer found information that Lassiter didn't have," Andre said. He looked at Melissa Carrier and nodded a thank-you. "Any information may prove useful when we're putting the pieces together."

"There's more," Melissa said. "Again, I don't know how much it will help, but…when Lassiter was in the car, I saw him mouthing words to someone. Someone watching while they took him away. And I'm certain he said, 'You must go on,' to someone. And then, 'See me.'"

Andre listened without taking his eyes off Melissa.

"Could that really help you? I never saw who he was speaking to—everyone was milling everywhere, and… I don't know. I just don't know more. But whoever it was, I know that they were here. That doesn't mean anything, I suppose, but…"

"Put together with other things, it means a great deal," he assured her. "I can't thank you enough." He paused just a moment and then asked her, "What about now—did you see anything here?"

She nodded painfully. Andre felt his pulse quicken with hope.

"What did you see?" he asked.

"A rougarou—I saw him carry her into that old building…but then I saw no more."

"We all tried to tell someone," Captain Bouche said.

"But no one hears us," Lieutenant Kendall finished.

"I hear you," Andre assured them, "and I thank you. And if you think of anything else…"

He couldn't hand them one of his cards.

"We'll come back here. And if, at any time, you don't see me, Cheyenne—Janine's cousin—can see you, too."

"Cheyenne. She was the one who screamed about Lassiter, right—because she heard you! And she was here earlier, and before?" Melissa asked Janine.

"My cousin, yes. She's gifted!" Janine said proudly.

"I'm going to get back up to the house," he said, "and talk to Guy Mason."

"He's fairly new," Lieutenant Kendall said. He sighed. "Not that I have much concept of time."

Andre smiled. With another sincere "Thank you!" to them all, he gave a wave and headed back up to the house.

As he walked, his phone rang, and he answered quickly.

"Rousseau here. Cheyenne?"

"I saw Emil Justine. I could be wrong, but I would swear he's innocent. I called a car service to get back to the Justine property, but we were passing the church and I heard the organ," Cheyenne said. "I told the driver to stop. I think that Derringer is in there—unless there's a new organist. I'm going in. I'll call a car again as soon as I've had a chance to speak with him, and I'll meet you there as soon as I finish."

"Cheyenne!" he said quickly. But she'd hung up without waiting for a reply. He hadn't been able to tell her Melissa's revelation, that ten years ago, Lassiter had definitely had an accomplice.

9

"Amazing Grace."

It was, in Cheyenne's mind, one of the most beautiful songs ever composed.

The sounds of it, played so smoothly on the organ, resonated from the church; the organist was truly talented.

Like most of the girls in the area, Cheyenne had spent years in the choir. Jacques Derringer had been a hard taskmaster. He wanted his harmonies perfect.

She entered the church and the sound seemed to fill the world.

The organ was behind the altar in a loft.

Even seeing him from the back, Cheyenne knew that it was Derringer. She could tell by the way his back, shoulders and arms moved as he played; he was dramatic in every way.

And as he sat, he did remind one of a strange mixture between Igor and the Phantom of the Opera.

A strange man, indeed—who would have access to a priest's wardrobe, she noted.

The deep, rich sound of the organ swelled…and then faded into the air as the sound became an echo in the mind.

He couldn't have heard her enter—not above the sound of the organ. But he turned as if he knew that she was there.

"Miss Donegal," he said, swirling around on his bench. The church had excellent acoustics; his voice boomed throughout it like the organ. "Or so I hear, it's Special Agent Donegal now."

"Hello, Mr. Derringer. Yes, I'm with the FBI," Cheyenne said. "I'd like to speak with you, if I may. If you have a moment."

"How courteous. You're going to speak with me one way or the other, I imagine."

She didn't reply. He stood and looked down at her from his lofty height. She stared back up. His hair was still long, but it was thinning, and there were gray streaks in the strands that fell around his face. He had always appeared almost gaunt, and his cheeks seemed even more cavernous than before.

Like everyone, he had aged.

"I'll be right down," he told her.

There were stairs on either side of the loft. They curved around and came down to either side of the pews. He chose the curving stairway to Cheyenne's right. She waited patiently at the rear of the church.

He was wearing a white shirt and black suit— she wasn't sure if she had ever seen him dressed any other way.

Sun beamed through the many stained-glass windows with their depictions of saints, the pigments creating differentiations in shadow and light. They made him appear sinister as he approached her, but there was a friendly smile on his face.

He extended his hand.

She took it and saw the way his eyes moved over her.

"Quite the grown-up. Quite the beauty," he told her.

"Thank you, Mr. Derringer. I'm here because someone is imitating Lassiter…and we're looking for any help we can find."

"Right. The way you were looking for help from Emil Justine," he said.

"Sir, the federal government does not have Mr. Justine under arrest, nor are we planning charges."

He surveyed her warily for a moment and then said, "Detective Vine is an idiot. And you know that, don't you? Ah, no, you won't say that about a lawman, will you? Are you going to prove that Emil is innocent, or do you think it's fine to lock anyone up, you know, just in case?"

"When we prove the truth, I believe that Mr. Justine will be proved innocent," she said. "But we do need to find the killer."

"I thought the killer was dead."

"We don't believe that the man we discovered dead in the alley was the Mortician, sir."

"Oh?" He didn't wait for a response. He nodded. "Oh…you think he had to be connected to Lassiter somehow. And I would fall in that category because…?"

"You were there when Janine was interred," she said flatly. "You knew Lassiter. And you knew Janine well."

"Janine had the voice of an angel," he said.

"Yes, she did," Cheyenne agreed.

He looked at her intently, and even when sounding sincere, he seemed a strange man. "I'd have never hurt Janine. She was a little wild as a teenager, testing the world, but I believed, one day she'd be my extraordinary soprano. I could see her in the future… recording music for the world to hear, joyous music that gave faith and hope to everyone."

"We know for certain that Lassiter killed Janine," she said.

"I knew him, yes, we all knew him. He taught our kids, he came to games—he acted as if he was about to run for city government. I would have reported him if I had known what he was in any way. I wouldn't have helped him. I wouldn't."

"A priest went to visit him in prison."

"I'm not a priest. And Father Mahoney, who gave services for your cousin, was transferred to Chicago years ago. Father Napier is here now, and he came in from Los Angeles. He never knew Lassiter. He wouldn't have had a reason to see Lassiter, and Lassiter wouldn't have known him from Adam," he told her. "I know there are people who like to blame priests for everything bad, but they were both very good men. Not just good priests. Good men."

"I don't think either man was ever a suspect," she said.

He took a step back. "I'm a suspect?" he asked her. The idea had obviously not occurred to him.

"No," she lied. "We do believe that this killer might well have been close to Lassiter. And we're asking everyone for help. We're asking if anyone can remember anything at all odd—someone who might have held secret meetings with Lassiter."

"If they were secret, how would anyone know?" he demanded harshly.

"You might have noted bits of interplay between Lassiter and someone else that you just shrugged off at the time—or thought of as Lassiter just being a good guy."

He was thoughtful a long moment. "So long ago," he murmured.

"I know. But still, if you think back, concentrate, maybe there was a moment, just anything that might have shown a special interest between Lassiter and someone else."

"From what I understood, Lassiter went to trial, prison and his death without ever suggesting that anyone else was involved," Derringer said, shaking his head with confusion. He looked at her, and then sighed deeply. "I saw him sometimes with the football kid… Mike. Mike somebody."

"Mike Holiday."

"Yes. He'd congratulate him at games and stuff like that. And then, of course, the man who was coach here back then. Rocky—Rocky Beaufort.

Think he was born somewhere near here—maybe Monroe, or somewhere fairly close by."

"Can you think of any specific incidents?"

"Well, I'd watch Beaufort and Lassiter together—standing there at games. And then, as I said, I'd see Lassiter talking with Mr. Football Hero, that Mike Holiday." He shook his head. "Quarterbacks and cheerleaders—they took people from my choir. Good people. And then Janine…" He shook his head. "I had great belief in her!" he finished.

"Well, thank you, anyway."

"Emil is innocent."

Cheyenne just nodded.

"I swear to you—here, in church—that I'm innocent, as well," he said passionately.

"Thank you. Should you remember anything else…"

She produced a card; he took it. And he smiled.

"You know where to find me," he told her.

She managed a smile herself. "'Amazing Grace' was—beautiful," she assured him.

"I live for my music. I'm glad you feel that way. You were always a good kid, you know. You could have gone far with me, too, but I know…after Janine."

"Yeah, well, thank you. I'd better get back at it," she said.

Out on the street, she called for a car—thankful that there were many ride share apps now, even out where she was, and drivers willing to take her to an old cemetery in the middle of nowhere. It was time to head back, whether she still felt ready to give a good right-hand blow to Andre's jaw or not.

She reasoned that she was also ready to pummel her cousin—but Janine would only laugh.

Good rights to the jaw meant nothing to the dead.

Guy Mason was still in his office when Andre returned.

Old Mr. Tybalt's family was gone, but Mason wasn't in his office alone—the embalmer Herman Peterson was with him. They'd been sitting; both men stood as he entered, Guy Mason behind his desk and Peterson by the chair he had taken in front.

Peterson introduced the two. Andre shook hands with Mason, and then also took a seat next to the embalmer.

Mason looked at him with what appeared to be sincere consternation. "I know why you're here. Herman has been filling me in." He ran his fingers through his hair. It was thick, sleek hair. Andre wondered if he didn't find that his hand was slick from hair products after such a motion.

"We're looking for any help we can get."

"And of course," Mason said, "I'd be on the list for suspicion—if it weren't that the detective leading the investigation wasn't fully aware that it would be ridiculous for me to be involved in any such...horror. I'm a lover, not a fighter," he said dryly. "I'm appalled and—unlike my cousin—I don't believe that Emil is guilty of anything, except for old age and wanting to retain some remnants of control.

Those outbuildings are far from the house, and farther from the cemetery. We haven't used them in years—maybe decades. Every so often the concept of either tearing them down or restoring them comes up...and then it's forgotten again."

"You enjoy working for Emil?"

"I like him, and I'm good at this—at helping people through bereavement. Death is a part of life, and especially in a case such as Mr. Tybalt today, it's a gentle goodbye from a family with faith, glad to see him move on rather than suffer here on earth. I seem to have the right personality for dealing with people," he said. "That's my job—people. I meet with them, I set times for viewings and interments, I see that we accommodate priests, pastors—you name it—and make arrangements for bands and whatever else. I have no real business in any of the outbuildings. I don't do maintenance, I don't go to the shed... I come here, to the house. My office is here, and all arrangements are made here."

"What about the keys?" Andre asked.

"I have a set of keys."

"Do you ever hand out the extra keys, or tell people where to find them?" Andre asked.

"I know where they are," interjected Peterson. "And I have my own set. I'm not here, usually, to greet people. Except for dead people. I come when there is someone to work on. Sometimes, no one else is working, and if that's the case and I do need to be working on a body, I know where to get keys if I've left mine at home. Sometimes, you need a lot of time…as with Janine Dumas," he said, glancing at Andre with a pained expression. "I had to make her appear to be at peace for her family. He cut her a lot—not in the face. He didn't cut his victims in the face. But still, the amount of damage he did… He left it up to chance or the embalmer to see that for a funeral, she remained pretty."

"Do you ever talk about the keys—where they were kept?" Andre asked them both.

"No, I mean, why would we? When maintenance is coming, I show them in," Guy Mason assured Andre. "And we've had different grounds' workers through the years. And they've had no business anywhere but in the old kitchen and maybe the smokehouse—gardening equipment is kept there. We don't give them keys. We're here, or, really now, *I'm* here."

"Have you ever been in public, talking about the keys?" Andre asked. "I don't know how or when, but the killer got into that shack somehow—at some time. I had to use the key to unlock it when I found Lacey Murton. I believe that Lassiter used it, though it may not have been known at the time."

"No, we wouldn't speak in public about the keys to the whole place," Mason said, frowning. "People tend to be respectful around here, but why invite trouble?"

"Why, indeed?" Herman Peterson asked. But he frowned suddenly and looked from Guy Mason to Andre.

"What is it, please?" Andre asked.

"We were at the diner—Academy Diner, down in town," Peterson said. "Remember, Guy? Emil had been saying that he'd run phones and do setup from his home during business hours, and after, he never minded speaking with his neighbors who were bereaved. But he wasn't going to be around all the time and he thought it would be a good idea for us to know about a set of keys he had stashed at the place. We were talking about him—saying he may as well have a doormat in front of the tomb with the word *Welcome* written on it. Emil is a trusting sort—and he's paying for it."

"I've tried to tell Bill—Detective Vine," Mason said to Andre, "that there's just no way that Emil is involved. He says we're all too close to the man. Bill is from the north of the state. Whole different culture up there. I don't think he's ever going to make this arrest fly. I mean, he has no evidence other than that Emil owns the property, and I keep telling him that he might as well arrest me. I'm here more often, though it's true I have nothing to do with the outbuildings. But Emil hasn't been in them in years, either. That's all so far-fetched, except that…" He paused.

Andre had heard someone coming in, too. He stood and walked toward the front door. Cheyenne had arrived.

It seemed to him that the quick look she gave him was still scathing. She hadn't really cooled down at all. He wondered if maybe he had been wrong not to speak up immediately about her ghostly friends.

That didn't matter right now; it couldn't get in the way.

Herman Peterson and Guy Mason quickly stood when they came back into the office.

"Gentlemen, you may know my partner," Andre said. "Special Agent Cheyenne Donegal."

There were already three chairs in front of the desk; Guy Mason had been helping three members of the Tybalt family. Mason quickly shook hands with Cheyenne, trying to give her a professional look. He had, however, noted Cheyenne's appearance—and he'd clearly noticed that she was extremely attractive.

Herman Peterson was bluntly staring—and smiling.

"My, my! Miss Donegal, you did grow up quite the lovely creature. I've heard around town that you've a fine reputation with your work, too. It's not good to see you under such circumstances, but it is good for an old geezer like me to see a young woman who was the youth of yesterday grow to be such an example for today!"

"Thank you, sir," she told him politely. "And forgive me, but..."

"I'm the embalmer. I don't live here. You wouldn't know me. But I saw you—years ago."

"At my cousin's funeral," Cheyenne said. She managed a pleasant smile.

"Yes."

"Forgive me, I don't remember. It's nice to meet you. And you were here. Well, that's a good thing. Perhaps you will be able to help us. Mr. Mason," she said, and then she smiled at Herman Peterson and shook his hand, too.

Then she said, "Please, sit down, and if you don't mind, forgive me for being late to this…meeting, and bring me up to speed?"

She looked over at Andre again.

"In a nutshell, neither of these gentlemen thinks Emil Justine capable of any kind of evil, especially aiding and abetting a monster of a criminal. And neither of them has been to the outbuildings—which, at this point, should probably be demolished for safety, whether historic or not. We're working on finding out how someone got a copy of the keys," Andre said. "When were the buildings last rekeyed?" he asked Peterson and Mason.

"Ah, not since I've been here," Guy Mason said.

"Before my time, too, I think. We've made copies of old keys," Peterson said. "I've had the same set for over a decade. Since before…" He looked at Cheyenne and his voice trailed.

"Before Lassiter—before the day of Janine's funeral?" Cheyenne said.

"Yes. And I had been about to say that we were sitting in the diner one day, Guy and I, talking about the place, and me saying I didn't need a big old handful of keys to carry around when I was here just when needed, and most of the time when I came in, either he or Emil was here, and it wasn't necessary. You called Emil right away, and that's when I started using the hidden set, only when needed."

"But to the best of my knowledge, Emil had those

keys in that tomb for decades, at the least. I think he took over for his father sometime in the early 1980s, maybe even back sometime in the 1970s," Mason said.

"So, someone could have heard you—or someone might have had a copy of them from way, way back?" Andre said.

"I guess," Guy Mason said. "From the time he hired me, those keys were there. I think that maybe Emil even just kept it up—because *his* father kept the keys there."

"Please, do keep watch. The killer's lair, so to speak, has been discovered, so he wouldn't be back to make use of it, but if the killer is still out there, this does seem to be a favorite...haunt," Andre said dryly.

Cheyenne gave him a quick glare and turned her attention back to the two of them. "Anything else you can think of? Anything at all?"

They stared back at her blankly.

She stood, and the men in the room stood, as well. "Thank you," she said. "We'll be in contact with you, and hope that you do remember something that just might help. No matter how small."

Before they could leave, Guy Mason turned to Andre. "He really isn't guilty of anything—I mean Emil. He's old, and he lived his life in a place in this world that's most unusual. People knew people and cared about them, and when he was a kid, no one even locked their doors. He knew the old legends, of course, anyone from the state does. But he's a good man, and he is innocent."

"I believe that, too," Andre told him. "If we can find out what did happen, what was going on, we can clear him."

They shook hands all around again, and Andre and Cheyenne walked out of the house together.

Cheyenne headed straight down the path to the gates at the side of the cemetery. She might think he had long legs and walked fast, but she was moving with real purpose.

He still kept pace, and when they came down the hill, he called her name. She turned to look at him, her features expressionless as she waited for what he had to say.

He tossed her the keys to the car.

"I'll be a minute," he told her.

She caught the keys, looking at him with a frown.

"I want to say thank you to Janine and Christian. They found…friends to help today. Two soldiers and a victim of the original Rougarou."

"And you didn't tell me?" Cheyenne demanded.

"I haven't had a chance yet. And I know that you're angry—"

"I'm not angry. All right, I am angry. But that has nothing to do with the case. I'd never let my personal feelings about anything—"

"I know that, but I do want to say thank you."

"I'll come with you," she said.

"Good. I'm glad you're not angry with Janine and Christian."

"Nope, just you," she said, stepping around him and heading toward the field of graves and crypts and family mausoleums. "Janine?" Cheyenne said aloud as she approached the Dumas tomb.

"Hey, guys, over here!" Janine said.

When they turned, the group of them were still together: Captain Bouche, Lieutenant Kendall, Melissa—and Janine and Christian.

Janine walked over and gave Cheyenne a ghostly embrace. She more or less went right through Cheyenne. She stepped back, and Janine did the introductions. Cheyenne smiled at the Rebel and the Yank and gave her attention to Melissa Carrier.

"I'm so very sorry," she said.

"Ah, well, I haunt the place with very good friends," Melissa said. "And Janine and I...it's fun to have a girlfriend amidst these menfolk."

Fun, of course, and they could commiserate. Life had dealt them both brutal blows that had led to their deaths.

"Thank you for trying to help us," Cheyenne told them, looking around the group.

"We are sorry only that we can't tell you more, and certainly, a bit angry with ourselves that we didn't know—that we didn't see," Captain Bouche said.

"We should have been aware, but we don't even know if Lassiter used the house," Lieutenant Kendall said. "I don't know if we could have stopped anything or not, but..."

"This killer seems to be re-creating the original's manner of accosting women," Andre said, looking over at Cheyenne. "The young lady who survived was abducted by a rougarou—and Melissa also was attacked by a man dressed as a rougarou. When Janine was taken…"

"I just fell like a pathetic lovesick puppy for charm and maturity," Janine said.

"But," Andre noted, "Lassiter did have that charm. He was able to slip away with you easily. You wanted to go, and you knew your parents wouldn't approve, so you certainly rather sneaked away with him. After the fact, people said that they saw you with him. That's made me think that neither the original killer nor our present killer has that same kind of charisma—and thus they used a costume, dark alleys, forest paths—places where he could wear a costume and get away with it."

"So, today's killer is not so charming," Cheyenne said thoughtfully. "He may look fine and normal, but he doesn't have what it is that Lassiter had—that Bundy-esque ability to make people want to be with him because of his smile."

"Ah, well, then, this man is most probably just— normal, whatever that may be," Janine said.

"There was something you said earlier that had me thinking," Andre said. "About kids. We came here as teenagers. Sad, but true, I think I had my first beer by the Duvalier tomb."

Janine laughed. "Hey, you just had beer. I have to say that I even shake my head at those…well, let's say I've seen a naked body or two in the cemetery that I never wanted to see."

Cheyenne was looking at him thoughtfully.

"Kids—you're right. We could ask for any help at the schools."

Andre nodded, and noted the sky.

The day was coming to an end. And in his mind, they hadn't finished all that they needed to do out here.

He looked around again, nodding to the five spirits who were helping. "We'll see you tomorrow. Cheyenne, we'll go ahead and stay the night and head to the schools tomorrow."

There were assents from all around.

Cheyenne said her goodbyes and followed him back up the path. As he walked, he put through a call to Jackson Crow.

His field director, he learned, had spent the day with the NOLA police and the local field office, trying to convince them that they might still have a serial killer on their hands.

"I can't control what certain officers do and don't believe, but the higher-ups have ordered that they be wary—and keep looking. I'm meeting with the coroner, and Angela has been heading around local establishments with pictures of all our victims," Jackson told him. "Eventually," he said softly, "we will find the detail that leads us where we need to go."

Andre stopped walking, looking at Cheyenne as he told Jackson about their day.

"Garlic and men's cologne or men's aftershave," she reminded him.

He nodded and passed on that information and then added, "Lacey told Cheyenne that she also saw something—someone, she thinks—out of the corner of her eye when the rougarou came to take her. Suggesting an accomplice."

"Interesting."

He explained how they had all used the cemetery at various times as kids, and that they were going to go to the schools to ask for help the next day. "I guess we'll also get to a department store and round up samples of aftershave and see if perhaps there's one particular scent Lacey recognizes."

"We'll keep in touch," Jackson promised, and they ended the call.

"You don't happen to have a family home here, do you?" Andre asked, looking at Cheyenne.

She shook her head. "Janine's parents moved away. Mine are long gone, as well—closest thing I have to a family home out here anymore is that large tomb with the name Dumas chiseled atop the arch."

"Any hotels or motels you like?"

"Sure, a nice—brand-new—little place just outside of Broussard. There's a little mom-and-pop Italian restaurant near it. I haven't eaten."

"I haven't, either. Food, place to stay. Are you planning on eating with me?"

"Of course." He started to smile, but her look remained hard. "We're partners on this. We will work it together, and we will bring it to a conclusion," she said tightly.

"Do or die," he murmured, and kept walking.

She definitely had a temper. She was trying her best to control it. He smiled slightly.

Cheyenne didn't offer the keys back; better that way. She knew where she was going.

She drove in silence, heading straight to the local hotel.

"The restaurant is just down the street, walking distance. I thought we'd park, get our things out," she said.

"Fine."

The desk clerk immediately thought they wanted one room. Cheyenne corrected him.

The place had forty rooms that all opened onto the central pool, and theirs were side by side on the ground floor. He rolled his bag into his room — basic, with a bed, dresser, TV and coffeemaker—and went out to wait for Cheyenne.

The water in the pool was aqua and looked refreshing. Tranquil, with flower and foliage artfully arranged around lounger chairs and small tables.

Cheyenne reappeared quickly. "Shall we?"

"Absolutely."

She still moved with her quick pace; he fell into step. They soon arrived at the restaurant, a small and adorable place called Angelina's with an Italian flag in the window and checkered cloths on the tables. It was evident that Cheyenne knew them well, because they were greeted at the door. She hugged the hostess, who was apparently an old friend, and then the hostess's parents—the owners—who came out. She introduced him, and the couple and the girl hugged him, too. Angelina—the mom and the restaurant's namesake—then assured him that they could prepare just anything that would make them happy, and he in turn told her that he believed that anything she prepared would make him happy.

The were shown a table and he gave his attention to the menu, which informed all diners that the staff was happy to make all kinds of substitutions.

"Nice place," he said to Cheyenne, and when their waitress came by, he opted for the lasagna and a house salad while she asked for chicken cutlets and a salad as well, both of them rounding out their meal with mineral water.

"You apparently know these people," he said lightly.

"Cassandra—the hostess—and her family moved here when I was in high school. My parents are supersweet people and they made them feel very welcome, and we even helped out here when they first opened," she said. "They were newcomers, and you know how people in small towns can be..."

"Communities can close ranks, it's true," he said. "Which makes it interesting how quickly some people have pointed fingers. Although almost everyone except for Detective Vine seems to think Emil Justine is innocent. I wonder what will happen to the cemetery. He is old. He probably isn't even sure what he plans to do in the future. He won't live forever, and his family seems to have moved on."

"They've moved on—that doesn't mean that they'll let the plantation and cemetery go," Cheyenne said. "They'll be absentee owners." She sighed.

Their salads and bread arrived, and they thanked their waitress.

Neither spoke for several seconds—they were evidently both really hungry.

Their hands brushed as they reached for the rolls at the same time. She glanced at him with surprise, and something like a flash of fire seemed to pass between them.

It was quickly gone. She withdrew her hand and he apologized. "Please. After you."

"No, no, go ahead."

"Cheyenne, it's a roll. We're equal partners on the job, but at dinner let me be a gentleman with some common courtesy, as I was raised. Forgive me—take one, and then I can take one, too."

She took a roll.

"We need to work on this eating-regularly thing," she muttered.

"We do," he agreed.

After a few moments of companionable quiet while they ate, Andre asked, "Is Angela coming out to stay with Lacey Murton? I just think it will be a lot better if one of us is watching her. Her mother is staying tonight, right?"

"I got that impression, but let me make sure." She pulled out her phone and called the hospital, identified herself. She was put through to Lacey's room. Andre heard her speak with Lacey's mother, asking her if she was staying and then—after apparently receiving an affirmative answer—assuring her that someone with the FBI, very well-known and completely trusted, would be there the following day, and stay with them in the days to follow.

"Okay, we're good on that end," she told Andre. Cheyenne was quiet for a minute and then asked, "Angela is way over me in rank and seniority, I imagine. She'll be okay to play watchdog and trust me to be investigating with you?"

"You're the reason the case has come this far. The Krewe is great. Those guys never micromanage," he said. "I've never been in a better working situation."

Their entrées came. They were silent again, and when the check came, he smiled at her as he picked it up.

"Your expense account or mine—no difference, right? Humor me. Let me do the paperwork."

She was silent as he paid.

Hugs with the staff went around again before they could leave. The family knew why they were there and wished them success.

"It's terrifying to think that such a man might still be out there," the mother, Angelina, said. She glanced quickly at her daughter. "I'm always begging Cassandra to be careful."

"And I am careful," Cassandra said.

"Be on the lookout and be doubly careful," Cheyenne told her. "Watch out for anyone in costume, or anyone asking you to go anywhere. If anyone comes near you, scream the loudest you can and create the biggest disturbance possible. This killer, I believe, is drugging or knocking his victims out—that's the only way he can handle them. Don't let anyone close enough to get to you," she said.

"You need to come home with us!" Cassandra's father said.

For a moment, it appeared that Cassandra would protest. "Hey, you know what, sure. I'll spend a few days bonding."

"Great," Cheyenne said. She hesitated. "We may be closing a noose, so…well, it's a good idea to be *exceptionally* careful right now."

"I wish I was you—an agent, not afraid of anything," Cassandra told Cheyenne.

"I am afraid—and I'm wary. I believe I know how to handle myself, but…"

"We work as partners," Andre said. "I have her back—and she has mine."

Cassandra laughed. "Well, Special Agent Rousseau, I'd be delighted to have you at my back anytime!"

He grinned and murmured a "Thanks," and they made their way out.

The night was shadowed; a moon, soon to be full, was lighting the sky.

"Big moon," Andre noted.

"Almost full," she said, and then she looked up at him. "Andre, do you think that will mean anything? We know this guy is dressing up as a rougarou, a version of a werewolf. Maybe he's just waiting for the full moon to strike again."

"Maybe. But I'd like to think he's not going to try anything here—his lair was discovered. Lacey was saved." He paused, looking up at the moon. "Hard to tell. His timeline has been haphazard, the way he's taken women, kept them and then killed them. I do think that Lacey surviving has put a few kinks in his plans for the future."

He looked up at the moon again, and his resolve hardened.

A man who dressed up as a rougarou just might think himself enhanced, stronger, invincible, when the full moon rose.

Cheyenne was right; time was against them.

10

When they reached the hotel, Cheyenne nodded to Andre and headed to her door without saying a good-night. She entered her room; he entered his.

Andre locked his door—double-bolted it—stripped off his jacket and tossed it on his bed, and then did the same with his holster, noting that there was a connecting door between his room and Cheyenne's. He stripped off the rest of his clothing, longing for a shower. He started into the bathroom, and then paused, taking the Glock with him. With everything happening, it seemed prudent to have the gun be wherever he was.

He was glad they were in a brand-new place; the water heated almost instantly. The shower running over him felt like nirvana.

But in the midst of his shower, he paused, going dead still, thinking he'd heard something above the rush of the water. Leaving it flowing, he stepped out, grabbed a towel—and then his Glock. He slowly and carefully opened the bathroom door farther, glad that he'd left it ajar.

He frowned. To his amazement, a woman also clad in only a towel was in his room. It took him a second to recognize Cheyenne because her long red hair was wet and darker plastered down her back.

She was at the window, looking out. He noticed she was armed.

He said her name softly—hoping she was expecting him to be there and wouldn't spin and shoot. Just in case, he'd kept the door halfway closed.

She beckoned to him; he walked out.

"There was someone here," she said quietly. "I heard them walking down the path in front of the rooms, and I thought it was just another guest…and then, I could swear they tried my door and moved down to yours."

He reached into the closet, hoping to find a robe. He did, donned it quickly, and he nodded to her and she flanked him. He opened the door to the outside.

There was no one on the path.

He lowered his hand and nodded to her. She covered him as he stepped out, as if enjoying a look at the pool.

Whoever had been there was gone.

He walked back into the room. Out of habit, he locked the door and put the chain on.

"It could have been a lost guest," she said. "Someone who forgot their room number."

"It could have been. I'm going to check with the front desk."

He dialed zero on the house phone. He was quickly connected, and identified himself as Special Agent Rousseau, and then asked how many of the rooms were taken.

All of them on the ground floor; only three were empty on the second. "It could have been a lost guest. It could have been... I don't know. The killer probably knows who we are, if he's been paying even a little attention to the news."

She nodded. "Do me another favor—it's late, but not that late. Can you call Jackson and see if he can find out who on our list of suspects is definitely still in New Orleans?"

"I can do that," he told her.

He called Jackson, who said that he and Angela were still out. They were on Frenchman Street.

"So Jimmy Mercury is there?"

"We just saw him playing," Jackson said.

"You see anyone else on our list tonight?"

"Angela went into the gym—acted as if she was just looking for a place to work out," Jackson told him. "Ex-coach Rocky Beaufort was there. That was about two hours ago, though. As to Mike Holiday, I can go check and see if he's on duty. The music store closed a while ago, but we went in earlier and both Katie and Nelson Ridgeway were there. But it's just a two-hour drive out to you."

He'd been concentrating on the moment, but—staring at Cheyenne in her towel—he asked quickly, "What about the note on the cocktail napkin we found in the cemetery? You went to the bar, right?"

"Yes. I brought pictures of all our suspects."

"And?"

"All right, Jimmy Mercury has played there—he still does sometimes. I showed them pictures of Mike Holiday, Rocky Beaufort and Nelson and Katie Ridgeway. They might have been there—the staff isn't sure. According to the manager, it's an extremely busy place, and people can all look alike. I also showed her and others on staff pictures of Emil Justine and Jacques Derringer. She's certain she would have remembered them, and doesn't recall seeing those men. So it seems we keep coming back to square one. But maybe we've eliminated the men most people would think to be the key suspects. Then again—that they weren't seen can only lead us on other paths, without closing those completely."

"Right." Andre thanked him and ended the call and gave his attention to Cheyenne.

"I can't say many things for sure, but that wasn't Jimmy Mercury. Jackson and Angela are cruising the city and they just saw Jimmy. They also saw Rocky Beaufort and Katie and Nelson Ridgeway earlier but can't guarantee any of the three might not have made it out here. They're going to head to Bourbon Street and see if Mike Holiday is working. And they checked on the threatening cocktail-napkin note—Jimmy has worked at the bar, and they can't be sure about the others."

She nodded. "The note on the tomb could have meant anything."

"And it could mean that the killer is gunning for you."

"Good—I'm neither weak nor vulnerable, and he tends to go after young women alone who fall for antics or are caught off guard. I won't be. I'm expecting him." She lifted the hand, still holding her Glock.

He suddenly heard the sound of the shower—water still streaming down in the bathroom—and murmured, "Excuse me," and went to turn it off.

When he returned, Cheyenne was still exactly where he'd left her standing. She'd drawn the drapes closed, and it was dim with only the light from the bathroom streaming into the room.

"So, here we are," he said. "You in a towel with a gun, me in a towel with a gun."

"Your robe is terry, but it's a robe. Technically, you're in more than a towel, so you're in a robe and a towel and carrying a gun," she said.

"Classy," he said dryly.

"I'm really furious with you, you know."

"I do know, though I don't think you have the right to be so angry. But hey, that's your call."

"You made me feel ridiculously foolish. You saw *ghosts* talking to me, and you let me pretend that nothing was happening, and you didn't say a word."

"I figured you would tell me when you were ready."

She stared at him. Her hair was still damp, streaming around her face. Her eyes were like embers slowly igniting into fire.

"By the way, I have to say…you look really great in that towel."

She didn't speak at first. She walked toward him. She stopped close in front of him. Arms at her sides—Glock still in her right hand—she rose on her toes and pressed his lips with a kiss. He felt the touch of that kiss, her lips moist and firm as they met his, and he was afraid that his instant arousal might well be seen or felt—despite the robe over the towel.

She lowered herself to flat on her feet and studied his face.

"You're still angry," he said, not moving.

Not daring to move.

"You don't want angry sex?" she asked him. Her voice sounded a little rough.

"Oh, I'll take angry sex," he told her. "I'd rather thought of myself as a bit more of a romantic, but… sure, angry sex is definitely better than no sex. If you're sure—"

"It's my idea, isn't it?" she asked.

"Yes," he said quietly, and his lips twisted into a smile. "However, despite the automatic safety mechanisms on the Glocks, we might want to put them down."

She nodded. "Which is your side of the bed?"

"Whatever side I end up on," he said.

That brought a smile from her, and she slipped away, setting her gun on the left bedside table.

He set his on the right, and then they moved back to the foot of the bed, where they met again, still a distance apart, looking at one another.

Then he stepped forward and lowered his face to hers. There was nothing subtle in their kiss.

Their mouths meshed together, tongues searching and clasping, and with nothing to hold except for the beauty before him, Andre pulled her tight against himself.

Her towel gave way first, and he relished the play of his hands over her bare flesh, his fingers running down her spine, hands caressing her buttocks, bringing her closer, flush to him, and there was no way she could miss the arousal she had created.

His towel fell. He broke away long enough to strip off the robe and pull her close to him again. They fell on the bed together.

He'd been fascinated with her, he thought, from the first time he'd seen her on the street. He'd become more entranced when she'd shown up at his house, when she'd talked and explained her feelings, when he'd started falling a little bit in love with her mind and the way that she thought and felt...

It wasn't her mind that occupied him at the moment, he knew.

She was deliciously damp and sweet from the shower. Atop her on the bed, he threaded his fingers through hers and kissed her again, and when that kiss ended, he drew his lips down over her body, discovering the exquisite beauty of her breasts and belly. He felt her fingers on him, dancing over his shoulders, the light scrape of her nails teasing him.

He kept moving. She writhed and arched beneath him, her breathing and heartbeat picking up cadence.

She twisted and came around, eager to touch his flesh with her lips, doing things with kisses and caresses that drove the desire screaming inside him. And still, as urgent as the hammering inside of him became, the need to prolong and savor each sweet taste of flesh was equally as strong, kissing and caressing the length of her, smiling at her strength as she rose, returning each searing hot kiss and stroke with a passion that was as sensually escalating as the rise of the wind in a storm.

Then there was the moment it could all be borne no more. He rose above her, and watched her eyes, the honesty and the hunger, and he was quickly deep within her. They held there, eager again to remember each and every moment and touch, as if they and they alone had experienced such exquisite ecstasy, as if they, and only they, in glorious rapture, had created original sin.

There were incredible moments in which the world went away, in which all that mattered was the appeasing of that delirious hunger that had burst between them.

And then climax. Volatile, delicious, seeming to cause all of the room to shake, but it was, of course, just them, as after-tremors ripped through their bodies... Maybe the bed did shake, as well.

And it was so damned good. He fell by her side, gulping in air—and praying that the thunder-loud pounding of his heart was a good thing, as well.

She curled against him, and for a moment, neither said a word.

Then he couldn't help himself.

"Angry sex. All right. Definitely better than no sex at all."

She whacked him on the chest, pushing up on her arms to stare at him.

He smiled, and she smiled at last, and fell back to his side.

"Why? Do you suck if your partner isn't angry?" she teased.

"Ow!" he replied, grinning and lacing his fingers behind his head.

She just laughed.

He pulled her closer to him, stroking back the dampness of her hair.

"I'm still really angry with you," she told him.

"That bodes well," he said.

It did, later.

As they lay together, he found that he was sated in a way he had never been before. Because he was fascinated by so much about her, even more so now that he held her.

He loved her mind, her earnestness—her toughness.

And all that they shared. Their strange history.

But there was so much in the present, and in the future, and in a shared look at the world. He had a feeling that she may have shied away from many men.

They might have been intimidated by her—or, she might have been afraid that she lived a lie, and that if they knew the truth, they would turn away in fear or bewilderment.

He lay awake awhile, and then he checked that both firearms were within reach.

Someone could have simply had the wrong room that night, or forgotten their room number.

Then again…it was best to be cautious.

He drifted off, grateful that he knew he slept lightly.

And grateful that they lay together through the night.

Cheyenne was spooned in Andre's arms when she awoke.

She was careful not to move for a minute, and barely opened her eyes. A moment of sheer delight at being held by Andre streaked through her. A man she found incredibly attractive and admired and liked more and more on a daily basis, a man who knew her past, her present and all about what she had always considered to be an extremely bizarre sixth sense.

His phone rang; the sound startled her so much that she leaped up, suddenly shy, dragging a pillow with her.

At that hour, it had to be Jackson or Angela calling, and she paused, waiting as he answered the phone.

She didn't hear anything but a lot of yeses and then a thank-you, and he hung up.

"Jackson got an assembly together for us at the high school, first thing."

"Great! I'll get ready. Uh… I'm fast. I just need a few minutes."

"Me, too." He grinned at her. "One room really would have been sufficient, but now, it's good to have two bathrooms. I can shower in five."

"I can shower in four!"

"Ah, but I'll be clean."

"Hey!"

"Whoever is ready first, come through for the other."

She started to run through the connecting doors, but then jogged back and procured her Glock. It didn't seem prudent to be anywhere, including the shower, without having it in arm's reach.

They were both ready within minutes and heading out to the car. "Jackson also has a hotline set up for kids to call."

"Shouldn't they call us in this situation?"

"He's afraid that there will be hundreds of calls. We have one of our people at headquarters on it. She's really an expert on fielding the calls—knowing when someone just wants attention or is playing a prank. If we give out our numbers, we may become paralyzed, doing nothing but answering the phone. Our agent will contact us immediately regarding any tips we should take seriously or anyone we really should speak to ourselves."

They didn't talk about the night before; they were back to business, finding a killer.

Except that when they parked in the teachers' lot

and headed toward the school, he grinned and said, "I sure hope you're angry with me again tonight."

She shot him a glare.

He laughed.

Then he grew serious as they entered the school.

Cheyenne suggested that Andre speak first. "You and then me—I had a cousin murdered, and people remember that. My coming after you might make a bigger impact."

Andre agreed. The principal introduced the two of them, and to Cheyenne's surprise, the students were attentive. The world had become a hard place. Young people knew it all too well.

"We're from here, you know—both Special Agent Donegal and myself," Andre said, addressing the students at the high school, who had gathered in the auditorium. "And it hurts when someone makes use of our community to perpetrate crimes, especially as heinous as these crimes have been. Now, to be honest, we know that many of you use the cemetery as a hangout—because we used the cemetery as a hangout."

Someone had a hand up, but Cheyenne knew Andre wanted to finish his plea before taking any questions. "Police and FBI have investigated the cemetery. I'm sure that you've seen news, and I'm sure the entire community has talked about the fact that a victim was found in the cemetery—thankfully, alive—and that Mr. Emil Justine has been arrested. We don't want to be anything but honest with you, and we beg you all to be honest with us. So, please remember, Mr. Justine is a suspect in collusion because he owns the property. There is no hard evidence against him. We're open here in this area—too open, when a case like this arises. We tend to be nice people, which is not a bad thing, but at times like this, we need to be alert and aware. And we're here asking for any help you can give us."

He looked at Cheyenne who stepped over to the podium and the mic. "You may or may not know— I went to this high school years ago, and my cousin Janine Dumas went to this high school before me. She became a victim of Ryan Lassiter, a killer known as the Artiste. Now, you are all well aware, I'm certain, that a killer known as the Mortician has been killing young women in our area on down to New Orleans—and he kidnapped one victim in Mississippi. We're here because we know you can help. It was friends who saw Janine with Lassiter who finally brought him down."

Andre spoke again. "No one will be in trouble for anything—as I said, we were kids here, too. You don't need to tell anyone if you wish to speak with us, and anything you say about being in the cemetery stays with us."

"Any little thing can help," Cheyenne said. "Something unusual you saw or heard. Someone who gave you a bad feeling, or was somewhere they shouldn't be. We need to know about it."

Andre opened the floor to questions.

One young man wanted to know why they didn't believe that Mr. Justine was guilty. "He's creepy—

like the cemetery guy in a horror movie," the kid said.

"Mr. Justine was out of town when many of the events happened. He's still under investigation, but the timeline doesn't fit," Andre said. And he went on, "Mr. Justine is elderly—and if you read up on Ryan Lassiter, you'll discover that the man was able to get away with so much because he was able to convince people he was the nicest guy around. Don't go by a person's exterior—go by what you might have witnessed or heard. Not gossip, or just thinking that someone is creepy. You have minds, and this area might be small, but this is one of the finest high schools to be found. You're highly capable of reason. If we didn't believe in you, we wouldn't be here asking for help."

The principal spoke again, and then thanked them for coming; Andre and Cheyenne thanked the students, and then headed out to the hospital. There they found Lacey's mom arguing with the doctor; Lacey could leave the hospital, but her mother was raging that they were being thrown out—and that the killer would come after Lacey again.

Cheyenne hurried into the fray.

"Mrs. Murton, please, it's going to be all right. One of the agency's top people is on her way here, and she'll stay with you night and day until we're able to catch the man who assaulted Lacey."

"Her!" the woman said. "Her? A giant man in a wolf costume attacked my daughter—and they're sending a woman?"

There was no way not to take offense at the woman's question, but Cheyenne controlled her temper.

"Mom!" Lacey wailed.

"Mrs. Murton," Andre said, stepping in. "Special Agent Hawkins has been in her current position for years. She's highly trained and has one of the best investigative minds in our field. There is no one to whom I would trust a loved one with the same whole-hearted faith."

The woman backed down. She still seemed perplexed, but it seemed she believed if Andre said something, it had to be true.

"I'm so sorry," Lacey said wanly. "Mom, we just need to be grateful."

"I am grateful!" her mother snapped, and then tears stung her eyes. "You're alive. I can't bear it if anything were to happen again. I'd lost you, you were found..."

She was going to break down completely any minute.

Cheyenne smiled at Lacey and then her mother, trying to assure them that everything was going to be all right.

Andre's phone rang, and he excused himself, stepping out to the hall.

"Do you know this woman? Special Agent Hawkins?"

"I do," Cheyenne said. "And she's the great leader of a very elite unit—Andre's unit—and she knows what she's doing, I promise. She's a crack shot,"

Cheyenne said, although, of course, she was only presuming that to be true. Still, she'd bet a lot on it.

Cheyenne was an excellent shot herself—one of her instructors at the academy had told her once that women tended to be excellent, patient and willing to listen and learn.

Andre came back into Lacey's room. "We have a few people we need to see," he told Cheyenne.

"Please don't leave!" Mrs. Murton begged.

Cheyenne glanced at Andre. He smiled and handed her a piece of paper.

"We'll divide and conquer. You take this one. Take the car—I'll wait until Angela's here, and then take her wheels. That way, Mrs. Murton, we're with you until Angela comes, and we know that you and Lacey are safe."

Cheyenne nodded and then lowered her head, trying not to smile. He was going to keep the peace here. Mrs. Murton just had more faith in a manly presence.

They were talking life and death. They just needed to move—and not deal with Mrs. Murton's prejudices.

He handed her the keys, his eyes on hers. "Be careful," he told her.

"Always," she promised.

It wasn't until she was out of the room that she looked at the paper, and of course, she knew right away what had happened…already.

Officer Rawlins of the police department would be escorting a Miss Eva Wilson to meet her at the cemetery, where Eva could show Cheyenne exactly what she'd seen when she'd been partying there with friends.

Cheyenne hurried out, found the car and drove the distance to the cemetery and plantation just as quickly as she could. When she arrived, there was a police car at the gate.

Officer Rawlins, a slightly broad man of about fifty, got out of his car as she approached with a quick nod for her. A young woman—just about Janine's age when she'd been murdered—stepped out of the car, as well.

"Special Agent Donegal," he called to her. "This is Eva Wilson. She slipped into the principal's office and said that she did see something unusual. I'm going to let you two speak with one another, and I'll get on. You'll see that Eva makes it back to school safely?"

"Yes, Officer, thank you. I will."

Cheyenne smiled at the girl; she was pretty, slim and tall, with long, smooth, dark hair, porcelain skin and large, dark eyes.

She had a feeling the girl was one of the popular students at the school.

She was wearing jeans and a tailored shirt, and a backpack slung over her shoulder. She looked at Cheyenne, and then back at Officer Rawlins. She thanked him nervously and started walking toward Cheyenne.

Cheyenne offered her what she hoped to be a reassuring smile. "Thank you so much for coming out here."

"I'm afraid that I may have nothing, but…"

"Anything may be something," Cheyenne said. "You were going to show me?"

"Well, I figured it might be easier if I tried to explain where I was, and what…what I was doing, and then what I saw, and you can… Well, anyway… I was over there, by the Dumas tomb…" She paused, looking back at Cheyenne with a little gasp. "Oh, I'm so sorry, that's your tomb, isn't it? Oh, I didn't mean *your* tomb, I meant your family's tomb."

"I know, and it's all right, really."

They went through the gates to the property and headed toward the tombs. The Dumas tomb was a fine one. Cheyenne knew that she was welcome there with her ancestors if she chose—when the time came. She rather thought that she might want to be cremated and thrown into the ocean rather than have a place waiting.

Didn't matter at the moment. Past the Dumas tomb, she saw the rise of the Broussard tomb, the finest in the cemetery—even larger and grander than that which belonged to the Justine family.

It was a bit higher on the slope of the hill, in a different row of the houses for the dead.

The Dumas tomb had a space toward the far-right edge. Walking alongside Eva, Cheyenne realized that from the far side of the tomb, she could look up the hill—not so much at the house, but at the outbuildings that stretched behind it.

Eva stopped walking. She swallowed hard and looked at Cheyenne.

"I was at a party—a party I wasn't supposed to be at."

"Hey, we've all been at a party we're not supposed to be at. And I promise, you're sharing with only me—I'm not running to your house to share this info."

"Well, if my folks find out I was here, they won't be happy, but that's not it."

"What is it?" Cheyenne asked.

Eva let out a long sigh. "I was stoned. One of my friends had this amazing grass, and we were…we were high as kites. There were about twelve of us here that night, kind of dancing around…smoking, drinking…if we pick up after ourselves, no one ever knows. Or maybe everyone knows and they just don't care… Anyway, I got tired, and I was leaning against the tomb, and… I saw it. And that's the thing, I was stoned, so I really didn't think anything of what I saw. Well, I did. I was terrified, but…maybe the grass was cut with something. I couldn't scream. I couldn't move… I couldn't do anything at all. I just sat there, and I was shaking and trying to hide behind the tomb. Oh, man, I really shouldn't have been here. It's so messed up…"

"Eva, it's okay. I'm not telling your parents or the school you were smoking pot. What did you see?"

"The Rougarou!" she said.

"You mean…from the 1860s?"

"No… I'm sorry, I don't think so. I guess, not *the* Rougarou, but *a* rougarou. He seemed to be very big, he was…furry. Like…full-figure furry. He had this big head and a big snout…and he was carrying a woman. It was like I'd entered a horror movie. He had a woman in his arms. He was running through the tombs, and he had her in his arms, and I freaked out, hid behind the Dumas tomb and just froze."

"Thank you," Cheyenne said, determined not to let Eva know how disappointed she was—they already knew that Lacey Murton's kidnapper had dressed up as a rougarou.

Eva was staring up the hill now, toward the outbuildings.

"He wasn't alone. The rougarou wasn't alone."

Cheyenne's breath caught.

"There were...two rougarous? Or did you mean, he wasn't alone because of the woman in his arms?"

Eva winced, shaking her head and turning to Cheyenne.

"No, no... I mean—" She broke off, grimacing again.

"Who was with the rougarou?" Cheyenne asked.

"The mummy!" Eva told her. "Oh, I know I sound ridiculous. And I didn't say anything because we'd been smoking, and... I thought I was hallucinating, for real. But I never said anything about the rougarou, and then that poor woman was found half-dead and..." She stopped and stared hard at Cheyenne. "Yes, I was smoking dope. But I know now that what I saw was real. There was a rougarou, and he was running through the tombs with a woman in his arms, just like a monster in a horror movie. But he wasn't alone—he was being followed by a mummy!"

11

Andre was grateful that Angela Hawkins arrived quickly, but he wished he could have warned her that she was up against a bit of a problem with Lacey's mother. It wouldn't matter; Angela would always handle whatever came her way.

As he'd expected, Mrs. Murton narrowed her eyes warily when she first saw Angela, who was a slim blonde, and could give the appearance of a Nordic princess, light and delicate.

He knew himself that Angela was anything but.

Mrs. Murton wanted a man—preferably an ex-heavyweight boxing champ.

Angela glanced at Andre with amusement, obviously well aware the woman was wary that *she* was supposed to be her daughter's guard.

"I know you're concerned about getting back to work," Angela said to Lacey. "For the next few days, if you're willing, however, we've arranged a safe house for you—we'd like to bring you back to New Orleans. There, we have special alarm systems in place, we have a number of agents, myself and Field Director Jackson Crow. Jackson has taken the liberty of speaking with Mr. Swanson, supervisor at B and G Oil Systems, and your job is guaranteed when you get back to it, Lacey. So, when your release papers are all settled, we'll take off for NOLA, with an escort from the city and an escort meeting us on the highway. You'll be perfectly safe, Miss Murton Mrs. Murton."

"Escorts...a safe house, yes, that's wonderful," Mrs. Murton said.

"Do you really think that you can catch him?" Lacey asked. "He's been out there a long time now!"

"We're closing in—because of you," Andre assured her. "He knows it. He's been disrupted. He's going to make a mistake." He glanced at his watch, anxious to go.

He was ready to meet with a young man—a football player who'd possibly seen something. The boy was afraid he'd be on the sidelines, in trouble for... well, he hadn't done anything, but he had been there, at the cemetery with others. "This field-managing-whatever man—Crow—he's...sturdy?" Mrs. Murton asked.

"As tall as Andre here, and yes, very strong," Angela replied. "You will be fine until we get to him—I excel in the shooting range, and thanks to the FBI, I have training in martial arts, as well."

If Angela wanted, she could toss most men to the ground.

Mrs. Murton was apparently very old-school.

"At any rate, I have an appointment," Andre told them. "Lacey, Mrs. Murton, I leave you in the excellent care of Special Agent Hawkins."

Angela nodded at him, still amused. She didn't take offense—she did what was needed.

"We'll be fine. Keep in touch," Angela said.

He nodded and hurried out before Mrs. Murton could worry again.

As he headed down—the keys to Angela's rental car in his hand—he called the principal and arranged to meet the football player named Jean Barre at the cemetery gates. A local police officer would be escorting him.

Jean Barre wasn't a particularly big kid; he was tall, and deceptively lanky. Left by his escorting officer with Andre, he quickly explained, "I'm the quarterback, Special Agent Rousseau. I'm fast as hell."

"I'll bet you are. So, what can you tell me?"

Jean looked uneasily toward the cemetery.

"Is this all confidential?"

"As far as possible, yes. We're not here to skewer you guys for being kids."

"And for doing the same things you used to do here, huh?"

Andre smiled. "I was gone by high school," he told him. "You want to go in?"

Jean Barre shook his head firmly. "No."

Andre realized that the young man was frightened by the cemetery.

"Okay, we can stand here. What can you tell me?"

Barre looked at him, biting his lip. "It's haunted."

"Okay," Andre said slowly. "In what way? Did you see…ghosts?"

"You're making fun of me."

"No, Jean, I'm not making fun of you at all." He hoped his voice rang with sincerity.

"There were voices that came from a tomb. I wasn't doing drugs or anything—well, I was drinking. I had a couple beers. I wasn't drunk, I wasn't hearing things—I swear it. I mean, that's why I never said anything. I can't afford for people to make fun of me. You can't…well you can't be quarterback, captain of the team, and have people think you're crazy. Half the old ladies in town think they're psychics or whatever, but for a guy…a guy in sports…"

"Gotcha. But I believe you, and I swear it will be between us and my partner. No one will make fun of you, and no one will tell anyone else."

Barre took a deep breath. His team jacket rose and fell on his shoulders.

"We were here, just a few nights ago, hanging out, drinking beer. Freddy and Ben were with me, and a few of the girls. Anyway, they ran off to read the etching on one of the single-tomb things. Belonged to a soldier, I think, and all the stuff about his bravery is chiseled into it. So I was just leaning back, thinking over some plays…and I heard the voices."

"Voices? More than one?"

He nodded very seriously. He inhaled deeply. "They were coming from the Dumas tomb. There was a woman's voice. And she was whispering, I think. It sounded so eerie. She was saying that it was lonely, so lonely, in the darkness."

"Lonely in the darkness," Andre said. He thought of the note that had been left on the tomb. *Tombs are lonely if no one enters after a decade.*

No ghosts had been talking; Jean Barre had heard the living.

"Then…there was an answer. I think it was a male ghost."

"And what did the male ghost say?" Andre asked.

"'Worry not, love, for love will come—and soon.' And then…"

"And then?"

"It was the oddest thing—I think that the ghosts were laughing. I was freaked—just a few beers, but man, you know…and I streaked out of there. Then, I thought I was an idiot—it wasn't ghosts. Ben came around and asked me what was wrong, and I said nothing, but I walked around the Dumas tomb and I checked the gate…it was locked. You know, there aren't, like, real spaces in some of the family tombs. The coffins just go in, and when someone else has to join the family, well, the ash is shoveled back into the holding area at the end. But the Dumas tomb is like a real mausoleum—not big, like some of the new ones, but I guess they thought there would be a lot of family in there. There's an entry and an altar and a pew…like the Broussard tomb and a few others. So, I had convinced myself that someone had been in there…but the gate was locked."

"Is there any way someone could have gotten past you?" Andre asked.

"No. I don't think so. Well, maybe… But I don't see how."

Andre glanced down the embankment that stretched in front of the estate.

His rental car was there; Cheyenne was still in the cemetery. He'd sworn that he'd see Jean Barre back to school and it seemed that Barre just wasn't going back in the cemetery.

"Thank you," Andre told him. "Thank you for coming to me. It could prove to be really important."

"I think it was Janine Dumas," Barre said, his voice barely a whisper. "We've all known all about her…and her killer. Maybe…maybe her killer has come back. He was executed, but I heard that voice… maybe he's come back. Anyway, I'm not going back into that cemetery."

Andre stood in indecision.

Cheyenne was capable; he knew that she was quick and alert.

But this was twice now: the note—which could have meant nothing at all, though he doubted it, and someone in the Dumas tomb, whispering and suggesting that Janine was lonely, waiting for a family member.

The only one still here was—Cheyenne.

He kept looking at Jean Barre as he pulled out his phone and dialed Cheyenne's number. He hadn't realized just how concerned he had been until she answered, and relief flooded through him.

"You're in the cemetery?"

"On my way out. With Miss Eva Wilson."

"I'm here in front with a Mr. Jean Barre. We'll speak in person and determine our next move."

She didn't protest; she didn't seem to think anything of his words.

He told himself it wouldn't have mattered if his partner was male or female—or if his partner had become someone who was rather suddenly the center of his life.

His partner was being threatened. That called for serious thought regarding further movement in the investigation.

Jean Barre was staring at him. "Is it possible?" he asked. "Is it possible for...for someone so evil to live beyond death?"

Andre was silent a minute.

I speak with the dead; I don't know the full scope of the universe.

But in his experience, the dead came back and remained for justice—or to help.

He told Jean the truth. "In every case I've known," he said, "the greatest evil we'll ever find is in men. I believe that Lassiter was sick, yes— and evil. And that someone has taken him up as an idol of sorts— someone who knew him, perhaps even helped him when he was alive. I don't know what you heard, but I believe that you might have been a little tipsier than you thought—"

"I didn't imagine it—really."

"No, I don't think that you imagined it. But I do

believe it's possible that what you heard…someone meant for you to hear, and they meant for you to be afraid. When I say a little tipsy—I think they slipped out when you were walking around. And—"

"I'm a coward for not going into the cemetery."

"No. You're an incredibly brave young man—you came to me, and you told me the truth, even when you thought that you might be ridiculed."

Jean Barre seemed to straighten, nodding at him, growing back to his normal size in his own mind.

"Thanks, man," Barre said, and then whispered, "Oh, my God!"

Andre saw that Cheyenne was walking out from the cemetery gates, a very pretty young woman in tow.

"Eva!" he garbled out.

"Jean!" the girl said.

For a moment, they were both silent—stricken.

Then Eva rushed over to Jean; Jean opened his arms wide, and Eva was in them.

"You, too? I knew there was something here. I was so afraid to say anything…anything at all. But I—" Eva began.

"You heard whispering, too?" Jean asked.

"Whispering? No," Eva said. "I saw them…the rougarou…and the mummy!"

Andre looked at Cheyenne.

"Eva saw people here one night—saw a rougarou carrying a woman up toward the outbuildings. The rougarou was followed by a mummy."

"I know I sound crazy!" Eva said.

"No, you don't. I believe that our people might play 'living statues,' here, or somewhere, like they do around Jackson Square," Cheyenne said.

"That's very possible," Andre said. "And, Eva, plausible, as well. You two have helped us tremendously."

Eva looked at Jean. There was already a romance going there, or one was being created.

Andre looked at Cheyenne and went on, "They've given us tremendous leads. Mr. Barre here was in the cemetery—by the Dumas tomb—when he heard two people whispering. He heard a woman whispering that she was lonely, and a male voice assured her that she wouldn't be lonely long."

Cheyenne didn't display fear. Her lips pursed slightly and she forced a grim smile. "My family tomb. I think I should check it out myself."

"We'll check it out," he said. "Right now, let's get these two safely back where they belong."

"Of course," she said, and added, "I'm assuming you think I should drive them back and you should do more investigation here."

"No, I was thinking we should both take them back, return Angela's car and investigate together."

Jean and Eva were still linked and looked at them with wide eyes.

"You're really not going to say anything about this to anyone, right?" Jean Barre asked.

"No," Andre said.

But he had to wonder just how many others might

have seen or heard this new rougarou and possibly a mummy in the graveyard.

"You were very helpful, and no, we won't say anything to your peers. But if you happen to hear one of them talking…we'd love to know," Cheyenne said. "People often don't say something because they're worried that others might think they're crazy."

"Or high," Eva murmured.

"Or…drinking," Jean said.

"You were both brave coming forward, and we sincerely appreciate it," Andre said.

"They can drive with me," Cheyenne said. "You can follow?"

He nodded and they headed for their cars.

Jean and Eva were returned to the principal at the high school, and they headed on to the hospital where they returned Angela's car.

Lacey had been discharged, and Angela was making final arrangements with the police officers who were to escort them to New Orleans. She stepped out into the hallway with them.

"Lacey will be in a safe house guarded by our best NOLA agents, and I'll stay with her, or Jackson will, until she's comfortable," Angela informed them. She studied their faces. "Anything else?"

"This killer isn't working alone," Andre said. "I believe that we're looking for two people, which makes it harder. One has an alibi for one event, while the other can have a cover for something else."

"I'd like to go back to the church," Cheyenne said.

"Have we made any headway on the video of the priest who visited Lassiter?"

"Experts have studied the footage over and over—the person must have known that he was going to kill, and that we would come around to studying the footage from that last prison visit," Angela said.

"We're going to go back and see Jacques Derringer again," Andre said. "And we'll probably head back to the city for tonight—hit all the spots you and Jackson visited."

"The killer likes to dress up," Cheyenne said. "I was thinking we should take a nice leisurely stroll around Jackson Square."

"I'm thinking Cheyenne should fly out to Wyoming—or maybe Fiji," Andre said.

"I'm thinking that I make great bait," Cheyenne said, turning to him. "You're not getting me out of here."

"Anyone can become a victim—I've seen enough agents go down," Andre said. "No agent, man or woman, is invincible by himself or herself."

Cheyenne smiled pleasantly. "I'm not by myself. I have you for a partner."

"We might just need an army," Andre said.

"We have an army. We have agents and police all over the city. Andre, forget it, I'm not asking to be excused from this assignment. If I'm key to it, then I need to be used—I need to be visible. The killer needs to know he can threaten all he likes. I won't be leaving this case."

Andre lowered his head, wishing he could make

her see the sense of his suggestion—and hoping that she'd understand that he'd make it no matter who the threat had been against.

But he didn't have the power to make her leave.

Jackson did; he could talk to Jackson. "Well, we'll have one another's backs for the rest of today," he said. He drew a breath. "I guess there were no usable prints on the cocktail napkin."

Angela shook her head. "Here's what we ought to be asking—who the hell wears gloves walking around NOLA all the time?"

"Well, we know that the killer can easily travel here from NOLA. He or she most probably has a job that allows for a lot of leeway," Andre said.

"And if one is occupied, the other can do whatever is necessary," Cheyenne finished.

Angela's phone buzzed, and she answered it. "Our cars are ready," she said. "I'll be in touch. I'll get Lacey and Mrs. Murton."

They left the hospital. Andre decided to ignore what was going to eventually be an argument between them. "What was your take on Jacques Derringer?"

"He's weird—he has always shown favorites. Now he knows that he's a suspect, and he's hostile."

"Think he'll be better with two of us?"

She shrugged. "You weren't in the choir, right?"

"I was too into my guitar and rock music when I lived out here," Andre told her.

"Then maybe, yes—he didn't know you. He did know me."

"I'll drive," Andre said.

"Ah, but I have the keys."

"So you do. Drive."

She tossed him the keys. "Never mind, I don't even want to drive."

They got into the car. "You know," he said, hesitating, the key in the ignition. "Just because Mrs. Murton is a jerk, you don't have to prove anything. Don't let her get to you."

She laughed. "She did! We keep trying to help them, and that woman…"

"You know your worth and that's all that matters."

"I even know that. Just drive, Special Agent Rousseau!" she told him. She leaned back in the seat, eyes closed, smiling.

They heard the swell of the organ music as they parked in front of the church. That day, Jacques Derringer was playing a beautiful rendition of "Ave Maria," a special treatment especially for the organ, one he had arranged himself, she imagined.

He finished his piece as they entered.

Andre applauded.

Derringer spun around on his chair and looked down at them.

"Ah, Miss Cheyenne, you brought your muscle, I see."

"I brought my partner," Cheyenne said.

Andre added pleasantly, "I don't really think she needs any muscle. We're just back to see if you might have thought of something else that could help us."

"And you want me to come on down there," Derringer said, irritated.

"Well, unless you want us up there," Andre said.

"Where is Father Napier, by the way?" Cheyenne asked. "I'd love to meet him."

"In the rectory, I assume. It's teatime for him," Derringer said, rising. "I'm coming down, I'm coming down."

Cheyenne glanced at Andre and said softly, "I'm going to go and meet the new priest, maybe find out if Derringer likes to dress up in his spare time—maybe play the piano as a mummy or something."

He nodded, watching Derringer. "Maybe best if I have a word with him alone."

"See if what he says matches up," she said very quietly.

"Yep." He looked at her. "He and Emil Justine—and our friendly mortuary manager, Guy Mason, and even the embalmer, Herman Peterson—are the ones who are around here full-time. With access. But still, I can't help but think that if there is a duo killing these women, they have to be close to one another. But someone did kill Braxton Trudeau in New Orleans."

He fell silent. Derringer was almost with them.

Andre offered Derringer a hand. "I don't know if you'd remember me. It's been more than fifteen years since I lived out here—"

"I remember you. And now you're Special Agent Rousseau. Yeah, I remember you."

"Well, sir, we are sorry to disturb you, but this

matter, as I assume you must know, is critical," Andre said.

Cheyenne smiled at Derringer, despite the fact that his expression was hostile. "Well, Mr. Derringer, we've already talked. I'm going to leave you with my partner. I'm going to meet Father Napier," she said.

"Why?" Derringer asked, his tone dry, "You're going to rejoin the choir? You coming to church?"

"Actually, I love the music at a church. Have you been to jazz mass in NOLA? Spectacular," she said. She turned and hurried around the side of the pews to a door in the back that she knew led out to the rectory, just past the Sunday school and meeting rooms.

She walked along the hallway that led to rooms she had known well when she'd been young. She had liked church and Sunday school—in their area, it had all been very social as well as religious.

Passing one of the large meeting rooms, she remembered potluck dinners and other events that had taken place there.

And she remembered Janine.

Mr. Derringer had always made her sing at events, no matter what it had been. He'd always found a reason to showcase Janine, as if she had been his creation.

Finally, Cheyenne crossed the little path that led from the church annexes to the small cottage that was the priest's rectory for the church.

The door was ajar, and she frowned, but knocked.

She could hear voices, and after a second realized they were coming from a TV or radio.

She nudged the door open a foot. "Father Napier? Hello—are you there? It's Cheyenne Donegal. I was a member here for years, but we haven't met."

She pushed the door open farther and noted that there were several magazines on the floor by a big recliner in the parlor.

In front of it, the television was on.

The weather station was informing them all that the southern Gulf region was going to be hot and humid.

Not a surprise.

"Father Napier?" she said.

She hated to intrude if he'd accidentally left the door ajar and he was taking a shower or doing something else of a personal nature.

"Father Napier?"

She stepped in.

Probable cause, she told herself.

Was it?

She moved into the house. There was also a glass on its side next to the recliner; it looked as if something had spilled over the hardwood floor and the rug between the chair and the television set.

"Father Napier!"

She drew her Glock and moved carefully from the parlor into the dining room, and through to the kitchen, calling his name. There was still no answer.

And no sign of the priest.

She returned to the hall and headed into the bedroom across from the kitchen. It was evidently a guest room, perhaps for visiting priests. It was neat and tidy, and no one was there.

She kept moving. A second bedroom was next, this one evidently the priest's. The closet door was open and she could see that he kept his vestments hung neatly, with his shoes aligned on the closet floor.

"Father Napier!"

She shouted that time, and still, to no avail. Her sense of something being very wrong increased.

Leaving the bedroom, she came to the bathroom.

Here, too, the door was ajar.

"Father Napier?"

And still, no answer.

She pushed the door open.

And found the priest.

12

Whether they were lead on the Mortician case or not, the situation at the rectory fell under the authority of the parish.

Andre watched as the body of Father Napier was wheeled out of the rectory, standing next to Cheyenne—and Detective Vine.

Cheyenne had dialed 911 first—and then had called Andre. He'd heard the sirens even as he responded to her call, rushing to the rectory.

Detective Vine had apparently been following their movements closely, because he'd arrived just minutes after the ambulance and the EMTs.

There was tremendous commotion. The neighbors had come out at the sound of all the sirens; cell phones were ablaze, and Father Napier's flock turned out in large numbers.

Watching the bustling crowd, Andre said quietly to Cheyenne, "Not a mark on him?"

She shook her head.

"Poison?"

She shook her head again. "I tried to revive him. Andre, there were magazines everywhere, a glass of water overturned…but I found him in the bathroom."

"He was sixty-six, I've been told. We question everything—especially now—but he might have had a heart attack and rushed to the bathroom for medicine, even an aspirin," Andre said.

Andre didn't think that Detective Vine had heard him, but he turned to the two of them. "No matter how one puts it, this is a suspicious death. There will be an autopsy tomorrow. Check him into the morgue tonight, and Dr. Michaud can give us all the details by tomorrow. He *thinks* it might have been a heart attack, but the house is in disarray, and I'm bringing in Jacques Derringer."

"You're arresting him?" Andre asked.

"He was the only one nearby, from what you're telling me. When you arrived, Mr. Derringer was playing the organ, right?" Vine demanded.

"Yes, well, I guess since you're not related to Derringer, you will hold him and determine if you can charge him with a crime or not," Cheyenne said.

Detective Vine stared at her coldly. "You found the man dead—maybe I should hold you."

Andre felt his temper soar; Vine, however, seemed to realize he had gone too far.

"We'll just need to finish the paperwork. If it's proven to be a natural death, Mr. Derringer will be released. Excuse me, I have to go speak with his pastoral council and see what they have to say and what they may need, as far as the church goes."

They were at the church at least an hour; the medical examiner had come for the body, and reported that he didn't know cause of death, but the priest had probably been dead at least an hour. He had suffered a hard blow to the head, but from his position, it appeared the blow might have been caused by the sink—meeting with Father Napier's head when he had crashed into it.

Due to the fact that the cause of death was unknown and suspicious, and Jacques Derringer had been the only person at the church, Detective Vine did intend to hold him for twenty-four hours—long enough to discern cause and method of death.

At the police station, Vine was annoying again, providing Cheyenne a pen and paper and demanding that she write down every moment since she'd entered the rectory.

She did; she didn't fight Vine in any way. Neither did Andre. They were just spinning their wheels; wasting time now. They could do nothing there—Father Napier was dead. Derringer was being held at the station.

Andre knew that Cheyenne was anxious to move—to head back to New Orleans.

Cheyenne was just finishing when Officer Brian Wilmette slipped into the interrogation room where she was writing her statement—Vine had said it would give her privacy. Andre was pretty sure that he put her there to prove that she was in his home, and he held all the cards.

"You okay, Special Agent Donegal?" he asked her.

"Can I get you coffee or anything?" He lowered his voice. "You know, you could have had your boss call our captain—there's just no reason... I mean, well, can I get you coffee?"

Cheyenne smiled at the young man. "I'm fine. Actually, I'm done. You can tell Detective Vine that we'll be back in tomorrow for the autopsy?"

"Driving all the way in and out so many times... I'm sorry," Wilmette said. "I'm sure you could get your rooms back at the hotel."

"It's okay. I like driving," Andre said.

But since Detective Vine was nowhere to be seen at that moment, Cheyenne stood and handed her paper and pen to Officer Wilmette.

"We could have done a lot of things," she told him quietly. "We do our best to get along."

Wilmette looked to the hallway to make sure that they were alone. "I think that...well, he's threatened by you. And," he added quickly, "he wants to believe that he's solved the whole thing, that he'll prove somehow that Emil Justine and Jacques Derringer have done all the killing." He shrugged. "I don't see it, but hey...he's the detective."

"I'm sure that one day, you'll be a detective, too," Cheyenne assured him. She looked at Andre. "Now we're leaving. We'll be back at the morgue for the autopsy."

Wilmette nodded, taking the paper. "He didn't have you type?"

"He didn't offer me a computer," Cheyenne said, smiling. "We'll see you."

"Um," Wilmette said nervously, once again looking down the hallway. "Maybe we should find Detective Vine and tell him that you're leaving. For now."

"Officer Wilmette, we are simply leaving. Now," Andre said.

They walked out to the car quickly. Cheyenne obviously didn't want to drive; she headed straight for the passenger's seat, nearly ripped the door from the car, and then sat with a hardened expression.

Once he'd pulled out onto the road, she exploded. "That man is…he is truly a gigantic dick! Ass, arrogant, self-aggrandizing—"

"And we're away from him."

"You know, I'm thinking about bringing him in to one of our offices!" Cheyenne said. "There's possible cause—he's trying to lay it all on Emil Justine and now Derringer—and as I've said, Derringer is creepy, but creepy doesn't mean guilty. And it's *his* kinsman who is managing the mortuary and the cemetery. Maybe he is guilty."

"He's definitely guilty of being an ass, but other than him being related to Guy Mason, we have absolutely nothing to suggest that he's involved in anything illegal whatsoever. Sadly, it isn't illegal to be an asshole." He was quiet a minute, and then glanced her way. "If he pulls anything again, we will let Jackson pull rank."

She glanced his way. "You told him what happened."

Andre nodded. "He suggested that we just stay here."

She winced. "Would *you* rather that we did that?"

"No," he said, watching the traffic before heading on to the highway. "I feel the way that you do. I don't want to let go. I want to find every stone and flip it over. Don't get me wrong—I don't know a better agent than Jackson Crow. He's making the right moves. I just think that the hotter we stay on this, the better we are. Asking the same people, and maybe different people, the same questions. And different questions."

"I keep thinking about Jackson Square," she said.

"Jackson Square—ah, the living statues. Have you ever seen a mummy on Jackson Square?"

"No, but I'm sure that way more has gone on at Jackson Square than I've seen. It's great, though—I've always loved walking around seeing the art."

"Selling the art," Andre said wryly.

"You sold art?"

"Of course—my folks displayed there before they were somewhat better off and well-known—not quite rich and famous, but doing well."

"Did you ever see a mummy at Jackson Square?"

"There's a first time for everything."

"We are going to need to get some sleep."

"Sleep will be good," he said, and then shrugged, keeping his eyes on the road. "I have to admit, I was looking forward to a little more private time during the night—and hoping that you were still angry with me."

"I'm angry enough about Vine being such a dick!" she assured him.

"Hmm. Should I be glad that Vine isn't around?"

He was glad he was driving—if he hadn't been, she might well have hit him.

"Vine. There isn't enough anger in the world. Not in this lifetime, not in my next lifetime, and not in any lifetime!"

Jackson called as they drove and let them know that he and Angela would be staying at the safe house that night, making sure that Lacey was comfortable and safe.

Andre told him that he and Cheyenne were going to head to Miracle Music and pay their respects to Nelson and Katie, stop by the gym, check on Mike Holiday, check on Jimmy Mercury and see what was going on down at Jackson Square.

"Careful burning the candle at both ends," Jackson warned him.

Andre smiled, glancing at Cheyenne.

"I think that many a tourist would find that a good schedule—other than Frenchman Street, which isn't far—we'll be in the French Quarter. And we'll call it quits early enough."

"What time is the autopsy?" Jackson asked him.

"Scheduled for nine. We'll be there." He hesitated. "I think that the medical examiner is going to find that Father Napier had a heart attack."

"Because?" Cheyenne, at his side, voiced the question.

"Okay, I think it is going to prove to be a heart attack that was cause of death—*manner of death* might have been something else."

"His vestments might have been borrowed, and he might just know by who," Cheyenne said.

"Can we have our people go in, find the father's vestments and wardrobe?"

"We can—and we will," Jackson told him. "I'll get all the paperwork we need."

They ended the call.

Cheyenne's mom had always talked about a "parking fairy," who was sometimes excellent in her life, and sometimes just too busy to come around and help.

Andre, she decided, must have had a personal parking fairy—always at his beck and call.

Once again, he found parking on the street quite easily, but even then, he glanced at her and said, "Too bad my folks didn't buy one of those houses with a nice courtyard and garage. Ah, well, now, that's just me being a whining kid—instead of just grateful they keep a place here that's at my disposal anytime."

"I wouldn't mind a place here at all," Cheyenne told him. "I miss NOLA. I mean, I never lived here, but it was the 'big city' and we came all the time and I loved it."

"There's something about it—just unique," Andre agreed. "Great history, amazing architecture, food—and the people."

It wasn't more than a half a block to the house. At the entrance, he said, "We'll just drop off and get going. But... There's someone you have to meet."

"Oh—here? I thought Jackson and Angela were

both with Lacey. And I met your neighbor. Maybe, if we get this solved—*when* we get this solved," she said, firmly correcting herself, "we should take her out for lunch or coffee or something. She seems a very nice woman, but lonely."

"She's on the board of a dozen charitable organizations," Andre told her.

"That doesn't mean you're not lonely—or that an afternoon with a kid you basically watched grow up wouldn't be nice."

"Good thinking. Thank you. We'll take her out."

"So, who am I meeting?"

He opened the door, lifted his bag over the threshold and reached for hers, and then called, "Louis? My friend, you here?"

A moment later, she saw a man coming down the stairs. Then she realized that he was dead.

He was extremely well dressed in a manner that would have well fit an eighteenth-century man of means, brocade vest and frock coat, stockings and black pumps. He'd been handsome in life, and passed away perhaps in his fifties.

"Thank goodness—the lady sees me! Oh, Andre, my man, this has been absolutely delightful, like a wondrous buffet! Such great conversations I had with your other friends, and now… I am meeting this vision of loveliness!" the ghost said.

"This is Special Agent Cheyenne Donegal, Louis. Cheyenne—"

"Oh, I know who you are, dear!" the ghost said. "It's such a pleasure."

"Cheyenne, this is Louis Marquette—" Andre began.

"Gentleman of New Orleans," Louis finished.

"Pirate," Andre said.

"Oh, buccaneer, my dear, and gentleman—and savior of New Orleans, I'll have you know!" the ghost said.

"He did sail with the Lafitte brothers," Andre said.

"And fought alongside Andrew Jackson!" Louis told her. "This was once my home, my dear. I do hope that you like it."

Cheyenne glanced at Andre, immediately aware that when she'd thought he'd been talking to Angela and Jackson, it had actually been the pirate.

So, they see the dead. They all see the dead. And more than possibly, that is what makes the unit so elite.

She looked at Andre. "I'm so sorry we didn't meet sooner."

"I'm so sorry we didn't meet in life!" he replied. "Ah, well…anything? I've been watching the television—I do love television, and I've learned to be quite adept with a remote control. But I haven't seen anything but rehashes of the same information."

Andre told him about their visit to the organist, Jacques Derringer—and how they'd found the priest dead on the floor.

"Then the organist was involved!" Louis said.

"We don't know that. He has been taken into custody. He was playing his organ when we arrived, but we'll know more tomorrow at the autopsy."

Louis winced at that. "Well, I have been here, and I have trolled the city." He shook his head. "Such entertainment to be had these days! I have watched—and watched—for a rougarou, but I have seen nothing."

"Did you go by Jackson Square?" Andre asked him.

"I did not. I wandered this street, watching and wondering just what I would do were I to see something…evil. I could scream…possibly frighten someone, maybe the wrong someone…but then, of course, unless you or someone with your vision was there, I would have to watch. I might be capable of tripping someone up, or…well, there is little action I can take. So, I watch the house and the television." He frowned suddenly. "One thing—I thought at some point that you'd returned. It was last night…after I came back here, returning from my stroll down Bourbon. I had turned the news on…and I thought someone was at the door. But it was not you—or your friends. They were already sleeping. I came to the door, but…nothing." He turned to Cheyenne. "They have an excellent alarm system here. It triggers the second someone tries to maneuver the bolts in the front door or the back door, and the windows, as well."

Andre turned his attention back to Louis. "But you do think that someone was trying to get in?"

"Revelers do wander down this way. I thought

it was Mr. Crow, perhaps, or his lovely wife, but by then, they were sleeping, and I assumed I must have imagined it. But now, in retrospect, I feel that I should have wakened Mr. Crow, but then again, I might have disturbed what sleep the man takes for naught."

"Thanks, Louis," Andre said. "If you do see or hear anything, wake me, please!"

"Ah, that I will, my lad, that I will. Ah, Miss Donegal—*Special Agent Donegal*—forgive me, mademoiselle, for I am still becoming familiar with new titles! But should you wish to know more about the glorious days when a city was saved, I will be happy to tell you much that you may not know!"

"That would be wonderful," Cheyenne said.

"But for now," Andre said, "we're heading out. Please, Louis—do keep watch for me."

A few minutes later, their bags were back in and Louis was seeing them out.

"So, you hid Louis from me—you saw Janine and Christian, but you hid Louis from me. You're a jerk."

"I wasn't being a jerk. I was trying to let you come to terms. I work with people who see the dead, but I was pretty sure that you didn't have friends who shared your talent, and I didn't want to…well, take you by surprise."

"How very altruistic!" she said.

He smiled and glanced her way. "Are you getting angry?"

"Furious! But alas, we're not alone in your house."

"You might have noted—Louis might have been

a pirate once, *buccaneer*, as he insists—but he did become a gentleman of New Orleans after the battle. He is very proper."

"Ah, well," Cheyenne murmured, determined not to be committal.

On the other hand, she didn't know how long this could last, being with him day and night, respecting more and more about him, and his ability to be a perfect partner, having faith in her strength...and knowing when a casual word from him might shut someone down who wasn't ready to offer the same respect.

He wasn't perfect; no one was.

He was incredibly close...

She wanted to sleep next to him, feel the warmth of his body, the touch of his fingers, breathe him in, the scent of his soap, his body...the sound of his voice, the look in his eyes.

They were agents, on the hunt for a truly heinous killer—or killers.

"What's our order of business? Gym first?" she asked.

"Gym, Miracle Music, Bourbon Street, and then Frenchman... No. I'm going to call Jimmy Mercury or text him, see if he's playing—if he is, we know where he is. And that will leave us free to head to Jackson Square."

"Sounds good."

They headed out, walking toward a block down Bourbon and then turning up toward Rampart Street.

At the gym, they found the pretty girl who had

been introduced to them as "Missy" at the front desk once again. She greeted them with pleasure, and then told them sadly that Rocky was out.

"That man works at least sixty hours a week—he loves this place!" Missy told them. "But even he needs a break now and then. He talked about needing a night to go a little wild. I think he was going to see music—I know that there's a really cool musician who is an old friend who plays down on Frenchman Street. Rocky could be there."

"Rocky really works a lot, huh?" Andre asked her, leaning on the counter and smiling.

The girl, Cheyenne noted, looked as if she was about to melt.

"Oh, yes, sir, he does. But then, of course, he deserves some time off—just like the rest of the world. I'm his assistant manager. When Rocky can't be here, I'm in charge."

She leaned on the counter, too. "I told him not to worry about a thing today. I could handle the place. He knows I'm great with our clients. And I am! Rocky, of course, is an amazing trainer." She looked at Andre and smiled coquettishly. "I can see he worked well with you," she said. "You know, I'm just sure that Rocky would be delighted to have you in here…nothing like muscle to show others that muscle can be forged!"

"Thanks," Andre told her. "So, Rocky was here last night, right?"

"Yes, he was." Missy frowned suddenly. "He left a little early—said he was tired. And when he called in this morning, I told him that he had nothing in the world to worry about."

"Rocky hasn't been in all day?" Cheyenne asked.

The girl was still staring at Andre, but she shook her head and answered.

"Well-deserved day off!" Missy said.

"Thank you," Andre said.

"You all come on back here, okay?"

"Oh, we will," Andre assured her.

They left the gym and Cheyenne said, "So he left last night. That would have given him plenty of time to get out to the New Iberia/Broussard area."

"And kill the priest," Andre muttered. He shook his head. "But that puts us back to Jacques Derringer. Rocky Beaufort might well have had a friendship going with Jacques Derringer, but...who the hell kills a priest?" he asked.

"Someone with no fear of hell. Except...we still don't know if anyone killed the priest. That will have to wait until tomorrow.

"Detective Fournier first thought that Braxton Trudeau had killed himself—I say that we need to just hope that the medical examiner can give us a definitive answer about Father Napier." She suddenly gasped. "Detective Fournier. I've left him out of the loop!"

"Don't worry about Detective Fournier. Jackson kept him and the NOLA police up to speed on anything that we've learned."

"He's not a bad guy—he's just...tired, I guess," Cheyenne said.

Their next stop was Miracle Music.

That night, they were greeted by Nelson Ridgeway.

He seemed to beam when he saw them, hugging Cheyenne and almost hugging Andre, but instead stepping back and shaking his hand profusely.

He was still Nelson, but he had matured; his face remained lean, but even his cheeks had filled out some, and his dark eyes didn't seem quite so large against the rest of his face.

"I heard you guys were here in town, hunting down that killer." He shook his head, looking at Cheyenne. "Man, this must be a bitch for you this guy is imitating Lassiter. To a T, huh? Are you getting anywhere?"

"We like to think so," Andre said. "We're asking everyone for help."

"Yeah, Katie told me, and I've been thinking and thinking...and coming up with nothing," Nelson said. "I mean, Lassiter was closest to Mike Holiday back then—you know, Mike was cool. Everyone loved Mike." He looked at Cheyenne, his expression sorrowful. "You know, back then, Lassiter would have gotten away with it, or maybe for a much longer time, if it hadn't been for you, Cheyenne. How the hell you suddenly knew...well, it gave the cops and everyone else a change of mind, held him until they got proof...but well, you loved Janine, she was your cousin. I can kind of see how the funeral might have gotten you thinking—or else, it was a tremendous insight. Maybe you'll have one again."

Cheyenne smiled. "Well, that would certainly help," she said.

"I heard they took in old man Justine," Nelson said. "I think that they're onto something. I mean, he owns the damned place, and he always seemed like something of a vulture to me. Anyway, we've been out of it for a while, Katie and me. Don't get back much. One of us is usually always here—except for in the dead of night. Which doesn't even really exist in NOLA," he added with a laugh. "Naw, I guess the dead of night is like five in the morning around here. Look, if you have time when you're not working— though you may always be working—we'd love to see you in a setting where we can just talk, lunch or something."

"That would be great," Andre said.

"Katie's out somewhere with her girlfriends to- night," he said. "Don't go leaving without giving us a chance to get together, huh?"

They assured him that they wouldn't.

Back out on the street, they moved down Conti, headed out to Bourbon.

Andre paused to look at his phone. He gazed at Cheyenne.

"Jimmy's working tonight. You'll never guess where."

"Yes, I will," she said, studying his face. "He's playing at The Last Cavalier, right?"

He nodded. "We'll have to get out there," he said. "Let's check on Mike."

They kept walking and she asked, "Do you think

it's unusual that so far we haven't seen Nelson and Katie together?"

"It could be unusual. Or it could just be that they cover for one another."

"I wonder where Katie is—out with her friends," Cheyenne said.

They had reached Bourbon Street, which was filled with couples, groups and even singles—just walking by with amazement at the neon and the hawkers in the street, all advertising the cheapest beer, the best band or the most beautiful people.

They didn't have to reach Mike Holiday's establishment to see him; he was on his stool just outside the door to the strip club, keeping a keen eye on those who would enter.

He saw them and lifted a hand to wave. "Still at it, huh?" he asked them.

"We are," Andre told him.

"Hey, I heard a priest out by home died today. I'm really sorry to hear it. My parents said that Father Napier was a truly kind man. Could that have had anything to do with what's going on?" Mike asked.

"Well, we'd like to think he died a natural death," Cheyenne said, stepping back so that Mike could take IDs from two young men. He waved them in.

He frowned at Cheyenne, shaking his head. "Hard to believe anyone from our little neck of the woods, turning into a monster. But then, obviously, Lassiter was a monster, so…"

"That's why we're trying so hard to find someone who might have been close to him," Cheyenne said.

"He liked me—well, I was the cool kid back then." His frown deepened. "You know, he tried to get me to spend more time with him. Said he had some football techniques I could use. But I was busy at the time. Girls—and being cool."

"So…he tried to kind of…recruit you into being a friend?" Andre asked.

"Sure. Remember? He was the cool substitute—we all thought it was great when he came in to teach our classes. He brought music in, talked about the hot bands. He was half teacher, and half that guy that everyone thought would make a great friend."

"That's true," Cheyenne said.

"Hey, Mike, what's your night off?" Andre asked him.

"Sunday—supposedly. They've been short-handed, and I can use the extra dough. I finally went back to school—online, but hey. I'm going to get a degree. In accounting. Imagine that!" he said.

"Good for you," Andre said. "Well, maybe, if you do get a night off, we can get together."

"There's always lunch," Mike said and grinned. "I'm pretty sure I haven't seen breakfast in years—when you work nights, late lunch is your first meal."

"Great. We'll see you, then," Cheyenne told him.

"You two a couple now?" Mike asked them.

"A couple of agents," she said quickly—maybe too quickly.

She started walking. Andre fell into step behind her.

"Jackson Square?" he said after a few long moments.

They turned off Bourbon, heading down to Royal Street and then cutting down another block to Chartres. It was growing later, but the square remained busy. The museums in the historic Pontalba Buildings were closed, naturally, and St. Louis Cathedral had locked its door, as well. But the square—with the magnificent equine statue of Andrew Jackson in the center of the grassy park area—remained busy. Diners were coming in and out of Muriel's and other restaurants. By night, though many of the artists who displayed their wares around the square had called it quits for the evening, tarot readers, mediums, musicians, jugglers and human statues were out in decent numbers.

"We'll do a full circle—I think I still know some of the carriage drivers," Jackson said. "Some of the best guides in the city. They wait down on Decatur Street, probably bored, chatting with one another and hawking themselves and their mules."

"Sure, sounds good."

Cheyenne approached one of the mediums at a table in the area in front of the cathedral—a Germanic-looking blonde with a dark bandanna, touting herself as Madame Morwenna. Cheyenne smiled, reaching in her bag for her credentials.

"Welcome, my friend—do you prefer tarot cards, or a palm reading? Hello, good sir!" she said to Andre as he joined her.

"Neither, I'm afraid. We're looking for help."

"Oh!" the woman said and shivered slightly, looking away. "Yes, that killer…" Her voice trailed, and she looked from one of them to the other. "They did catch him—they didn't catch him. What the hell are you people doing? Everyone is still so scared."

"We came to see if you'd seen him in your crystal ball, perhaps," Andre said.

She glared at him, eyes narrowing. "I need the sense and feel of a person, and so help me, I pray I never get the sense or feel of that man! If you're not customers, please move on. This is how I make my income."

Andre reached into his wallet and laid two bills on her table. She looked at him with surprise.

"We need help—information," he told her.

She glanced at Cheyenne, as if a little amazed. Still looking at Cheyenne, she nodded. "I, yeah, sorry... I just... I hate being afraid. This is how I make my living. Some of us out here—artists, musicians, mediums—we all watch out for each other, try never to leave alone, and still, it's nerve-racking!"

"We understand that," Cheyenne said. "And we're trying—the police are trying. Trust me, there's nothing we want more than the truth about this killer, getting him locked up and behind bars."

"Skinned alive and boiled in oil would work for me," Madame Morwenna said. "What can I tell you?"

"You see a lot of the human statues, right?"

"For sure—there's a guy who stands on a little pedestal he brings himself just over there, left side of the square facing the river. He's all in gold and I think he's supposed to be one of the Grecian gods.

And we have a kid who does an amazing creepy clown. Oh, and there's a fantastic fashion doll, and it's hard to think of New Orleans without conjuring a vampire novel in your mind—vampires roam around in fantastic costumes. There's a guy who does a version of King Kong, and—"

"What about a rougarou?" Cheyenne asked.

"A what?" Madame Morwenna asked.

"You're not from here, I take it?" Andre said.

"Minnesota," Madame Morwenna said. "But please, don't pass that around. Locals seem to do a lot better. People seem to think that anyone from New Orleans has to have some special contact with the other side."

"Your secret is safe," Cheyenne assured her. "A rougarou is like…um, a werewolf, would be the closest."

Madame Morwenna was silent for a minute. "I don't think so… I've just seen King Kong."

"What about a mummy?" Andre asked her.

She brightened. "Oh, yes, I've seen the mummy. Whoever does the mummy is great—white bandages and an incredible headdress. Perfectly still, arms crossed at the chest, and then sudden movement and robotic gestures—kids shriek, and everyone is amazed."

Cheyenne glanced at Andre quickly.

"Have you seen the mummy tonight?" Andre asked.

Madame Morwenna shook her head. "Not tonight…but last night! Maybe the mummy will show later."

"By any wild and bizarre chance, do you know the actor who does the mummy?" Cheyenne asked her.

"No, I'm sorry. I can ask around. My friends—many of whom have already gone in for the night—and I were impressed, and we asked each other and none of us knew him, or her, not sure. The bandaging job is fantastic. Great makeup over the white bandages on the face, too, giant dark eyes…really cool."

They thanked her. She nodded, fingering the bills Andre gave her.

"Thank you—I've never been paid just to talk before."

They smiled, waved and left her.

"A mummy," Cheyenne grumbled. "A rougarou and a mummy. There has to have been a rougarou—on the night that Lacey Murton was taken. How easy to slip into a dark alley after playing a statue on the square. Who would notice?"

"Frankly, much as I love the city, I wonder who would notice much of anything here," Andre said. "But you're right. I think we'll find out that there has been a rougarou working the square. This killer, like the Civil War killer, needs a costume."

Cheyenne was thoughtful. "I think that leaves out Mike Holiday," she said. "And surely, Jimmy Mercury. He's working most nights way too late to sideline as a human statue."

"No matter what Vine wants the truth to be, I'm also leaving out Emil Justine. I don't think that he has the strength or health left to drive into town and play a character on Jackson Square. That would make our possible suspects remain as Derringer, Katie and Nelson Ridgeway—and Rocky Beaufort. Unless we're totally off base, and I don't think that we are."

"Let's talk to the carriage drivers," Cheyenne said.

They turned to their left kitty-corner from Muriel's and started down the street, toward Café Du Monde. They turned right again on Decatur.

It was a busy night; only three carriages remained lined up in front of the square. One of the drivers was in his rig, head back—resting. One was standing by the fence, talking to an artist who still had his wares displayed.

"I know that guy," Andre said. Absently taking Cheyenne's hand, he strode quickly along the sidewalk, bringing her along.

"Nathaniel!" Andre called out.

The man by the fence, tall, graying, but maybe in his forties, turned at the sound of his name. He smiled, seeing Andre.

"Hey, there! Great seeing you—oh, maybe not. You here on fun?" He grinned at Cheyenne. "No, you're working, aren't you?" he asked Andre, his face growing serious.

"We are. Nathaniel Rocket, this is Special Agent Cheyenne Donegal."

"Saw you on TV," Nathaniel said.

"Cheyenne, my old friend, Nathaniel. He used to

help out sometimes, when I'd be with my folks and they had art out here," Andre said.

"Very nice to meet you," Cheyenne said. "I love your mule. May I?" The carriage waiting on the curb—obviously Nathaniel's—was drawn by a beautiful white mule.

"You'll make Jezebel very happy," he assured her. "Best mule ever—she's like a puppy dog. I keep her at my place—have property up in the Treme area." He looked at Andre proudly. "I bought the carriage company from an old fellow who just wore out and wanted to spend his days sipping café au lait. It's mine now. Oh, here's a carrot. Jezebel will love you forever."

Cheyenne took the carrot and thanked him and stepped over to the mule. Jezebel was a beautiful creature and very affectionate, nuzzling Cheyenne as she fed her the carrot.

She was stroking the mule's nose when Andrew asked Nathaniel about a rougarou and a mummy.

"Yeah, strange as all get-out, huh? But then, what's strange here, huh? Guy does a fantastic rougarou—stands up on a little box he carries and unfolds right there on the corner, and freezes at first, then shocks tourists, and then does some robotic things. Don't see him all the time—just now and then."

"Do you know when you saw him last?" Andre asked.

"It's been a bit," Nathaniel said. "Fantastic costume, though. How the man in it endures it, though, in our heat, I have no idea. Of course, I've only ever seen him come out at night."

"What about a mummy?" Cheyenne asked, leaving Jezebel.

"Oh, yeah. Actually, I've seen the mummy more often. I saw the mummy last night, as a matter of fact. Right there, right on the corner, across from Café Du Monde."

They thanked him.

"Hey, you two are locals, or kind of local," he told Cheyenne. "I give the best tour in the French Quarter, and I'd love to give you one on the house—or on the carriage, as that may be."

"And I would love to take you up on that!" Cheyenne said.

"I'm sure you know the history and our legends… but hey, I can do my best. I know a lot about a little-known pirate who became a gentleman after Andy Jackson and the boys took a victory at the Battle of New Orleans—thanks to Andre here. Looked up all kinds of stuff, and it was amazing. With a little digging, I learned that everything he told me about the man was true!"

Cheyenne glanced at Andre, grinning. "I'll just bet. When this is over…hopefully very soon, we'll take you up on that offer," she told Nathaniel.

Andre had started to walk back the way they had come. Frenchman Street and The Last Cavalier were a bit out of the French Quarter, but still—though she wouldn't recommend it to unwary tourists at night—the walk for her and Andre would be easy enough.

They were also armed against trouble, and certainly after the FBI academy, street savvy.

But something drew her attention; there was a crowd gathering on the other corner.

She started walking toward the crowd, searching for the reason they'd collected there.

And then she saw it...

The mummy.

13

"Andre!"

He heard his name shouted and turned swiftly. He'd thought that Cheyenne was at his side—and was surprised to see she was not.

Even as he turned, he saw her running—and he also saw the mummy atop the small box, entertaining the crowd.

The mummy apparently saw Cheyenne just as she'd seen it—and in a split second, the mummy was off the box. And running into the crowd, down Decatur Street. Cheyenne was running, too—as fast as the wind.

He took off in their wake, pulling out his phone as he ran. He called Jackson, who would put out a bulletin alerting every law enforcement officer within the area that a mummy was on the run.

Jackson didn't ask questions; he said he'd set things into motion and be in the area himself within minutes.

There were too many people on the street, coming

and going from shops and restaurants, trying to get out of the way as he shouted, "Move! FBI!"

They only managed to create more of a knot and greater hurdles as he raced after Cheyenne.

He saw her, and then lost her. He couldn't see the mummy at all anymore.

He caught a glimpse of Cheyenne—she was halfway down Decatur, heading for Canal. He kept running, and lost her again, somewhat stalled as he leaped over a woman in an electric scooter, ignoring her comments about his manners. He had no choice at the moment.

There were sirens and a mounted officer came up to him, assuring that they were all on the lookout for a mummy throughout the city.

He thanked the man and ran on, frantically scanning the crowd.

He'd lost Cheyenne.

He stood dead still, swearing. There were dozens of restaurants and bars she might have slipped into; music poured from the old property he stood before—most of the corner bar/restaurants offered access from the side streets as well as from Decatur.

For a moment, he caught his breath, damning himself. He could call Cheyenne, but if she was in hot pursuit, she wouldn't answer her phone. He didn't know what the hell side street she might have taken.

"A mummy? Has anybody seen a mummy?" he shouted, his tone so loud he managed to drown out the music for a moment.

Some people looked at him as if he was insane—even for New Orleans.

But one man stopped and told him, "Hell, yeah, the idiot nearly toppled me over—that way, heading toward Royal."

Andre thanked him, even as he ran, swerving down the side street and heading toward Royal. But once there, he paused again. He was looking in both directions when he heard someone running behind him; he spun around again, hand on his Glock, and then relaxed.

It was Jackson.

"I can't find Cheyenne or the mummy," Andre said.

"The info is out—every cop in the city is searching for the mummy."

"A guy pointed me here," Andre said, "but now—nothing."

"I'll go left, you go right," Jackson said.

Andre nodded and started running again. Halfway down the street, he was startled to see people holding up sheets of off-white, coarse fabric.

He slowed to a halt.

The one man holding on to most of the fabric was very drunk.

"Sir, where did this come from?" he asked.

The man looked at him, bleary-eyed. He made a face at Andre and said, "Ancient Egypt?" and laughed.

The people with him seemed to have been celebrating just as heavily. They all thought that the man's reply was hysterical.

"Hey, mister!" A waitress slipped out from the bar, a pretty girl in a skimpy black outfit. "Someone went flying by here, and this stuff was blowing just about everywhere," she told Andre.

"Which way?"

She pointed toward Canal.

"Thanks—can you hold whatever of this you can? Cops will come by for it."

The waitress looked confused, but at least she was stone-cold sober. "Yes, yes, of course."

"Ancient Egypt!" the drunk chortled again.

And this fellow thought it just as funny a second time. The waitress rolled her eyes.

Andre began to run again.

It was one thing chasing a mummy when it was still a mummy—even in New Orleans, people noticed a mummy running through the streets.

But the city was crowded, and people were everywhere. Cheyenne had noted there was a major pharmaceutical conference going on at the convention center, and that had drawn in thousands of people who now appeared to all be out exploring, on top of the general influx of tourists. And the mummy was fast, twisting and turning.

She paused; mummy wrappings seemed to be falling out around the streets. People were picking them up. She nearly went over a young woman who had been attracted to the discarded material and paused to pick it up.

It appeared that the trail led back toward Bourbon; Cheyenne ran up the street, on Bourbon to Canal.

She was almost there when she saw the headdress in the garbage can.

The "mummy" had tried to press it down; a bit of gold foil remained visible.

Gasping for breath, Cheyenne paused long enough to retrieve the headdress, holding it with the edge of her jacket and looking around.

She caught the arm of a man who was standing near the garbage can, chatting with a friend.

"Sir, did you see who cast aside this headdress?" she asked.

"Um, someone just did. Yeah, he ran that way," he said.

"No, man, he ran that way."

"Dude, you're wrong—all way around. It was a woman, and she ran that way."

"Thanks!" Cheyenne murmured, looking around for anyone hurrying away in any direction, and for someone who might have actually seen something.

There was a luggage shop on the corner: suitcases, roller bags and computer sleeves were displayed in the large windows. Perhaps a clerk had looked out.

Cheyenne hurried up to a young woman behind a counter. She flipped her badge out quickly and said, "I'm looking for the person who was wearing this headdress. It was thrown in a garbage just out there. Did you happen to see anything?"

"I did!" the young woman told her. "It was very odd—I don't know if it was a man or a woman. They were wearing a skintight black bodysuit kind of thing. You see all kinds of wild things on Canal, but I was about to call the police. I'm pretty sure that he—or she—snatched a shirt or a hoodie from a woman who wasn't paying attention and had it slung over her shoulder."

"Did you see which way the person went   the person who threw away the headdress?"

"Toward Harrah's...and maybe they crossed the street, toward the CBD."

Cheyenne handed her the headdress and said, "Hold this, please. A police officer will be by for it, or another government agent. Please, slip it behind the counter and hold on to it."

"Oh! Okay!"

Cheyenne ran back out—and almost straight into Andre.

"I lost him—or her. I lost the damned mummy!" she told him, angry with herself. "How the hell do you lose a mummy—especially one unraveling all the way down Bourbon Street?" Then she remembered they were still on the quest. "Toward Harrah's—or, possibly across the street, heading into the CBD. Now in tight black clothing, and possibly a hoodie."

Andre instantly pulled out his phone and repeated her words.

"How the hell!" she muttered angrily again.

"The mummy was desperate," Andre said, "and obviously knows the city."

"I'm desperate and I know the city, too. Harrah's? Or Central Business District?"

"Cheyenne, wait—just wait. Police and agents are combing the area, and if this person does know the city and they've managed to blend in with the flow of humanity, you running yourself ragged isn't going to change anything. Breathe. If you want, we'll go down the street, but you have to realize, we can't be everywhere. And we do have help out there—cops and agents have been called in."

She stared at him, unable to curb her anger—with herself.

"I have to keep looking."

"Let's head toward Harrah's. There will be cops all over the CBD by now."

He walked at her side. "We've collected wrapping. The headdress?"

"The clerk at that store is holding it."

"We'll get it to the lab, Cheyenne. This may still be one of our biggest breaks. They may find something."

She stopped walking and turned to stare at him.

"And what? Eventually, they'll get skin cells or a hair…and we'll need to have something to compare it to, and…" Her voice trailed.

He smiled, pausing, and took her by the shoulders. "We can easily manage that. We know our suspects. We can meet them all, collect coffee cups… we can do it without needing any warrants. Cheyenne, if this mummy really was involved—and why would they run from you unless they've got something to hide?—we're moving forward, and moving forward well."

"How do we explain that a teenager told us about a werewolf and a mummy?" she asked, frustrated.

"There is something we can fall back on whenever needed," he said with a wry grin.

"Oh?"

"Ye olde anonymous tip," he said.

She sighed.

They started down the street again. He continued, "They've also procured something like a hundred different fragrances. Angela is working with Lacey—she's going to see if she can identify one of them."

Cheyenne nodded, still feeling deflated.

She'd had the mummy in her grasp—and the mummy had eluded her.

By now, Andre didn't need to tell her, the person could have stolen clothing out of a shop, changed to a T-shirt—even doffed what had already been pilfered.

They crossed the street by the mall to get over to Harrah's casino and mounted the steps to the Canal Street entry. The place was overflowing, or so it seemed. People were even waiting in line for select machines. Poker and craps tables were full. People laughing, playing, meeting new friends at the gaming tables...

Some dressed up, and some dressed down. But none in a skintight black bodysuit.

They parted ways and walked around the central Masquerade showroom and bar and met up on the other side.

"Anyone remotely familiar?" Andre asked her.

She shook her head.

"No one remotely dressed as the shop clerk suggested," Cheyenne said.

"We'll find the mummy," he assured her.

As they headed back out, they met up with Jackson, just coming in. "We have an agent picking up the headdress and bits of mummy wrap—they'll go straight to the lab. And of course, everyone on the city is on alert, but…"

Cheyenne understood too well.

The mummy had now blended in.

"You have an autopsy in the morning, after a two-plus hours' drive. I suggest you give it up for the night. We have to trust in our fellow law enforcement officers, you know. We're aren't waging this battle alone," Jackson said.

Cheyenne just looked at him. Jackson nodded. They still just stood there.

"Go home," Jackson said.

Andre took her arm. "Cheyenne."

"Yes, of course," she said.

But she couldn't help herself. She turned back. "I lost a *mummy*."

Jackson smiled. "We'll find the mummy," he insisted. "Trust me. In fact, I believe you and Andre will find the mummy. But first get some sleep."

They left at last.

It seemed a longer walk back—probably because she was so disheartened.

"Tomorrow, we'll set up a dinner with all our old 'friends.' We'll have it at my house—and we'll use paper plates and paper cups. We'll get fingerprints and DNA and rush it all to the lab…and between the headdress and wrappings, we'll find the mummy."

"And when we find the mummy," she said, "the mummy will give us the rougarou."

"Yes. Are you angry?"

"Furious. With myself."

"Hey, I was there, too, just feet away. I didn't just lose the mummy—I lost you, too. Does that make you feel any better?"

She glanced over at him. "No, it just tells me that…you lost a mummy, too."

He laughed. "So—you're angry."

She finally realized he was teasing her. She gazed at him and managed a smile.

"Well, definitely too distraught to sleep for a while."

"I like it."

They reached his house, but before they could enter, Andre's next-door neighbor came out. "Andre, dear, it's you, right?" she called, coming out to the little porch in front of her door.

"Hi, Rita, yes, it's me. Is something wrong?" Andre asked her. "Do you need anything?"

"No, dear, I'm fine, but…but I wanted to tell you. The strangest thing happened last night."

"What was that, Rita?" Andre asked her.

"There was someone here last night—I mean, at your place. Ajax carried on and I looked out the window."

"I had friends staying here last night, Rita," Andre told her. "Actually, my field director and his wife, another agent."

Rita waved a hand in the air, pausing to smile at Cheyenne, and then going on. "Oh, no, no, I don't mean that handsome young couple. I saw them go in before this... I was in bed myself, but Ajax was upset. I didn't go out, but I did nudge the curtain open just a bit. And that's when I saw...now, don't laugh at me, dear, but I saw a mummy. A mummy was at your door... I thought that...well, I don't know what I thought. I was actually about to call the police, but then the thing went away. I did want to tell you, though. Even though I know that your alarm system is as good as Ajax, though, trust me—he warns me before people try a door."

Andre looked over at Cheyenne. "Well, it seems that if we can't find the mummy, it will come back to us."

"You know whoever it was, dear?" Rita asked.

"No," Andre admitted. "No, I don't."

"But," Cheyenne said, "Rita, look out a curtain, but don't ever come out if you see anything strange, anything at all."

"Oh, honey, I see the strange all the time," Rita replied. "And don't you worry—I never come out if I see strange, especially stranger than the strange we always get around here."

"Rita, we'll be gone for a while," Andre told her, "starting early in the morning. If you see anything unusual, definitely don't get involved, I will truly appreciate you telling me."

"Absolutely, Andre. Does this have anything to do with the monster you're hunting? I guess a mummy is a monster, but…"

"We are hunting a monster. A human monster. And you be careful," Andre said.

They bid her good-night; Andre opened the door to his house and once they were in, locked it and set his alarm.

"So, last night…the mummy came here. Andre, I guess it's not so hard for someone to know that we're working the case, but…this someone knew where you lived, and was…testing the lock? I don't know."

"That's just it. Whoever it is knows us," Andre said. "But for now…"

He paused and looked into the parlor. The ghost of Louis Marquette was there; he was seated on the love seat and he had the television on low.

He glanced over at Andre and Cheyenne and stood politely.

"Anything to report tonight?" Andre asked him.

"No, nothing," Louis said. "And you must get some sleep. You mustn't fear—I will be watching through the night, and this time, I will not hesitate to waken anyone, I will bang on your door immediately."

They thanked him and started up the stairs to the second floor.

"I need a shower and sleep," Cheyenne said. She was tired; she was uneasy.

She could use his company. But she was also a little uncomfortable. They really weren't alone. Well, they were alone on the second floor. But they hadn't really set any parameters for how this was going to work between them.

She was relieved that Andre didn't tease her or make demands—or suggestions.

"Good night, then," he said, heading down the hall to his own room.

It was best this way, Cheyenne thought, hurrying in, stripping her gun, jacket, clothing and shoes, and heading into the shower. The hot water felt so good after the length of the day. It seemed to soothe the muscles she had abused, running through the French Quarter, dodging tourists, leaping over a few here and there.

Stepping out of the shower, she wrapped herself in the huge bath towel left in the guest room bath. She pulled out her travel bag and opened it, thinking she'd find a large T-shirt.

But then she hesitated.

To hell with it.

What if there were no more nights with Andre?

She suddenly didn't want to wonder. She clutched the T-shirt to her but stepped out into the darkened hallway in her towel and skittered down to Andre's room.

She could hear the sound of the television drifting

up the stairs; still a news program. Louis Marquette must have gone from one report to another.

She had barely touched his door before it opened. He was in a towel, as well.

"What took you so long?" he asked her.

"Hey, I told you…"

"Yes, you did."

"You're very presumptive."

"So I am."

"And… I mean, it's all right, isn't it?"

"Way more than all right," he told her. He pulled her into his arms, and it seemed, if anything, the sensation created by his lips on hers was even more electric and wild, and when he lifted her and held her, when she felt their bodies together, it all just felt combustible.

Anticipation…knowing…and anticipation. Feeling his kisses cover her body, knowing where they would go…how she would hunger to touch him in turn, taste him, know his scent and lie beside him, filled with his strength.

It was much later when they slept, but even as she dozed, Cheyenne smiled.

If she hadn't taken those few steps down the hall…

She'd probably still be lying awake, wondering just how she had managed to lose a mummy.

"You might want a mask," Andre warned Cheyenne as they donned paper suits to join in on the autopsy.

She grimaced. "I've been in autopsy before, you know."

"I know." He considered then that he had never dated an agent before—or even a cop. Someone who understood what he did—who did it, too. With Cheyenne, it had been a rocky start, and they'd had some major hiccups along the way, but she could actually understand just about everything about him.

Dating.

Can this be called dating? he wondered.

Then he gave his mind over to the matter at hand; Detective Vine had arrived, and he had a sour expression on his face.

"What is it about you two?" he asked, grabbing his own paper gown from the supply on a shelf in the prep room. "I can go months and months without a body—and you have come up with two."

"Lacey Murton wasn't a body—she was a living, barely breathing human being," Andre reminded him.

"No trouble in this town, though, until the federal government noses in."

Andre was going to keep his temper—no matter what kind of a jerk Vine was determined to be.

He needn't have worried or considered a reply.

Cheyenne handled it. "You're forgetting, Detective Vine, I'm from this area. And so is Andre. And I know that bad things have gone on for a very long time. Very bad things. You might want to thank Special Agent Rousseau. Because of him, you have one dead body—not two. Oh, yes, and by the way, this is our investigation. And we were talking to a person

deeply involved in all those events when we found
Father Napier. With any luck, Detective Vine, he
had a heart attack. But if we believe that there was
foul play, well, we will be down your throat like
June bugs!"

Vine looked at her, startled. "Well, look at the
Southern belle, will you?"

"I'm not a Southern belle, Detective. I am a well-
trained agent—head of my class, as a matter of fact.
Please, remember that."

Vine looked at Andre, as if seeking help.

Andre smiled and grinned. "I'd remember that,
if I were you."

The door opened; it was a young woman named
Sandy Powell. They'd met her when they'd come
in, and she was the medical examiner's assistant, a
competent and pleasant young woman. "The doctor is progressing with the autopsy, if you're ready."

They filed in. The three of them stood to the side
and back, watching as the ME, Dr. Michaud—a serious man who merely nodded to them all in ac-
knowledgment that they had arrived—continued
with his work.

They might have all been to an autopsy before,
but there could be nothing pleasant in watching a
man who had been by all accounts a very good and
loving man, flesh and blood and breath, being sliced
open, ribs cracked, body torn apart.

No matter what manner of empathy a medical examiner might feel.

The man's internal organs were weighed. Dr. Michaud spoke to his recorder throughout the proceeding. And in the end, he looked at them all. "A heart attack, I believe." He shrugged. "I know that Father Napier was under the care of Dr. Philips, in town. He was a good man who didn't smoke or drink, but he loved our rich foods and grew up on fried…everything. His eating habits apparently did him in."

"Thank the Lord!" Vine said, looking over at Andre and Cheyenne.

"He died of a heart attack—but could he have been frightened into the attack?" Andre asked.

"I don't think any of us will ever know," Michaud said.

"His parlor was in disarray. It appeared that he jumped up and ran into the bathroom," Cheyenne said.

"Exertion…possibly. At this moment, all I can tell you is that the man had a heart condition, and that he died of a heart attack," Michaud said. "He took a good knock on his head, crashing into the sink, judging by where he was found. But that wasn't what killed him."

"Fear?" Andre asked.

Michaud shrugged. "I don't know. Men and women have died of fear—the body is a precious shell for all that lies within humanity, made up of many components, including chemicals and more. The brain is an amazing receptor, but what it receives can cause absolute havoc on other organs. I will, naturally, be checking his stomach contents for any toxins, but he ate some time before his death. I don't know if that will help you in any way or not. You're the investigators."

As they filed out, Andre noted that Detective Vine had grown somber. He turned and looked at them when they reached the sidewalk outside the parish morgue.

"His heart gave out. His parishioners will receive some solace in that. The good Lord called his own back home. For us—all of us—that isn't so good."

"Why is that?" Cheyenne asked him.

He looked at her. "I'm going to have to release the organist. I have nothing on him."

"Well, Detective, our office should have informed you. We have agents going into the rectory and the church, mainly searching through Father Napier's vestments and clothing because someone with the ability to obtain false ID good enough to fool the prison system visited Ryan Lassiter several times before his execution. That person was dressed up as a priest. If we discover that anything matches up, you may well have a reason to see Jacques Derringer brought back in."

"Your people?" Vine asked.

"Your captain knows all about it. He didn't inform you?" Andre asked. "I'm sorry, our field director made the arrangements yesterday."

Vine pursed his lips. "Trouble is on you—and blood is on your hands—if that Derringer does anything else."

He turned and headed for his car.

"What do you think?" Andre said lowly to Cheyenne.

"I think he's on the outs with his captain," Cheyenne said. "Maybe over this."

"He needs to learn to be a team player," Andre said. "Most of the time, we all do just fine—even being Krewe, with what many people consider a different method of working." He let out a long sigh. "Well, we've made a long trip out here and we could have gotten this information over the phone. While we're here I thought that we should stop back by the cemetery, pay another visit to Detective Vine's kinsman, Mr. Guy Mason."

"That's a fine idea. We can also stop by and see how Emil Justine's lawyers are doing."

"And check in with your cousin," Andre said softy.

She nodded, her lips curling just slightly. "And check in with my cousin."

"And maybe I'll make some calls."

"Oh?"

"Yes, every one of our old 'friends' has said they'd love to get together. I want it to be tonight. We'll have to see if Mike Holiday can take a night off, and we'll be early enough for it to be late lunch/early supper. I'll ask the caterer to make sure we have paper cups and plates. We'll get Jackson and Angela there, too, and that way, one of us can make sure we have a paper cup from everyone discreetly stashed away and we'll have DNA. It will be a lovely evening."

"On to the cemetery," Cheyenne said. "Nothing like looking for a mummy—and of course, a rougarou."

"Right," he said. "With the help of a few ghosts, of course."

14

The gates were open when they arrived. Andre drove the car up to the house—there was only one other vehicle there—the business car driven by Guy Mason.

The door to the house was open; Mason evidently wasn't worried about anyone coming to cause him harm.

They found him in his office, going through paperwork.

"Special Agents, hello," he said, seeming surprised to see them, but not annoyed.

"Please, sit. What can I do for you?" he asked, indicating the chairs in front of the desk.

"We're just following up," Cheyenne said. "Hoping you might have thought of something that could help us. I'm not sure what you've seen on the news, but Jacques Derringer will be released today. The medical examiner is ruling Father Napier's death as natural—he died of a heart attack."

"Ah, poor fellow," Mason said, and shrugged. "I

mean, the man is dead. And once you are dead, can it really matter to you how you got that way? Believe me, this I know, even though I am not an embalmer. We are like all animals. Once the flicker of life is gone, we are all but dead meat."

"Interesting," Andre said, folding his hands idly and appraising Mason. "You're not much of a believer in the hereafter, or in the soul going on?"

"If it goes on, it's not in the body. You take Mr. Tybalt's family—they loved the man. Really loved him. But his life is over. The body rots—burns here, in our sun. Our tombs and crypts and 'cities of the dead' make fast work of the circle of life. When the pain of death, however it occurs, is over, then a man or woman is at peace. Whether there is a hereafter or not, the body has no purpose. Funerals are for the living, not the dead."

"I believe that to be true," Cheyenne said, "but I also do like to believe there is a hereafter. And I wonder how many people believe that the dead go on, and—perhaps from some lofty perch, a heaven in the clouds, as many artists depict—look down and watch. Perhaps they watch to assure their loved ones are okay, or to make sure they are given a fond farewell." Smiling, she leaned forward. "Perhaps, in some small way, all the people who believe in ghosts are right and some stay behind to see that justice is done."

Mason grinned at her. "Trust me—it's all just dead meat. Anyway, how is that young woman who was rescued? Has she been able to help at all? I guess not, or you wouldn't be here again." He sighed. "Look, I know I'm a suspicious character. I'm here and Emil is still trying to get out of jail. He will— they have nothing but circumstantial evidence. And so you know, Bill Vine isn't a bad guy. He just knows that I wouldn't hurt anyone—don't want to say that I wouldn't hurt a fly since I've swatted hundreds of them in my lifetime. Part of bayou life in Louisiana."

"Really," Andre said, "we just came hoping that something else might have occurred to you. We hope you've tried to think of anything unusual you might have seen—or anything else you might know about. We know that kids are in here all the time, but there are still no guards around the property, no way to keep people out."

"We can't afford to build a better wall," Mason said. "Yes, there are a lot of graves and crypts and larger family mausoleums, but you have to remember that this began as a family graveyard. In the early 1800s, there weren't many public cemeteries—not in this area. Once the back-then Justine opened it to all his neighbors and the nearby communities, it became big. We still have a number of families in the area making use of their family tombs, but…the money isn't really coming in. We can't afford to hire full-time guards. The police watch, but you know yourselves that it's easy enough for kids to sneak in and hide between tombs when patrol cars go by. We can't afford to stop it. Justine can barely pay me. Right now, I'm here because there's a funeral the day after tomorrow. Half the time, I don't even come in. I supplement what I make here by selling vintage and antique stuff online."

"Mr. Tybalt's funeral is Saturday," Andre said. "I believe you mentioned that the other day."

"Yes. Did you know him?"

"Not well," Andre said, and he stood. Cheyenne rose as well, and Guy Mason did the same. "I believe you might need some help for that. You'll have people coming out of the woodwork for that."

"He was elderly. Most of his friends have already passed. The family will be here, of course, but I'm not sure it will be busy. They're off today speaking with the priest who was sent in by the diocese yesterday to...well, to take Father Napier's place. Temporary right now, I understand but...well, you can imagine. Napier was loved in the community. People need...consolation."

"People will come," Andre said, "because they'll want to see where Lacey Murton was found. They'll want to rehash the Rougarou, and the Artiste—and wonder about the Mortician. People can be ghoulish when the horror doesn't touch them personally."

"I'll mention this to my cousin. He'll see that he has cops out for the funeral, maybe a man to specifically watch over the outbuildings," Mason assured them.

They thanked him and left.

Out by the car, Cheyenne looked toward the cemetery.

"We can wander down," Andre said. He watched her with a touch of humor. "Interesting theories you were exploring with our Mr. Mason. Is that when you first saw Janine after her death?"

Cheyenne nodded. "She was suddenly next to me, insisting that I tell the world that Lassiter killed her." She glanced at him. "You—you never saw anyone here, in this cemetery?"

"That day? I was playing my guitar, glad to be in the jazz band. I wasn't paying attention to anything else—I just ran after Lassiter when Jimmy shouted to me to flank the man."

They walked among the tombs. She looked at him. "When did you first realize that you saw the dead?"

"I was a kid—small. My dad was fine thinking that I had imaginary friends. My mom...she just let me talk to them. She never saw them, but she was open to anything." He glanced her way. "As I got older...well, I learned not to mention it."

Cheyenne saw Janine and Christian slipping out from around the Dumas family mausoleum. Cheyenne knew that the two had been watching them since they'd arrived.

"Anything?" Janine asked anxiously.

Cheyenne told the two ghosts about Father Napier and seeing the mummy in New Orleans. While she asked them if they had ever seen a mummy running around the cemetery, Andre stood aside to make phone calls. "Like an Egyptian mummy?" Christian asked.

"Yes."

"No. I'd have noticed a mummy," Janine said.

"Have you seen anyone in here lately—anyone at all?" Cheyenne asked.

"No," Christian said. "It's been so empty…it's creepy. No one visiting the dead. I think everything has freaked people out. They don't bring flowers, they don't come to cry or pray or anything. It's been weird. But we'll stay and keep watch as long as you need."

"What about Melissa and Captain Bouche and Lieutenant Kendall?" she asked.

"They've been watching, too," Janine said. She smiled grimly. "All these years…poor Melissa. I don't think she'll ever know who killed her."

"My friend Keri researched in every way that she could," Cheyenne told her. "She had some ideas, but she's a good writer—she'll put forth ideas, but unless she can completely substantiate them, she won't say they were fact. Maybe she can come down for a few days and talk to Melissa, help her."

"That would be great. Melissa is very sweet. And…she wants to move on," Janine said. She smiled at Cheyenne. "I've been fine. I've had Christian all these years."

"And I've had Janine," Christian said. "We would have never found one another in life, and I believe—obviously—that there is a higher power, and that I have been forgiven. So, we're doing okay, but… Melissa. She's so sad."

"She has friends—I mean, she's got Lieutenant Kendall and Captain Bouche, right—and you two," Cheyenne said.

Janine shook her head. "They are friends, yes. But it's not the same. She wants to be with her family, with those who have gone on. She's miserable. I think that the captain and the lieutenant believe that they stay in the name of peace and unity." She smiled. "They haunt those who are fighting or bickering, and either try to straighten them out or scare them into getting along. Melissa is just…so sad."

Andre walked over to them. "It's set. We're having a dinner party. Catered by one of my mom's favorite places on Magazine Street—Your Cajun Uncle Sam's."

"You really think this could be someone we knew?" Janine asked.

"Yeah. We really do," Andre said.

"We'll keep watch!" Janine promised.

"And we'll be back for the funeral the day after tomorrow," Andre told her.

They left the cemetery and headed to the jail to see Emil Justine. They started with Detective Vine, who was not happy. "Justine isn't here—no indictment. We're investigating—oh, yes, of course, you're lead on the case, but we are still investigating."

"Do you know where he is? Did he have one of his children come for him, or did he return to his home?"

"Went to his house—in Broussard. I'm assuming you can get his address. I heard you were out to harass my cousin again. He'll slap a lawsuit on you if you don't stop," Vine told him.

"Interesting," Andre said, looking at Cheyenne. "We go to your cousin for help, and you think he'll throw a lawsuit on us. You've gone after Emil Justine like a determined dog, but he should just say thank you for the room and board?"

"They teach you to be a wiseass in the academy?" Vine asked. "Justine owns the property."

"Guy Mason manages it," Cheyenne said.

"Well, Justine's not here—and I have nothing from the church, or on the organist—and I have nothing from the rectory. Your people were in there, so…"

"Yep, thanks," Andre said. He had set his hands on Cheyenne's shoulders; she wasn't sure if he felt they had to get out of there because she'd lose her temper—or because he'd lose his.

As they walked out, he told her, "I'm starting to think that he might be guilty of something—he's an ass."

"Yeah, and…"

"Being an ass isn't illegal. But really…"

He stopped walking again.

"One more phone call,"

"Okay?"

"I want Angela to get someone looking at the financials—both business and personal. Maybe there's money being passed from someone to someone else."

"For?"

"For turning a blind eye," he said. "Come on—let's pay a visit to Emil Justine, and head on back. We don't want to be late for our own dinner party."

Cheyenne easily found Emil Justine's home address. It was listed online, along with his phone number and the welcome to call anytime when a loved one passed away.

Emil Justine appeared to be older and even more tired than he had before. Still, he welcomed them in.

His home was a new house, a small two-bedroom ranch, and Cheyenne noted everything in it was brand-new and modern in style.

Maybe having grown up in a historic house—with historic plumbing, electricity and pipes—had made him crave what was new and always worked.

"I'm sure that Detective Vine is going to keep looking for evidence against me," Justine said once they'd settled into his living room. "But for the time…here I am. I'll probably head up to Pennsylvania—my kids want me out of here. They think I'm too old to deal with everything going on. But Rusty Tybalt was a friend of mine, so I'll be at that funeral. Then I'll make my arrangements. I won't be leaving the country. Vine will know right where to find me."

"He does seem to be determined to charge you," Andre told him. "Do you know why? Does he have something against you?"

Justine shook he head in bewilderment. "I don't understand. Unless, of course, Vine is worried about Guy. Maybe, in his mind, someone had to know what was going on. And he's never going to believe it might have been his cousin. So, it had to be me."

"How well did you know Guy Mason when you hired him?" Andre asked.

"He's from Shreveport, but moved down here for

a girl. He and the girl broke up, but he'd invested in a small home, and he'd worked for one of the big funeral companies when he'd been up in Shreveport. We met at church. Oh, actually, Father Napier introduced us. Anyway, I checked out all his credentials, and he's for real. He's been a good employee, especially considering that I can't pay that much and a lot of responsibility is on him. I like Guy. He loves antiques, and when he's not at the funeral home, he's out scrounging the countryside, buying up things he knows he can get some good prices for on the internet. I don't wish him any harm. Detective Vine's behavior is not his fault. He's trying to do his job. But at least now I'm out."

"Well, sir, I hope it all works out well for you," Cheyenne told him.

"I swear to you again, I have had nothing to do with kidnapping or murder," Justine told them.

"And you're doing all right?"

He nodded. "And how's the young lady who was saved?"

"Still doing well," Andre assured him. "We'll be checking on you this weekend—we're coming out for the funeral, too. Help keep an eye on things."

"That will be fine. You're welcome to be anywhere on my property, crawl the house—look through the attic and the basement...you're welcome anywhere there."

They thanked him and left.

"Nice man," Cheyenne said, and Andre smiled.

"Well, being an ass doesn't make you a murderer

and being nice doesn't mean that you're not—but still, I don't see how Justine could have been involved. He was away too much."

"Unless it's money," Cheyenne said.

"Money. That's why I'm having everyone's financials checked and double-checked."

"So, what are we having tonight?"

"Down-home cooking!" he told her. "Boudin, jambalaya, cheese grits, turnip greens—I decided to go as stereotypical as possible. I mean, what would a rougarou like? Cajun!"

Andre and Cheyenne made it back to the house by four, and when they parked and walked up, they found that the caterer was arriving, as well.

Andre remembered his board—with all of the guests' pictures on it—and started to move into the parlor, but Jackson told him, "I've taken care of it. The board is upstairs in the closet. Someone would really have to be prying to get into it."

"And," Angela said, "we've got everything coming in—just as you ordered."

"Paper everything," Jackson confirmed.

"Guests should be arriving shortly," Andre told Jackson. "Every one of them said that they could come." A thought had been mulling in his mind. "I've been forming a plan, and it's something that might just be out of the question. First, have you had any luck? You were trying to see if you could find the scent that Lacey said she smelled on the rougarou."

"So far, we've been through at least a hundred,"

Jackson told him. "We have to give her time in be-tween, or she could ignore the right one or come up with a false positive. I've been smelling a lot of different aftershaves lately! Okay, what do you use?"

"Me?"

"Yeah. Just curious after all the ones I've been through today," Jackson said.

"I wear the same thing all the time. An aftershave by a small company in Virginia. They're growing—but for now, I like the company a lot, and they fit a government employee's budget. What about you?"

"I use one from a department store," Jackson said. "I never switch. Guess I found what I like, and I stay with it."

"And Angela?" Andre asked.

"She loves a scent that's by Versace. It's all she wears."

"Some people switch up now and then, but perfumes, colognes and aftershaves mix differently with different body chemistries, and we all have a tendency to be creatures of habit. I'm not sure what Cheyenne wears, but I have noticed that it's the same every time."

"I'm beginning to see where you're going with this—you think that if we had Lacey here, she might recognize the person who snatched her by his scent?"

"She remembered it. Plus garlic, well…just about anyone might have garlic breath at some time or another."

Jackson was thoughtful. "Putting a victim into further danger is not something that we do."

"She wouldn't be in danger. Four good agents are part of the evening meal."

"We can ask her," Jackson said after a moment. "She may say yes. Her mother may say no."

"We'll have Cheyenne go and talk to her. Lacey really seems to respond to her."

"You stay and welcome the guests—I'll go with Cheyenne. We want Lacey's mother to know that if a spot-on markswoman isn't enough, we have some brawn going for us, too. Angela is getting the kitchen set up. We'll be as quick as possible."

"The safe house is close?"

"Just Uptown—and by a police station. You never know when you may need help." The two of them headed back to the kitchen to share the plan with Angela and Cheyenne. The aroma of the freshly delivered food was tempting, but they'd wait.

It was a dinner party, after all.

"It's dangerous," Angela said. "The plan—using a civilian. It's dangerous."

"But actually kind of brilliant," Cheyenne said. "I know you've been letting Lacey smell scents all day, and that she hasn't identified anything. And scents smell different on different people, so, having her here with those we suspect could work. Lacey may recognize whatever someone is wearing right away. Or it could be a bust. We may wind up with nothing."

"And our killer might have changed his scent," Jackson said. "We are creatures of habit, but then again, sometimes we change our habits. But if the killer is among our guests, he won't be expecting Lacey here and could just be wearing his aftershave.

"It's a chance all the way round, but maybe, if Lacey is willing, one that is worth taking," Jackson said. "Fine, let's go for it. Cheyenne?"

"We can ask," Cheyenne said. She glanced at Jackson. "And He-man here can deal with her mom!"

She and Jackson left; Andre walked into the kitchen where the ghost of Louis Marquette was seated at the table, enjoying the fact that he was being seen by someone other than Andre.

"I'm thinking of ways to secure our cups for DNA that won't be noted," Angela said to Andre. "I couldn't think of anywhere that someone else might see them and discard them or become suspicious because we were hoarding cups. But I think—and feel free to offer another suggestion—that it would be easy enough if we take turns, running upstairs with empty cups. I have name tags for them all up in your parents' room."

"I haven't a better plan. I'd like to think that people wouldn't go through my cupboards, but you never know. But even with the bedroom, we have to make sure that no one goes in and discovers what we're doing."

"Oh, excuse me, lad, but that's covered!" the ghost said, smiling. "I shall be upstairs in the bedroom. Thankfully, your dear parents did see fit to purchase that wonderful large-screen television. And of course, the door will be closed, and it's really no one's business if you choose to run your televisions throughout the day!"

"Okay, great," Andre said.

The doorbell chimed as he spoke.

"Our guests are arriving," Andre said. He left Angela and walked to the door.

Jimmy Mercury was the first to arrive. "Hey, buddy!" Jimmy said, giving him a warm hug. "So, you're getting some free time in, huh? I guess no one can work 24/7, but…hey, honestly? I wasn't expecting any off time with you for a while."

"Well, we are working this case hard, coming and going from the Justine place," Andre said. "But my immediate supervisor and another coworker are here, and they think that you're no good at your work if you don't take some time to kick back. Come on in. Angela is in the kitchen."

He led Jimmy Mercury back and introduced him to Angela.

Louis had apparently headed upstairs, and today, Andre had a feeling that he was both glad to be of assistance—watching over the bedroom—while also getting in one of his favorite pastimes: the Saints were playing that day, and Louis was a fan.

Jimmy accepted an iced tea. He didn't want a beer or anything stronger because he had to be at work that night by eight.

"I'm at The Last Cavalier tonight—and through the next month, really. But I was thinking, if you all finish up early here and want something to do, come on by. Actually, maybe some of the others will join—it's a cool place. And if I do say so myself, the band is great."

The door chimed again. This time, it was Mike Holiday; he greeted Jimmy with a big hug, and said that he'd have to leave for work, too. "Don't have to be in until nine, though, so I have a little time. This is nice—you actually meant it when you said that we should get together."

Andre smiled. He had always meant it. He found himself hoping that Mike was moving along well in life; he had his old days of small-town fame behind, found life hard in the real world and was trying to make a good go of it. He'd turned into a nice guy. Or so it seemed.

He'd barely let Mike in before Katie and Nelson came walking down the street. He welcomed them, and the way they greeted Mike, it was difficult to believe that they'd suggested they'd ever been anything but the best of friends.

"Where's Cheyenne?" Katie asked him, after meeting Angela and greeting Jimmy Mercury.

"With Jackson. They'll be back any minute. Come on into the kitchen—we went for down-home stuff, you know, turnip greens, grits…oh, yeah, we've got crawfish, gumbo, jambalaya…went the whole nine yards."

"Bread pudding?" Katie asked. "It's always been my downfall."

"It is her downfall," Nelson said.

"I'm really glad you could both come," Andre told them.

"The kid who works for us is great. He'll hold the fort," Nelson said. "So, Mike, you still bouncing back the teenagers trying to see big boobs?"

"That I am!" Mike replied.

The doorbell chimed again; their last guest, Rocky Beaufort, had arrived; he greeted Andre at the door with a big grin. "What, I'm the old man here, huh? Former students here, there and everywhere. Mikey!" he said, seeing Mike Holiday in the hallway. They shared a big hug. "You need to come around. You know, you have the right stuff to be a great personal trainer. Sure, that would mean classes and training yourself, but hey, could be a good thing for you."

"I'm actually going to college online," Mike told him. "But I appreciate the offer. And who knows…"

Nelson walked up to him and slipped an arm around his shoulders. "Hey, Mikey could flunk out of college—and then he'll need you, Rocky!" he said cheerfully.

"Well, it's online, but I've got straight As right now," Mike said.

Andre stood with the group. "Food is in the kitchen, and I'm starving. We were out—didn't stop for lunch once I knew you guys could make it." He hoped they didn't realize that he was sniffing them, as well—everyone smelled like something. Aftershave, Louisiana sun and maybe soap.

They all made their way back to the kitchen and Andre said, "We figured we could fix plates and take them into the dining room."

"Where's Cheyenne?" Rocky asked. "Hey, have you two become a thing? That's kind of cool—you know, like that show… *Bones*…or one of those others. There's a private eye one out now, too, and way back when, *Moonlighting*— Hey! That's where Bruce Willis got his start."

"Well, we've quickly become very good friends, at any rate," Andre said, trying to be noncommittal.

"You were the class ahead of us—but you'd been gone awhile when Janine…died," Katie said, munching on a piece of corn bread. "But back then Cheyenne would have been just a kid. A pretty remarkable kid, though—the way she got you and Jimmy going after Lassiter. Wow, still hard to believe. We all thought he was so…cool. And studly."

"There you go with studly," Nelson said with a moan.

"Oh, sweetie, you're kind of studly," she assured him.

Nelson made a face and shook his head.

"Cheyenne should be back any minute. What would you guys like to drink? It's beer or tea, really—not so easy to keep a great choice in a place when you're not really living in it," Andre said. "She headed out with Jackson, trying to see if a new friend wanted to join us today."

"Is it a he or a she? No one we know, huh?" Mike asked.

"No, we just met her ourselves. It's Lacey Murton, the young woman who had been held by the guy we're hunting, the Mortician," Andre said.

"Oh! Wow!" Katie said. "You all became friends? Is she all right? She's not from here, is she?"

"From the area," Andre said vaguely. "We're hoping she'll come out. She's a sweet girl—afraid right now to be anywhere. So we thought we could get together—and get her going safely out into society again."

"Good plan," Jimmy said. "We'll be on our best behavior."

"Mike, no flirting—it's too soon!" Nelson warned.

"Hey, I was never a flirt!" Mike protested. He shrugged with good humor. "I couldn't help it if girls fell all over me."

Angela laughed softly. "Well, I can see that," she said. "I've got to run up—I'll be right back. Hopefully Jackson and Cheyenne—and Miss Murton—will be here soon."

Angela grinned and moved on past them. She already had her first cup for their collection; Jimmy had put down a paper cup and she had casually scooped it up, slipped it into a pocket and was sliding through the others to reach the stairs.

She had barely gone before there was a knock at the door. Cheyenne and Jackson were back, and Lacey Murton was, miraculously, with them.

"Lacey, thank you for coming," he said quietly, looking from Cheyenne to Jackson, who did their best to remain expressionless.

"I'm here to sniff, it seems," she said softly. Then she squared her shoulders and flipped her hair back. "There'd better be some good food!"

"This way," Cheyenne murmured, looking at Andre as she walked through the foyer and to the left, toward the kitchen.

"You're armed, right?" Lacey asked.

"Every one of us," Cheyenne assured her.

People were setting up in the dining room, putting down plates and plasticware, cups, hot sauce, butter and more.

They stopped when Cheyenne led Lacey in. "Guys, this is Lacey Murton," she said in a casual tone. "Lacey, Jimmy Mercury—musician extraordinaire. Katie Ridgeway—she and her husband own Miracle Music on Conti. The big dude is our friendly gym owner, Rocky Beaufort, and Mike Holiday there is working on Bourbon Street and back into college online."

Andre arrived just behind her; it gave him the opportunity to study the faces of his friends as Lacey made her appearance.

"Hello, everyone," Lacey said.

"Hey, if you like music, young lady, you come be my guest any night!" Jimmy told her, beaming gallantly.

Katie laughed. "If you like music, come to our store."

"I can't offer much," Mike told her, grimacing. "Unless you like boobs."

Lacey laughed at that, delighted.

"Well, we play music at the gym," Rocky said. "Stirring, get-your-feet-moving music. So, you are welcome to come by my place anytime, too. Get a personalized fitness assessment."

Lacey smiled and thanked them all.

"I love music—and food," Lacey said. She turned to look at Cheyenne and back at Andre. "I could eat," she said.

"Right this way." Andre caught her elbow and lead her toward the kitchen. "We're leaving room at the table to eat and we have it all like a buffet in the kitchen."

"Sounds good," Lacey said, following his lead.

Nelson Ridgeway was still picking through the offerings. He looked up at Lacey and smiled and said, "Hey, welcome. I hear you're Lacey. I'm Nelson. Nelson Ridgeway. Katie's better half."

"Nice to meet you," Lacey said, shaking the hand he stretched out to her.

"It's a pleasure. Hey, you know, if you need anything at any time around here, you can ask any of us for help," Nelson said.

"Thanks," Lacey said easily.

"Plate, silverware. Sorry—plasticware. Help yourself to what you like," Andre said.

Mike popped in his head. "Hey, Andre—can we take the tea out to the table? None of us is drinking tonight, going through a lot of tea!"

"Sure," he said, and handed Mike the gallon. Mike grinned at the others and let the swinging door close behind him.

Lacey was filling her plate. Her hands seemed to be trembling.

"Maybe double up on the plates," Andre said, helping her.

She nodded quietly, head down. Nelson went out; Mike Holiday came in.

"Hot sauce?" he asked Andre.

"Right there," Andre said, pointing to the table.

Cheyenne looked in. "Everyone okay? Lacey, I've got a place for you—we gathered up some other chairs. Come on, I'll get you seated."

Andre knew that she'd have Lacey sit right next to Jackson or Angela.

Casual conversation went around the table, all of their guests too caring—apparently—to quiz Lacey about her terrifying experience.

Mike laughed at one point and said, "How about those Saints, huh?"

Then they argued about the name for the home basketball team, all saying that "Jazz" had really defined NOLA best, but hey...they'd root for Pelicans, too.

"Jazz should be us—nothing against Utah, but I like Jazz," Mike said.

"Well, we do have pelicans," Katie said.

A moment later, Lacey excused herself, asking Cheyenne for the ladies' room.

"I'll take you up—two of them upstairs, none of them down," Cheyenne said.

The two stood, and Andre did so, too, saying, "Let me just check them out first, think we're good here, but...haven't been in the guest bath in a while."

He headed after them.

Before she reached the top of the stairway, Lacey collapsed. Cheyenne caught her, but Andre hurried up to help before they could all tumble down the stairs.

In his arms on the landing, Lacey looked up at him.

"He's here," she said.

15

Cheyenne glanced over Lacey's head at Andre. They were both startled—they'd had some hopes for the event but had barely dared dream that Lacey could and would name her kidnapper so quickly and easily.

"It's okay, Lacey, breathe," Cheyenne said quietly. "Who is it?" she asked.

"The one named Nelson. He smells just like I remember the rougarou," Lacey said. She took a deep breath. "It's him, it smells just like him, I know that it was him. Yes, yes, it smells just like him—except for the garlic. He doesn't smell like garlic just the aftershave."

"You're sure?" Cheyenne asked.

"Positive," Lacey said.

Andre looked at Cheyenne again. "Okay, we need to get Lacey out of here, back to the safe house. We can say that her mother just called—had an accident or something. I'm going out the front door with her. Send Jackson or Angela out to go with me, and for the moment, keep the night going—see if we think Katie is in this with him, or if it might be one of the others."

"Arrest him! Just grab him and arrest him!" Lacey whispered urgently.

"Lacey," Cheyenne said, "we're going to arrest him, but to keep him locked up, we're going to have to have more evidence. A prosecutor can't go to trial without more, and we don't want him getting out on bail. You're going back to the safe house—you'll be fine. I promise."

Lacey nodded, trying to stand. Andre helped her down the stairs and Cheyenne followed quickly. Luckily, Jackson was on his way into the hallway and met her there.

She quickly told him what Lacey had said, and he hurried out to join Andre and Lacey.

Cheyenne walked into the dining room. Nelson seemed to have become best friends with Mike Holiday; they were head to head at the table, talking away. No one seemed to be disturbed by Lacey's departure, or they hadn't realized it yet.

But Angela looked up at her, a question in her eyes.

"Poor Lacey," she said, loudly enough for the others to hear her. "She finally gets out—and then gets a call. Her mom slipped and wants her home, won't let anyone go to the hospital with her except for Lacey."

"She's gone?" Mike asked. "Pretty girl—I was trying to get to know her."

"Very pretty girl—I'd give you some competition if I was younger," Rocky said.

"It wasn't us, was it?" Katie asked, sounding concerned. "I mean...well, we were careful about what we said, didn't want to bring up what happened... I mean, we were fine, right?"

"You were all charming," Cheyenne assured them.

"I'm going for more grits!" Nelson said. "This was really nice of you guys to set up—a chance to see one another again."

"A pleasure," Cheyenne said.

"Okay, so now it's just us— and Angela—who is kind of like just us," Jimmy Mercury said. "So tell us, what's the real scoop—are you and Andre together?"

"I'll bring the grits in, Nelson," Angela said, hiding a smile.

"So?" Jimmy pressed.

"Slow down. We've just seen each other for the first time in...years," Cheyenne said. She stood, pouring herself more tea.

And wondering how she was going to get through the rest of the dinner.

"Anybody need anything? I'll just refill this," she said.

In the kitchen, she asked Angela, "Are we bringing him in? Do we call Detective Fournier and let him bring him in? I have to admit, this is new to me. I mean, we learn things about people this way, but I've never had to tell a prosecutor that a suspect has been identified by smell."

"Jackson and Andre will make arrangements to have Nelson picked up as soon as he leaves here. We'll have Fournier hold him—he'll have twenty-four hours. And we'll need to get something on him in that twenty-four hours. We'll need search warrants for his home and the store. We can go looking for a rougarou costume and whatever else. We'll need to figure out the time lines, add them up. Right now, well, at least I have four cups. Still need one."

"All right. I'll work on that," Cheyenne said.

"And just keep being charming!" Angela said.

She did her best. Tried to pay attention to the small talk and contribute when she could. In an odd way, it was like being back at home.

Yet, all the while, she wanted to scream. Nelson. Nelson Ridgeway. Brainiac and computer nerd. Was it really possible? Did Katie know? Did she have any idea of what her husband was doing?

Eventually—and especially without Lacey there anymore to make people tiptoe in conversation—talk turned back to the past.

And Janine.

"How did you know it was Lassiter?" It was Nelson asking her—looking straight at her.

She smiled. "Janine told me."

"What?" he asked, frowning.

Let them all wonder.

"She'd been secretive, but dropping hints. And then I heard other people talking—she'd been seen with him. Flirting. And he had flirted back, and they'd obviously made arrangements... I didn't have proof. I just knew."

"It was pretty amazing," Nelson said. "It was almost as if...as if she was there, shouting out somehow through you."

She stared back at Nelson.

"Yes, it was as if she was there."

Eventually, Jimmy stood up and said, "Well, it sucks to leave when we're just really getting it together after so many years, but I have to go to work."

"Thanks for coming, Jimmy," Cheyenne told him, and the group stood, all hugging Jimmy goodbye, including Angela. He asked them all to come by when they could.

Next to leave was Mike Holiday. "Well, you all know where I work. We have good dancers and pretty girls...so."

There was laughter, and more hugs.

Rocky Beaufort said that he needed to go by the gym.

And Nelson and Katie wanted to go by the store before closing. They offered help in picking up; Angela and Cheyenne assured them that everything had been on paper it was easy to toss.

Cheyenne was standing at the door as Nelson and Katie went out, the last to leave.

They barely reached the sidewalk before Detective Pierre Fournier, dressed in a casual suit, walked up and asked Nelson Ridgeway to identify himself.

Nelson did so.

And Fournier began to read him his rights; in seconds, Katie was screaming and crying and protesting. But Nelson Ridgeway was in handcuffs, being taken away to a waiting squad car.

There should have been something that night—a sense of completion, at the very least.

But after Lacey had been taken back, Nelson had been taken away, and Katie had been calmed down and escorted home by an officer, Andre still felt the sense of something being missing or incomplete.

He wanted to believe that Nelson had played the rougarou and the mummy, but he knew that wasn't right. The mummy had been with the rougarou in the cemetery, and while Eva might have admitted that she was high when she saw what she was afraid she had imagined, he didn't think that she was wrong. Maybe a second person hadn't done the actual killing, but they had been involved in what had gone on. And it might have been Katie.

He and Cheyenne were alone in his room; Jackson and Angela were resting across the hall.

He was also sure, though, that they were awake, as well—going over just who might be the accomplice.

"Katie, of course, she's the obvious one," Cheyenne said. "Maybe we should have made arrangements for her to be taken in, as well—they could have questioned them both separately and maybe tripped one of them up. As it is—"

"As it is," Andre said, "we're pushing it. We need to come up with something else—and quickly. Tomorrow, we'll take a crack at Nelson. It's an easy way to play good cop–bad cop."

"Who is good—and who is bad?" Cheyenne asked, carefully setting her gun and holster on the bedside table and stripping off her cotton shirt.

He walked over to where she stood, pulling her around and into his arms.

"We both get to be good. Fournier is bad cop—he's the one who brought him in. We get to go and ask questions as if we're trying to straighten it all out for him. That's tomorrow. There's nothing we can do right now."

"What about Katie?"

"She'll stew in fury and misery tonight, and she'll have an attorney in there by tomorrow. But we can spend some time with her—bewildered and trying to help."

"All right. But—"

"Tomorrow! That's tomorrow. For tonight…"

She looked into his eyes and he watched the slow curl of her lips and felt the sensual touch of her fingers as she teased him through his clothing.

"Tonight…is for us?"

"Tonight is for us."

They'd quickly become so comfortable with each other; it was so easy to be together, to laugh and tease… But comfortable took nothing away from hunger or excitement. He knew her better and better, and with each little nuance he learned, he needed another. Her feet were ticklish, she was exquisitely sensitive at the nape of her neck, she moved as fluidly as the most graceful ballet dancer, and with the heat and passion of a salsa pro.

And in his life, he had never known before that just holding someone after could be as emotionally sating as the act of making love was physically fulfilling.

She lay beside him, still awake, and he knew that she was uniquely with him—and still back on the case, happy to lie in his arms, feel his touch, as she pondered what they knew, and what they didn't know, and what all their steps in the future would be.

Somewhere in there, they slept.

He woke to the sound of his phone ringing.

It was Detective Pierre Fournier. "We've got a problem."

"A problem? Did Nelson confess—and swear that he did it all on his own?" Andre asked skeptically.

"No, and his attorney is screaming about us holding him. There's been a new development," Fournier told him.

"And what's that?"

"While we were holding Nelson Ridgeway, the killer struck again. A picture of Katie Ridgeway was found this morning on a table when the cleaning crew went into a bar on Frenchman Street—a place called The Last Cavalier. It's the 'before' picture. With any luck, he hasn't killed her yet. But you found his hideout, so...where he's taken her now, well, it's anyone's guess."

* * *

Fournier was furious when they reached the police station.

Nelson Ridgeway was already out—and threatening the police with every lawsuit known to man, while telling his story on every conceivable form of media.

While he was being held, his *wife* had been taken. She'd have never become a victim if the police hadn't been holding him. "These people must learn that citizens have rights, that we have a constitution!" he had railed. "And if my wife dies…"

He broke off on a sob. It seemed very convincing.

"What made you think it was him?" Fournier demanded.

"Lacey Murton identified him."

"Eyewitness identifications have been known to be faulty. We needed more," Fournier said. "My captain is ready to rip me a new one where the sun don't shine! The chief is in an uproar and I thank God that whatever happens with this—it's on your hands."

"And we take full responsibility," Jackson assured him. He and Angela had gone to the station with them as support. "I'll take care of your captain."

"I can head over to Miracle Music, and then The Last Cavalier," Angela said, "though the picture is definitely Katie Ridgeway. When the hell did he get her—right after they took Nelson in?"

"Lacey Murton said she saw—definitely saw Nelson Ridgeway?" Fournier demanded.

"She smelled him," Andre said.

"She *what*?" Fournier demanded.

"She knew his scent. He was dressed up when he took her, but she knew his scent," Andre explained.

"Oh, come on, how in the hell—"

"Trust me, she knew!" Cheyenne told him. "She knew—when something like that happens to you, things like that trigger in the mind. I know that she was right."

"Then who the hell just took his wife?" Fournier demanded.

"Whoever the hell his accomplice is!" Andre snapped. He drew in a deep breath. "We should have taken him last night—the FBI."

"It wouldn't have mattered who took him—the law wouldn't have allowed any of us to keep him as it was. His wife was taken. Her picture was left—just as the other pictures were left before. We have this little thing called a constitution. We enforce the laws, we don't make them, and we can't keep people locked up because of the way they smell!" Fournier said.

"All right, sorry," Cheyenne said. "We need to move, figure out what our next steps are."

"We'll go out to the cemetery," Andre said. He looked at Cheyenne. "Whatever the hell is going on—"

"Rousseau!" Fournier said. "You are the ones who cleaned out the killer's lair. He can't go back there—he knows it."

"He can't go back to the old shack, but I'm willing to bet he will go back there, somewhere."

"Why?" Fournier asked.

"Because he thinks he's the rougarou—that he can't be just talk. That he's got it right—he learned from the original, he learned from Lassiter. He's going back there," Andre said.

"Jackson and I will be here, following everything in NOLA," Angela said.

"All right. Let's get out and moving," Cheyenne said. She touched Andre's jacket. "Let's go to the bar—see what they can tell us there. And if the clerk can help in any way. And then we can head out."

Andre nodded and told Fournier, "If you can find Nelson Ridgeway after all this, keep an eye on him. I'm assuming he's going to close his business down for the day, but… I'm telling you, Lacey Murton didn't make a mistake."

Angela caught up with them before they could leave the building. "I'm going to get on those financials—if you think that the killer has been paying someone to look the other way, we need to follow the money. And we're up against the clock again now. We have to find Katie Ridgeway. If it's him…"

"Do we really think he'd kill his own wife?" Andre asked her. "I just don't know. But this might have been their plan all along. If Nelson should get locked up, snatch his wife and leave a picture— then the police would be forced to let him go."

Angela looked at Cheyenne. "You know these people. What do you think?"

"I think that, one way or the other, Katie is missing. I don't know… How could this have happened? I mean, how could Katie not have known what her husband was doing, and then again…an accomplice wouldn't have snatched her if he didn't know that it was what Nelson wanted. One way or the other, Katie is in trouble. And yes, I believe this killer has embraced the legend—he is, in his mind, not the Mortician, but the Rougarou."

Angela nodded. "Get going, then. We'll be in touch."

They headed to Frenchman Street and The Last Cavalier. It was locked up; too many members of the media were milling around outside.

Andre showed his badge through the window, and they were both let in.

The manager, a little man with a full beard and whiskers, met them and introduced them to the man on the cleaning crew. All he knew was that when he was mopping up the floor, he saw the picture on the table. Knowing what it was because of the recent press about the kidnappings, he'd immediately called the police. Andre wanted to know who had last been in; the night manager and two of the waitresses had left together.

They hadn't noted the picture when they left.

"When did the band leave?" Cheyenne asked.

"Right after last call—they get out, and that helps us get the customers out," the manager told them. "God, am I sorry, that poor woman, gone. While they were holding her husband."

She noted that Andre kept his temper.

When they reached the Ridgeways' store, Miracle Music, it was locked up. They tried banging on the window, but no one came; if the clerk was inside, he was adept at ignoring them.

"Call Angela—they can get a search warrant," Cheyenne suggested.

"They need to search the Ridgeway home, too," Andre muttered. He swore softly. "No one even knows when the hell Katie Ridgeway was taken. A patrol car drove her home from my house last night because she was having such a hysterical fit about Nelson."

"Someone she trusted took her," Cheyenne said. "She let them in—and they took her."

He stopped and called Angela; he wanted people watching Mike Holiday, Rocky Beaufort—and even Jimmy Mercury.

Especially Jimmy Mercury, he told Angela. Cheyenne could see that it hurt him; Jimmy Mercury had really been his friend.

"All right, are we heading out to the cemetery?" Cheyenne asked. She frowned. "They've let Jacques Derringer go. Maybe they've been paying him... maybe he stole the priest's vestments for whoever went in to see Lassiter before he was executed. It's possible."

"I just don't believe that Laccy could have been wrong," Andre said, looking at her. His eyes were tormented.

They were both personally involved. Too involved, and they probably should have been taken off the case.

"Andre, it's almost three. We need to get out there.

Now. It will start getting dark, and if we're going to search places…"

The distance between New Orleans and their old part of Cajun country had never seemed greater.

They went by the church, but there was no sign of the temporary replacement priest or the organist, not in the church or at the rectory.

As they headed to the cemetery, Andre received a phone call.

He let Cheyenne answer it and asked her to put it on speakerphone.

Angela's voice came through clearly. "All right, we're still working on this, but over the last months, your friendly cemetery manager, Mr. Guy Mason, has indeed received some nice sums of money. We're having a tough time finding details—it's cash into an offshore account. We're working on it."

"Great," Andre said grimly. "We're on our way to see him now. Anything else?"

"We have a tail on Jimmy Mercury—he's at home. We haven't been able to locate Nelson Ridgeway or Mike Holiday. Rocky Beaufort is at his gym— smiling behind the desk and setting up appointments. We've had people in the music store—they're still searching. And I've gotten our DNA samples to the lab."

They both thanked her, and Andre promised to report back after they'd seen Guy Mason.

Cheyenne studied the old plantation as they drove through the gates. Darkness would be upon them soon. It was that time of day when the sun was going down, and the dying colors streaked across the old stone wall, the gates to the drive and the tombs, so many cast in that strange golden light that added to their decaying splendor.

Andre parked in front of the house—right behind Guy Mason's car, the one with the words *Justine Plantation Mortuary Home and Cemetery* advertised in black paint along both sides.

"I'm going to find Janine and Christian," Cheyenne told him. "See if they know anything."

Andre nodded. "Watch your back."

"Definitely," she said.

She wandered down through the gravestones, many long forgotten, chipping and peeling. A large angel wept atop a tomb marked Marquette, and she wondered if it might have belonged to a family member of Andre's ghost, Louis Marquette.

"Janine?" she whispered her cousin's name, and then, realizing she was alone, she said it more loudly.

Her cousin might have been by the Dumas tomb where her remains, nothing more than bone and ash now, rested.

"Janine?"

Her cousin suddenly popped out from between two crypts.

"Cheyenne, I wondered when you were coming—there's another note. On the tomb, and I... I'm hearing things from there!"

"What?"

"Come on, come on..."

Cheyenne hurried after her. "Did you see who

left the note? You heard things—you didn't go in?"
Cheyenne asked.

"We were on the other side, dividing a patrol between the five of us—you know, Melissa, Lieutenant Kendall, Captain Bouche, and Christian and me.
And those old war buddies thought that they needed
to watch the outbuildings, and Melissa was taking
the house, and…it was here when we got back. Cheyenne, be careful, be careful…the note…it says, 'Welcome, Cheyenne'!"

Cheyenne headed with long strides to the tomb,
smoothly drawing out her Glock as she did so.

The note was there, once again written on a napkin taken from The Last Cavalier.

Two words, just as Janine had said.

Welcome, Cheyenne.

The gate to her family mausoleum had a broken
padlock. She swore softly, Glock at the ready, and
opened the gate. It creaked as if in agony on hinges
that needed oiling.

Theirs wasn't a grand family tomb—there was a
narrow alleyway that allowed for coffins to be interred on both sides and at the rear. There was an
altar in the center, crusted with the dirt of the ages.

And on the altar, there was a body.

A woman.

Still holding her gun, Cheyenne stepped forward,
her heart sinking. It was certainly Katie Ridgeway.

And possibly…

She was dead.

Katie let out a groan and twisted. Her wrists and

ankles had been bound, and she was now covered in the same dust and dirt and death that coated the tomb.

"Katie!" Cheyenne holstered her gun and went to her, working frantically at the ties that bound her, helping her to sit up. "Katie, you're all right. I'm going to call an ambulance, we'll get someone here right away."

"Oh, Cheyenne!" Katie cried, throwing her arms around her rescuer, starting to slip from the altar.

Cheyenne stumbled a bit under Katie's weight, trying to balance the other woman.

And then someone rose from behind the altar.

"Welcome, Cheyenne," he said.

Cheyenne reached for her Glock again, but froze. It was too late; a snub-nosed Smith & Wesson was point at her face, just inches away.

"You're back!" Guy Mason said, smiling. "Have a seat, but… I've nothing more to tell you."

"Interesting. I do have something to tell you—or talk to you about."

"Oh?"

"Money," Andre said. "Specifically, the large amounts you've been receiving. You see, I realize you have an offshore account, and you've been careful about the way you filter it through…but you know, the FBI doesn't just have field agents—we have staff you wouldn't imagine, some of the finest accountants and technicians in the world. Anyway, they found your money. And what I want to know is, where did it come from?"

Mason stared at him blankly. "I—uh—don't know what you're talking about."

"I think you do. And I really suggest you cooperate. You know that Louisiana does have the death penalty, and there are federal cases in which the death penalty might be dealt out, as well. Conspiracy to commit murder—"

"I never murdered anyone, I swear!" the man told him.

"But someone paid you to ignore what you saw or heard at the cemetery," Andre said.

Mason swallowed.

"I…uh… I don't know who."

"Now, Mr. Mason, how in the world would that be possible?"

Mason had lost his friendly air; he didn't look much like the dignified funeral director anymore, either. He was flushed and grimacing.

Andre smiled. "Not to mention the IRS. In comparison, that will be nothing."

"I swear, I never murdered anyone, and I never knew—I swear I never knew—that there was a woman being kept in the outbuildings. I received a call…and I needed money…and…he left the money for me at the Broussard tomb. He'd leave it where we leave the keys."

"I see. And you have no idea who was paying you?"

"He—he had to know that Justine hired me. He…

he didn't call me here. He had my cell. Easy enough to get… I have it on my business cards. But he said he just needed some space and he didn't want to be bothered. If I saw lights or heard noises…he said it wouldn't matter, because kids were in the cemetery all the time, and this wouldn't be any different…but he'd pay me. A lot. He seemed amused. Said something about having money now. And I thought…"

"You thought what? He was some kind of a ghoul who just wanted a place in a cemetery and maybe hang out in old slave quarters?" Andre asked harshly.

"I didn't know he was holding a woman, I swear it! I thought maybe he was selling drugs." Mason seemed to slump in on himself. "Maybe even selling drugs to kids. I was just paid…not to notice. I stayed away from the outbuildings, and I drove right by the cemetery night and day. That's all. Please, you have to believe me. I would never hurt anyone."

"Really? Even if it was 'just' drugs—you didn't think that a pusher could hurt the kids around here?"

"I think kids will buy drugs no matter what I do," Mason said bitterly.

Andre was about to tell him that he was going to have to come in—that he would likely face obstruction charges. But to his surprise, he wasn't alone with Mason anymore.

Janine, with Christian at her tail, came racing in. Her ghostly arms wrapped around Andre's arm and she tugged at him—futilely.

"Come, Andre—now! Quickly!"

He jumped up, scaring the hell out of Mason.

"Don't leave," he warned the funeral director. "I'll be back."

"Drop the gun, Cheyenne, or I'll kill Katie," Nelson Ridgeway said.

"You'll kill your own wife?" Cheyenne asked.

He smiled. "I'd kill anyone. Lassiter was a great teacher. You make friends, you can have lovers— even wives—as long as you know that you may have to say goodbye at any minute."

"Oh, God, he'll do it! Drop the gun, please," Katie begged.

Cheyenne's eyes flashed to Katie, and she noticed something. Something she'd seen before, and stared at for a long time before she'd realized what it meant. Katie was wearing a tiny cross pendant. The same small cross from the Mortician's pictures.

Thoughts racing, Cheyenne was careful to keep her expression stoic. She said flatly, "Andre will be down here any minute."

"Not soon enough, I'm afraid. He's talking to that idiot Guy Mason, and Mason is probably caving like a toddler in trouble," Nelson said. "Now, carefully— set down the gun and the holster."

Cheyenne unclipped the holster from the waistband of her suit trousers from the back. She placed it on the altar. It was now almost completely dark inside the tomb.

Katie suddenly let out a shrill cry of laughter. "I told you, Nelson—I told you she'd fall for it! Great big special-FBI-agent, tough girl, who brought down Lassiter! Yes, our girl Cheyenne—so good that she'd risk her life for mine. I told you!"

Cheyenne's breath caught in her throat. "It doesn't matter—you won't get out of here. Andre will stop you." She forced herself to shrug, and then smile. "One way or the other, he'll probably kill you."

Nelson smiled back. "No, he won't. Because he'll drop his gun to save your life, and...well, you both have to go. First, you ruined Lassiter's life—you sent him to his death."

"A jury sentenced Lassiter to execution by lethal injection."

"He was an inspiration!" Katie cried. "And he's dead—because of you!"

"He was a killer, and he justly died—just as you'll die, too," Cheyenne said, amazed that she could sound so calm.

Where are Janine and Christian? Have they gone for Andre? Certainly, they must have.

"So, that was it? You weren't in the popular crowd—and you must have been jealous as hell of Janine. So you became Lassiter's disciples. But wait! Neither of you had his charm or his looks, so you had to take a look at history. Dress up as a rougarou— keep the legend going!"

"Nelson has plenty of charm!" Katie said.

"And my Katie is beautiful!" Nelson protested.

"Not bad, and you were smart—you could always cover for each other," Cheyenne said.

A shadow moved in the tomb. It was Melissa Carrier, Cheyenne saw, sliding silently around behind Nelson. Melissa blew a cold breath at him; Nelson used his free hand to swat at his ear, thinking, perhaps that an insect had entered the tomb. He shivered.

"We set out to take care of all the Janines in the world," Katie said.

"Oh, you mean all the women you thought were cuter than you— No, I figure it was Janine's voice— she was so adored at the church. Lassiter killed her for you, didn't he, Katie? He knew she was falling for him."

"She was a bitch!" Katie snapped.

"She'd be interested to hear you say that—she's here, you know."

"Yeah. She's dead and rotting in the wall," Katie said.

Cheyenne shook her head. "No, she's *here*. Didn't you ever really wonder how I knew Lassiter killed her? She was right there—her ghost was right there. She told me. And now you've gone and called her a bitch. She's not going to be happy."

"She's not here!" Katie spat out.

"Not next to me, not at this minute. Melissa Carrier is, though. She's right behind Nelson. She's still seeking justice, or…peace. Maybe she'll get it once you're dead."

"You're the one dying!" Nelson assured her. "You and Mr. Perfect. FBI agent, musician, football player…jerk! And we will go on."

"Which one of you killed Braxton Trudeau—and why?" she asked.

"Oh, come on—he was going to steal all our glory," Nelson said. "I am the Rougarou! And Katie has created a new persona. She's the Mummy!"

"Of course she is. And they'll know it. Her DNA is all over the headdress and bandages she shed," Cheyenne said. "And all over the cups you left at Andre's house. Everyone will know."

The two looked at each other.

Melissa Carrier, victim of the first Rougarou, murder unsolved, bless her, chose that moment to wrap her ghostly arms around Nelson.

He twitched in alarm. Cheyenne took her chance. She used her elbow in a hard shove right into Katie's gut, stealing her breath and shoving her back. Cheyenne made a dive for Nelson, and his gun went flying.

Katie wasn't down long. She leaped on Cheyenne's back. Cheyenne slammed hard back into the wall of crypts, against Janine's crypt, and Katie let out a cry of agony and slumped to the floor. Nelson was diving for the gun.

Cheyenne dived for her own. She grabbed the holster and Glock just as Nelson fired. She fell on the altar and rolled over it, panting.

"You're dead, you're dead, you're dead!" Nelson screamed.

And then, though the last of the dying light was gone, the full moon had risen. And Cheyenne realized that she could see faintly in the shadows of the tomb.

She was not alone. Captain Bouche and Lieutenant Kendall had joined Melissa Carrier inside the crypt.

"Dead, dead, dead!" Nelson screamed.

"Janine!"

The ghosts ran fast—glided fast—all but flying over the terrain. Despite his desperation, Andre couldn't move as fast.

They hadn't told him anything; he didn't know what he was running into.

He didn't know who he was facing!

He raced down to the cemetery, trying to keep the ghosts in view—his weapon pulled and ready.

Then, he almost tripped. There was a body on the ground. He stooped down.

He'd found the organist, Jacques Derringer.

Andre checked for a pulse, seeing that the man was alive. Barely.

Blood was pooling by his head. He'd been crushed by a brick taken from a decaying tomb; a piece of it, covered in the same blood, lay nearby.

He paused to call in for help, praying that the seconds it took to try to save this man's life did not cost Cheyenne hers.

And in that moment he knew he never wanted to live without her again.

He stood; Janine was coming back for him. "Andre, Andre...he's going to kill her!"

He stood, and then he knew exactly where they were going.

The Dumas tomb, where Janine lay...

Where Cheyenne was welcome to rest, as well.

"Where is she?" Nelson called out to Katie.

"Behind the altar, but..."

Nelson rose, and Cheyenne could see him as a silhouette, but that silhouette was a shadow that seemed to change in the shadowy depths of the tomb. She was a good shot—but she couldn't take aim.

Still, she fired.

She heard Nelson swear.

"I told you I should have a gun, too!" Katie snapped.

"Shut up!" Nelson told her.

"Idiot! You know what, Cheyenne—he thinks he's the big Rougarou—but guess what? I've been the brains behind this thing from the beginning. I got to know Lassiter. I became friends with the priest and managed to steal robes. He caught me putting them back, but...hey, I didn't kill him. I was just there... okay, I was wearing my mummy wrappings...and he fell over dead! But hey, I killed Trudeau, and I set up Nelson as the Rougarou. Okay, so he loved it— our secret—but guess who loved cutting up and torturing those women? Me—I'm the man!" she said, and laughed.

"Bitch!" Nelson said quietly. His gun went off; the sound was deafening. Cheyenne blinked and breathed hard. She hadn't been hit.

And then she realized that although Katie had thought herself smart, she hadn't been smart enough to realize that Nelson *would* kill her.

Katie wasn't making a sound anymore.

"Cheyenne!" She heard her cousin's voice. "Are you okay?" Janine was in the tomb.

Cheyenne kept her place behind the altar and spoke to Nelson. "Janine is here now. Janine, and Melissa… and Christian. Oh, and two gentlemen you never met, one a Reb, and one a Yank. They fought a war, they saw a lot of bloodshed, and now they're all about peace—and life, Nelson. They're going to see that you're arrested."

"No," he said. "I am the Rougarou! The police will come. They will find you dead, and Andre dead—and Katie dead. And the Rougarou will go down in history as he did before."

He fired again; she couldn't see him, he couldn't see her.

It was a game of Russian roulette.

It was impossible to miss the sounds of gunfire.

Janine threw herself at him before he could enter the tomb.

"Christian and I will go first—you can't help her with a bullet hole in you."

"Lure him out…do your best, I can take him by surprise."

"There are two of them…it's Nelson…and Katie, I think. She was moaning and all, but I think she was faking, just to get you two in there somehow," Janine told him.

"Get him to the gate, let me take him, and then... then I'll worry about Katie," Andre said.

He looked up at the sky.

The full moon was out. If he could just get the man out into the moonlight...

"If Janine is here, Andre is here, and he knows what you're doing. He'll get you before you get him. You should have kept Katie alive awhile longer; she might have helped you. But now...well, he's out there."

Nelson was slipping. He began to fire at her, wildly. She hunched down as stone and cement shattered around her, and when she could, she twisted and shot back. But just as he was firing blindly, so was she.

He swore, and she heard movement over the ringing in her ears. She thought he was headed to the heavy gate, determined to throw it open. Cheyenne started to rise, determined to fire at him.

Another barrage of bullets came her way.

She would lose her cover soon.

She heard the creak and risked peeking her head out. Nelson was hunched low, pushing at the gate. And as he did, Cheyenne saw Janine slip up behind him, pushing at him with all her strength.

He started to stumble, and Andre rushed him. He toppled him over on the ground, taking a solid swing at him and then rolling some distance away.

"Get Katie!" he shouted.

Cheyenne leaped to her feet and raced to him. He remained straddled over Nelson.

Nelson was just staring at him. "I am the Rougarou," Nelson said.

"What you are is a pathetic, sick killer—and under arrest," Andre told him. He looked up at Cheyenne. "You got Katie?"

"I didn't have to," Cheyenne said. "She was his last kill."

They both looked around; Captain Bouche, Lieutenant Kendall, Melissa, Christian—and Janine—had circled them.

"This will be the end," Melissa said, and looked at them hopefully. "The end of the Rougarou. No more can he come around—you have proven that killing can be stopped." She smiled at them. "Twice," she said.

They heard sirens in the distance.

It was Detective Vine who first came running onto the scene.

Andre got up, letting Vine cuff and take Nelson Ridgeway.

"I am the Rougarou!" Nelson screamed again. And maybe he was—he was a monster, howling out in fury beneath the full moon.

"Special Agent," Vine began.

"Take him and go ahead—deal with this!" Andre said. "He'll face federal and state charges. But for now…he's yours. Oh, by the way—bring your second cousin in, too. He has to answer for his part in this, no matter how small. And see that Jacques Derringer gets to the hospital pronto."

Andre reached for Cheyenne's hand and then looked back. "And, oh. We're not doing any paperwork. Not tonight. Deal with that, too."

He led her out of the cemetery, and Cheyenne smiled. "The car is at the house," she reminded him.

"We'll go back," he told her. "For now..."

He pulled her into his arms. She felt the way that he was shaking and she knew that he'd been terrified that he would lose her.

He held her so tightly and yet so tenderly.

"You love me," she said, looking up at him.

"Yeah, well—you love me!" he replied.

She shrugged. "No argument there."

She kissed him.

The night, and she was sure the days to follow, would be theirs.

All theirs.

"How do you feel about the Krewe?" he asked her.

"The Krewe?"

"After this, you can't go back to Miami."

"Well, I can."

"But you don't want to. And you do want to be Krewe."

"I can talk to Jackson, but I don't know..."

"Yes, you do. And I've already talked to Jackson."

"Hey!"

He smiled at her. "That's why we're great partners. We can read one another's minds. Seriously, you know you want to be Krewe. It's the only way to go."

She turned back, and she was surprised to see that the moonlight was framing a strange tableau.

Christian and Janine were together, standing with Captain Bouche and Lieutenant Kendall. A little distance away was Melissa. The young woman seemed to be caught in a strange pool of the moonlight, suddenly so bright, it might have been the sun. Then the light faded, and only four ghosts remained.

"Melissa's gone on—hasn't she?" she asked Andre. She couldn't stop the tears from forming in her eyes.

He nodded, and he pulled her to him again and whispered, "You do want to be Krewe, right? I mean, I could transfer, too, but…"

She smiled.

An ambulance had come, and it seemed that the night was alive with sirens and flashing red lights. She didn't give a damn.

She kissed him.

And then she whispered, "Yes, I do want to be Krewe. But right now… I just want to go…home."

"Ah, and they say you can never go home!"

"We can," she said. "Because…well, I was thinking…"

"What?"

"Well, first of all, we can handle home. And then…home is where you are for me now," she told him softly.

"Are you feeling angry?" he asked her, walking to the car.

"No, but…"

He grinned at her. "Oh, well. I have a long drive to try to really piss you off."

"What?" Then she saw his eyes, and she laughed. As she turned and looked over her shoulder one last time at the cemetery, she thought that, strangely, she had truly come home.

Tomorrow, she would thank Christian and Janine.

Tonight, well…tonight was a gift her cousin had helped give her. Tonight was life.

A life she knew she would get to share with an extraordinary man.

Yes, it was possible to go home.

* * * * *

New York Times **bestselling author**

HEATHER GRAHAM

returns with the next story in her thrilling Krewe of Hunters series.

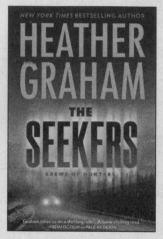

Keri Wolf has joined the crew of *The Seekers*, a show that searches for paranormal phenomena, as they explore a supposedly haunted old inn. The place is infamous for being the site of an ax murder rampage. They've barely begun when a dead body is discovered. As a nonfiction author, Keri is supposed to be the rational one, but she can't explain a terrifying apparition that seems to be both a threat and a warning.

Former detective Joe Dunhill knows what she's going through—the strange gift of being able to see and talk to the dead is a struggle he shares. A new member of the FBI's Krewe of Hunters, he's on the team investigating the disturbing death. The deeper Joe and Keri plunge into the dark secrets of the inn, the closer they get to a devastating truth.

Available now wherever books are sold.

Be sure to connect with us at:

Harlequin.com/Newsletters

Facebook.com/HarlequinBooks

Twitter.com/HarlequinBooks

mira

Harlequin.com

MHG6879